Cornelius Conway Felton

Familiar Letters from Europe

Cornelius Conway Felton

Familiar Letters from Europe

ISBN/EAN: 9783744765916

Printed in Europe, USA, Canada, Australia, Japan

Cover: Foto ©Andreas Hilbeck / pixelio.de

More available books at **www.hansebooks.com**

FROM EUROPE.

BY

CORNELIUS CONWAY FELTON,
LATE PRESIDENT OF HARVARD UNIVERSITY.

BOSTON:
TICKNOR AND FIELDS.
1865.

To

Rev. A. P. PEABODY,

THE VALUED FRIEND OF THE WRITER,

These Letters

ARE GRATEFULLY INSCRIBED

BY

M. L. FELTON.

FAMILIAR LETTERS.

I.

On board the Ship Daniel Webster, Boston Harbor,
Saturday, April 9, 1853.

AFTER lying by a couple of hours, a sufficient number of sailors has been mustered, and the ship is now getting under way. Dinner is preparing, and the passengers are prepared. The wind is favorable, and we shall make a good distance before night. There seemed some danger of our being detained here, for want of these men, until to-morrow, and perhaps longer, without the possibility of going ashore; but the actual starting is an omen of good success throughout.

Wednesday, April 13. —Since I wrote on Saturday we have had excellent weather and fair winds. All the passengers except myself have been sick, but to me every moment since I came on board has been full of enjoyment; my only drawback, the seeing how shockingly the rest were suffering.

16th. — We are getting on at the rate of ten or twelve miles an hour. With you, it is now about half past nine o'clock; with us, a little after eight.

Sunday, 17*th.* — We had a good run last night, with much less motion.

Last evening I read some passages from the Midsummer Night's Dream to the Captain. When I came to the description of the mermaid riding " on a dolphin's back," he pronounced it a humbug. " The dolphin's back is as sharp as a razor, and no mermaid could possibly ride the beast, unless she had first saddled him." So Shakespeare is caught napping here.

Our company were all at breakfast this morning, except Mrs. ———. We are now a little more than half over. They tell me that the sea has been unusually rough, but I have not suffered in the least. The Captain repeated to me yesterday, that he had never known any one to bear the sea so well, on a first voyage. But the truth is, I have found nothing to bear; everything around me has excited, so far, an unflagging interest.

Thursday, April 21*st.* — After a day of the most painful experience, I sit down in the evening to continue my brief notice of events. I rose, as is my wont, at 5 o'clock. Went on deck, and took the usual rounds of the ship. The

weather was a little overcast, and the sea ran high.
After a while, Mrs. L—— came up, and we sat
talking in the wheel-house, from which we looked
over the whole length of the ship. Suddenly,
about twenty minutes past eight, the terrible cry
of "A man overboard!" came from the forecastle.
He was lowering the foretopgallant-sail, — about a
hundred and ten feet above the deck, — and fell,
striking one of the lower sails, and then bounding
into the sea. The Captain was just coming up
with his quadrant, to take an observation. He
sprang forward, and gave his orders like lightning.
The ship was hoven to, but with a tremendous
strain upon masts and rigging ; one of the boats
was lowered, and three men jumped in. The sea
was heavy, and the motion of the ship violent ;
the boat capsized, throwing the three men into the
sea. One, the boatswain, caught hold of the tackle
by which the boat was still held to the stern of the
ship, and was drawn on board. The other two
were struggling in the waves. A fourth stripped
himself and clambered down into the boat, which
had righted itself, but was nearly full of water.
Just at that moment a tremendous lurch of the
ship dashed the boat against her, broke the tack-
ling, tore off the davit, and she again capsized,
with such a weight hanging underneath that it
was impossible for her to right herself again.
The brave sailor managed to get upon her keel,
but she floated away, at one moment poised on

the top of a wave, and the next sinking out of
sight. Another boat was lowered instantly, and
the second mate, the boatswain who had already
come within a hair's-breadth of losing his life,
and two young sailors, volunteered to man her,
and attempt the rescue of their shipmates.

Away they went. But the waves seemed to
rise higher and the wind to blow stronger. We
watched both boats with straining eyes, and the
most painful, even agonizing feelings. I assure
you, those noble fellows had not one chance in
a thousand of ever reaching the ship again in
safety. All the rest — four in number — had disappeared from sight, and there was not the shadow
of a possibility of their surviving. Two awful
hours passed, and then the Captain called his
crew aft, and asked them if they thought it best
to continue the search. After a moment of sad
silence, they said, " No, there is no hope "; and
the signal was given for the boat to return.

But this was a difficult matter, in such a sea.
Without the most consummate seamanship, and
the most absolute self-possession, as well as des-
potic command over others, on the Captain's part,
it could not have been done, and four more gallant fellows would have followed their companions
to the bottom. His presence was everywhere;
his voice seemed to fill the ship; the men were
puppets in his hands, and did exactly his bidding.
As the boat neared the ship, he ordered the men

on board what to do. They obeyed implicitly and instantly, though the orders, as one of them has since told me, were directly contrary to their own rapidly formed plan. Ropes were thrown to them, and they were safely got on board, amidst the joyful congratulations of sailors and passengers. So unexpected was this marvellous rescue, that we, for the moment, forgot the poor fellows who had two hours since passed into eternity, under our very eyes. Then returned the solemn and awful sense of what had happened; and then the ship made sail, and all was over.

I need not say that this spectacle, which passed before my eyes, was the most terrible ever witnessed by me. But the skill, devotion, and energy shown by the Captain, officers, and crew were sublime. In the midst of the horror, I could not help feeling *this*, too. I looked at the poor fellow, keeping his seat bravely on the keel of the distant boat; then at the four men in the second boat, struggling to his rescue; then upon the Captain, as he went aloft and gave his orders with the clearness of a trumpet, with a kind of spell-bound awe. But the might of the elements baffled the utmost that human skill, unconquerable devotion, and the noblest humanity could do. At eleven o'clock, a meeting was called in the cabin; and we passed resolutions and raised a subscription to procure some testimonial for these noble fellows who went out in the second boat.

There has been a strong wind and a heavy sea all day. At this moment the ship is pitching tremendously, (as you may judge by my writing,) and driving at the rate of a dozen miles an hour. During all this, there has not been an instant of danger to the ship, except when she was suddenly brought round, at the moment the first man fell overboard. Had she not been most strongly built, every mast would then have been snapped off; but, as I have told you, the noble ship rode the waves like a king.

We are about 390 miles from Cape Clear, and 700 from Liverpool. We already notice a change in the clouds, indicating that we are approaching land.

Friday, April 22d. — Last night was the roughest we have had. The ship pitched and tossed and groaned tremendously. For the first time my slumbers were broken in upon. Crash went a basket of crockery; bang came a tremendous wave against the side of the state-room. This last seemed to suggest the idea of a quarrel. I dreamed I was abusing somebody for a badly cooked ham, and it ended by my throwing it at his head. I awoke, and was rather glad to find I had not been guilty of such an absurdity; for, you know, I never did such a thing in my life. The tumult still continues; but we are approaching Cape Clear at a prodigious rate.

Saturday, April 23d.—We are now in soundings, and expect to see Cape Clear to-day. If the wind holds, we shall reach Liverpool next Monday. The passage has been rough, but, in point of speed, a very good one. It is only a fortnight to-day since we embarked, and here we are, almost within hail of land. The sea is discolored, and the sea-birds multiply. The clouds look differently, and everything betokens the approaching end of the voyage.

Sunday Evening.—We have had a pleasant day. We passed Tusca Rock before sunset, and near enough to see the lighthouse very distinctly. The coast of Ireland is bold and hilly. We have been able to see some of the buildings, and a flagstaff on a headland. A windmill was at first mistaken for a castle, and called out a good deal of enthusiasm.

I find, to-day, that there is, among the second-cabin passengers, a colored man with a white wife, going to Europe for three years' study. He has been appointed Professor of Greek, Hebrew, and German in some interior college of New York. I am sorry I did not know this before; I should like to have become acquainted with him. I have noticed him and his wife—a pretty, delicate little woman—several times; but the lines of demarcation are so strictly drawn, that no intercourse occurs, except by some special effort, between the first-class and second-class passengers.

Monday, 10 *o'clock.* — The wind and weather continued propitious until we reached the Holyhead Light, about four o'clock this morning. There we suddenly encountered a gale from the northeast, which made it necessary to put about, and shoot off to the Irish coast.

Evening. — The gale has subsided, and we are again upon our course, hoping to get by Holyhead to-night. You cannot imagine the contrast between the clear sky and calm sea and favoring breeze we are now enjoying, and the terrible uproar which lasted ten hours.

Tuesday, April 26th, 10 *o'clock.* — We have signalized to Liverpool by way of Holyhead, and expect to meet a steamboat, to tow us in, in the course of the day. The mountains of Wales have been in sight; and, in particular, we had a perfect view of Snowdon, which I hope to ascend in a few days. I have not been idle during this voyage; have read half a dozen novels, half a dozen plays of Shakespeare, written a good many letters; and have got well acquainted with the officers, which is worth a good deal, for they are downright good fellows, every inch of them. The rough-looking mate, W——, has the courage of a lion and the heart of a woman. He told me the other day all about his courtship and marriage. The Captain has promised to draw on a chart the line of our voyage, and take it to you on his return.

Wednesday Morning. — Here we are at Liverpool. We got round Holyhead yesterday before noon; had a pleasant run up; ships multiplying the nearer we came; then steamers plying about. At one o'clock, the pilot — a pleasant-looking John Bull — boarded us. We had to remain outside the bar till ten o'clock, for the tide, so that the ship did not reach the dock until midnight. We stayed on board all night. I have just been on deck to take my first look at Liverpool. It is a busy scene; and here ends the voyage, — a long story about a short matter. Voyage exactly sixteen days.

1*

II.

CHESTER, April 29, 1853.

WE stayed in Liverpool one day only, but I saw a good deal of the city, and quite enough to understand its commercial importance. I was amused, interested, and instructed every moment; but two or three things struck me much, — the pleasant voices, and low, distinct pronunciation of *all* classes of people, and the universal disposition to oblige. On the other hand, in the obscure streets, the wretchedness and rags were deplorable. The stolid-looking little donkeys, with their carts, driven by just such ragamuffin boys as Dickens loves to describe, who whacked them over the back without exciting any other feeling in the shaggy little beasts than the most profound indifference, made me laugh twenty times. Our hotel itself was just such a rambling building as Mr. Pickwick lost his way in.

The next day we came by railroad to this old place; the most interesting city in England for its antiquities. Immediately after our arrival we turned our steps to the Cathedral, once an abbey, but on the dissolution of the monasteries converted into a cathedral church. It is the most extraordinary historical monument of its kind in Great Britain.

In the afternoon we drove over to Eaton Hall, the new and splendid seat of the Marquis of Westminster. We walked through the park by a winding road, from which opened the most exquisite views of lawn, wood, and stream; the river Dee, here and there glancing on the sight; old trees, of a thousand years, stretching their aged arms overhead; thousands of rooks cawing and clamoring, high up in the tree-tops, where their nests were built, and, underneath, thousands of other feathered singers giving their softer notes to the concert. The afternoon was very fine, — cool, and partly overcast with clouds, which gave a most enchanting softness to the landscape. The road is so made as to bring the Hall in sight from just the most picturesque points of view. It took two or three hours to make the circuit. We passed close by the Hall in returning to the road; but it is not open to visitors, and so we did not see the interior.

The next morning early, I went to the Cathedral and attended the morning service. How many do you think were present to share in this act of devotion, in this wonderful old place? Just eight, including the sexton and myself. After service I ascended the tower. The day before I had gone upon the tower of Trinity Church with considerable difficulty. The stairs reached only

to the first landing; from that up to the summit
a series of ladders furnished the only means of
mounting. The doors, or traps, were so small
that I could scarcely squeeze my body through,
and the accumulated dust of centuries was almost
smothering. The view was beautiful, but too
much overshadowed by showery clouds passing
over at the moment. I was not sorry to get down
again. I said to the sexton, " It seems to me you
have not calculated correctly for Englishmen ; the
ladders and passages are scarcely large enough
for an American." " Why," said he, " very few
Hinglishmen goes up 'ere."

But the Cathedral tower is higher and more
central; the ascent is by a winding stone staircase, a great part of the way pitchy dark and narrow, though not quite so narrow as Trinity. The
dust and heat were severe. I took a peep into
the belfry on the way, and at that moment the
peal of the organ floated up from below. Con-
tinuing the ascent, the stairs still narrowed ; but
by and by the light broke in from above as if
straight from heaven. Curiously enough, just
below the last step a rook had built her nest,
which filled up the whole width of the stairs.
With some difficulty scrambling over it, without
much damage to the nest or myself, I emerged
upon the summit, and was almost overwhelmed by
the first magnificence of the view. The quadrangular summit is very spacious, and well fenced by

a parapet. I stayed as long as I could, looking over the immense prospect and listening to the sounds that came up from below. If I were to linger over this indescribable scene, I should fill up my letter with this and nothing else.

After breakfast we bade farewell to our hotel and took the cars, with the purpose of getting to Leamington and visiting Warwick Castle and Kenilworth. We passed the wonderful vale of Llangollen, the most delicious landscape in Wales, and perhaps in the world. Of course we had only momentary glimpses of its magical beauties, but enough to stamp the picture on my memory forever. After a succession of rural scenes such as only England can present, we came suddenly upon a mining district! What a contrast! The earth torn up; heaps of rubbish; fires blazing up from tall chimneys.

We reached Leamington, a part of the ancient parish of Warwick, in season for an early dinner. In the afternoon we hired a carriage and drove to Warwick Castle. We reached the spot after the hour of receiving visitors. I was advised to send my card in to the Earl of Warwick, and ask permission to enter. The old porter took the card to the groom of the chambers, the groom of the chambers took it to his Lordship, who most courteously granted permission. The consequence was, we saw the Castle under the most favorable circumstances, — no other visitors being there, —

and passed leisurely and quietly through all the apartments, except some of the smaller ones occupied by the family.

This castle is one of the oldest and finest in England. Every part of it, except "Guy's Tower," is fitted up with perfect taste and comfort, for the residence of the family and their guests. The rooms are crowded with the most precious works of art, — antiquities of the rarest description, — all arranged with admirable skill. We spent a long time in giving even a hasty examination to these treasures, not one of which but has its historical interest. The grass was delightfully green, and the turf soft within the extensive enclosure. Crossing over to the other side, we ascended Guy's Tower, and, the weather happening to be uncommonly fine, the prospect over the lawns, park, forests, and the winding Avon, which flows just under the walls, was enchanting. Next we passed out of the castle into the conservatory, where stands the world-renowned Warwick Vase. Here again I cannot undertake to describe anything I saw; but I will say, that Warwick Castle more than repays a voyage across the Atlantic.

Returning, we visited the Parish Church of St. Mary, and saw the interesting monuments of the Beauchamps, Dudleys, Leicester, &c. We got back to dinner about seven o'clock, a little fatigued by the labors of the day, but filled with the highest enjoyment.

May 1*st*. — This morning, early, we took post-horses for Stratford-on-Avon. We drove first to Kenilworth Castle. It is the first of May, and the English May. Captain Howard joined us at Chester, and will continue with us to Oxford. You would have smiled to see us; — a pair of horses; a trim postilion, with buckskin breeches, white-topped boots, spurs, a leather leggin on the right leg to guard it against the pole, white jacket with silver ball-buttons, a jaunty cap, white gloves as clean as a lady's in a ball-room, an elegant whip, mounted on the near horse; the Captain and I on what we should call the driver's seat; the girls and P—— in the carriage (a post-chaise), with the top thrown entirely back. Such was the style in which we departed from the famous Leamington, on the 1st of May, 1853, — a most beautiful morning, — on our way to Kenilworth and Stratford-on-Avon.

Another succession of English landscapes, enlivened by the singing of thrushes and other birds. A drive of three or four miles brought us in sight of the castellated remains of Kenilworth. We stopped at a little alehouse, and then walked over the grounds, and all around this venerable and romantic ruin. I read Walter Scott's description aloud, and it is very interesting to notice with what fidelity he has followed the details as far as they go, and with what life his pages are animated as you read them on the spot. We walked entirely round the walls, tracing the ancient moat, and gazing with a delight, mixed with something of sadness, on the heavy masses of ivy which hang over the ruins like natural tapestry. We remained here for a considerable time, studying the scene, and conversing with an intelligent farmer whom we found near the spot. I shall send by the Captain a quantity of cards with views of this and other places we have already visited. Here again was more of the beautiful English turf; and innumerable birds making the ruins vocal with the first songs of May. Having spent as much time as we could spare, we went on to Guy's Cliff, of which we had only the front view; but that is beautiful enough. We passed through a delightful country, every inch of which is like a garden, having views, near and distant, not only of consummate beauty, but of great historical interest.

About eleven o'clock we entered Stratford-on-Avon, and stopped at an excellent inn in the same street with the house in which Shakespeare was born. It was not many minutes before I was looking upon that insignificant building, — one of the most interesting spots in the world.

I called on Mr. F——, to whom I had a letter, and was most courteously received. We attended the afternoon service in the church where Shakespeare attended. After service we stood before the monument, and read with reverence the inscription on that and on his tombstone. Then we crossed the Avon, which flows directly under the church, and walked over the delightful meadows, spangled with the first flowers of spring, — " the daisies pied and violets blue." I felt that here Shakespeare breathed in his inspiration; here he watched the wild-flowers, and learned to embroider his poetry with their amaranthine colors. I fancied I felt whence his poetry was drawn, and recalled Gray's lines on Shakespeare with a clear perception of the fitness of every epithet.

> " In thy green lap was Nature's darling laid,
>   What time, where lucid Avon strayed,
>   To him the mighty mother did unveil
>   Her awful face : the dauntless child
>   Stretched forth his little hand, and smiled.
> ' This pencil take,' she said, ' whose colors clear
>   Richly paint the vernal year :
>   Thine, too, these golden keys, immortal boy !
>   This can unlock the gates of Joy ;
>   Of Horror that, and thrilling Fears,
>   Or ope the sacred source of sympathetic Tears.' "

We also went into all the apartments of the Shakespeare house, saw the room in which he was born, and inscribed our names there. Our walk extended over the most beautiful part of the Avon meadows, and just before we left them to return to Henley Street, a nightingale — the first, Mr. F—— said, he had heard — struck up *two notes*, and only two, of the most liquid sweetness.

Now can you imagine a more beautiful group of poetical circumstances? The first of May; a morning visit to Kenilworth Castle; a drive through the garden scenery of England; arrival at Stratford-on-Avon, after having crossed the winding stream at many picturesque points; a visit to the house where Shakespeare was born; attending religious services in the fine old Gothic church, approached by a beautiful avenue of lime-trees, interlacing their boughs overhead, through an ancient burying-ground, — the church where Shakespeare worshipped, where he was married, where he was buried, where the only authentic bust exists, where lies the tombstone over his dust with his own epitaph, —

> "Good frend for Jesus' sake forbeare
> To digg ye dust encloased here
> Bleste be ye man yt spares yese stones,
> And curst be he yt moves my bones," —

where his "bones," in consequence of these singular lines, have been allowed to remain undisturbed, and will now remain so long as the world shall stand, — where his wife lies buried by his side, and two of his sisters; — then a stroll over those lovely meadows, which his footsteps had so often printed; gathering daisies, where he so often saw them, just as we did, in the fresh beauty of the spring; listening to the nightingale "pouring his throat," just as he listened; returning, just as he returned, over the old arched bridge, built long before his day; walking up the street where his father lived, into the old market so familiar to his eyes, again by the house where he was born. I say, can you picture to yourself a finer or more interesting combination of poetical circumstances than were pressed together in these few hours?

But this is not all. Mr. F—— made us all come and take tea at his beautiful place. After tea we strolled towards Henley, through a rich meadow on a path between hedgerows, with thrushes singing the whole distance, — to Clifton Manor, a house of Shakespeare's time, — then, by a footpath through the fields, to Anne Hathaway's cottage in Shottery, — the very path where Shakespeare walked in the cool of the evening, — just at the time Shakespeare was wont to visit Anne; and while we walked, another nightingale poured out a succession of notes which would have enchanted your very soul. Mrs. F—— drove the girls in a pony carriage. We reached the cottage early in the evening. It is still occupied by one of the Hathaways. She showed us over it. We sat on the settle where Shakespeare and Anne used to sit and talk together, at the same hour in the evening. We stood within the old huge fireplace, where he had so often warmed himself in winter, after a cold walk from Henley Street.

We looked over the old family Bible; went into the chamber where there is a richly carved bedstead of oak, that has come down from the age of Elizabeth; sat on the seat of a spinning-wheel once used by Anne; came down and drank a glass of fresh, sweet, delicious water, drawn by the representative of the Hathaways from the old well covered with a broad stone, and bought some printed sheets, containing the verses on Anne Hathaway, popularly ascribed to the poet.

How beautifully the first stanza applies to the scenery and circumstances,—the evening, and the song of birds, and the delightful spot!

> "Would ye be taught, ye feathered throng,
>   With love's sweet notes to frame your song
> To pierce my heart with thrilling lay,
> Listen to my Anne Hathaway.
> She hath a way to sing so clear,
> Phœbus might, wondering, stoop to hear, —
> To melt the sad, make blithe the gay,
> To charm all hearts, Anne Hath-a-way:
>   She hath a way,
>   Anne Hath-a-way,
> To breathe delight, Anne Hath-a-way."

And again : —

> "To make grief bliss, Anne Hath-a-way.
> Talk not of gems, the Orient list;
> The diamond, topaz, amethyst,
> The emerald mild, the ruby gay, —
> Talk of my gem, Anne Hathaway
> She hath a way with her bright eye,
> Their various lustres to defy ;
> The jewel she, the foil they,
> So sweet to look, Anne Hath-a-way :
>   She hath a way,
>   Anne Hath-a-way,
> To shame bright gems, Anne Hath-a-way."

We walked back to Mr. F——'s, and passed a most agreeable hour with his family. Was not this a May-day to be remembered?

III.

LONDON, May 13, 1853.

WE left Stratford-on-Avon, after one of those memorable days of association with the past, under the most agreeable present circumstances, that so seldom happen to men. We travelled thence to Oxford, stopping at Woodstock on the way, to visit Blenheim palace. It is a wretched building, disgraceful to the taste of the times when the nation's gratitude expressed itself with ostentatious profusion to the first Duke of Marlborough. It has a glorious park, however, and noble collections of works of art, by the best of the old masters. I shall not take up time by any minute descriptions of these or other similar objects; but it was a great pleasure to me to see them.

Early in the afternoon we reached Oxford, — the city of monastic colleges and monastic men. The impression made on me was not quite agreeable, even at first. I delivered a letter to one of the heads, for the purpose merely of getting a general view of the University, as we intended to pass, for the present, only a single night there. He received me with the greatest courtesy, but, being unwell, excused himself from personally attending us, and gave me a written paper which seemed designed to open to our inspection everything which we might desire to see. It was rather late, and the Bodleian Library was shut for the day; but the Gallery, he said, we could visit. We presented ourselves at the entrance, having inquired the way of one of the servitors of the University, and on my showing the pass, " Sixpence for each member of your party," was the salutation we received before a single picture was exhibited. Next we went into some of the public Examination Rooms, and thence into Divinity College, which was shown to us by a drunken porter. He had to be paid; and finally, the man who showed us to the other two had to be paid. Thus, in less than an hour we paid three fees for seeing two or three only of the public buildings of the great university city of England. I felt so indignant that I would not proceed further. We returned to our lodgings, and after tea strolled by ourselves through some of the grounds and the beautiful quadrangles, which are so delightful in Oxford.

In the evening, Mr. C——, a Fellow of Wadham College, came in. He is one of Mr. ——'s friends, and a most amiable and accomplished gentleman. He proposed taking us over his College the next morning. We were charmed with his conversation and manners. The next morning it rained; but he came punctually, in his academical costume, which they all wear, and showed and explained everything belonging to Wadham. I presented my circular letter at the Bodleian Library; the Librarian received us most courteously, and took us over the apartments himself.

We left Oxford at two o'clock, in a dismal rain, and reached London in about two hours. We entered this great metropolis with a storm and fog; coal-smoke mingling with them, and reducing the thing called here the atmosphere to a sooty consistency as thick as molasses. P—— and I were on the top of an omnibus, and had the full enjoyment of this brilliant aspect of London. Nelson's monument and that of the Duke of York were dimly discernible, as we drove within a hundred yards of them. The houses — called mostly *huses* — looked spectral as castles in the air. We had engaged lodgings at John Chapman's, on the Strand, — the busiest part of the city, — where we found Mr. B—— and his family living in the American boarding-house style. We made ourselves as comfortable as we could, until the next morning. The first thing I then did was to drive to ——'s with the package I had for her. She is as charming as ever. Having despatched this 'important piece of business, I drove next to Dickens's. He was out, but I saw Mrs. Dickens, who asked me to come and dine with them that day.

At the appointed hour I went to the house again, — having in the mean time seen Dickens himself, and taken a long stroll with him about

London ; visiting Gog and Magog in Guildhall ; the Monument, which we ascended ; Bolt Court, and other notable places. Forster had already promised Dickens that he would dine with him that day, and there I met him, — so old a friend, though now seen for the first time *in propria persona*. I need not say that he was cordial as a man could be, nor that we had a most agreeable time. I have since then been with him almost every day, and find him genial in the highest degree, and one of the best-informed men on all matters of literature that I have ever seen.

In the evening we went to see Mons. Houdin, the French conjurer, and were much entertained by his admirable sleight of hand.

Next morning breakfasted with Forster alone, and had a long talk with him on the slavery question in the United States. I think I succeeded in explaining its constitutional bearings, so that he has now, what few Englishmen have, a fair understanding of the whole matter.

Visited Westminster Abbey, and was deeply impressed by the grandeur of the interior, as well as by the hallowed associations of Poet's Corner. The Parliament House is beautiful, but not impressive, except the old Westminster Hall. The courts do not strike me as in any respect more dignified than our own ; and in some particulars, dignity is the last attribute I should think of applying to them. The wigs and scarlet robes of the judges form to my eye the most atrocious masquerade that ever disguised the natural figure of man. The judges are good-looking persons, but when on the bench they and the counsel cut such absurd figures, that the most skilful caricaturist could not add to the grotesqueness of the scene.

May 20th. — I have been now two weeks and a half in this great capital; busy every moment of the time, and not, I hope, unprofitably so. I have passed much time in the British Museum, studying the Greek and Assyrian sculptures, — an admirable preparation for Greece. Tell Agassiz I have seen Sir Philip Egerton twice, and breakfasted with him once. He is kind, simple, and cordial in manners; so young-looking that I thought he must be his own son; but he persisted in saying he was himself.

Yesterday, dined with Forster. Have seen many of the artists and some of the politicians. To-day I go to Rogers's with Mrs. Dickens, and then to the Zoölogical Gardens, then to the French Theatre.

IV.

Sherborne, Sunday, June 5.

YOU see by the date I am with Mr. ———.
Here he lives, in a lovely spot; a large, old-
fashioned house, more than two centuries old, —
of stone, but nearly covered with ivy, and rose-
bushes now in full blossom. Five minutes' walk
from here are Sherborne Castle and one of the
most beautiful parks in England. The grounds
about this house are not extensive, but are well
laid out, with a variety of trees, which at this moment are vocal with the song of birds. The air is
soft and delicious; the turf of the richest green,
and like velvet to the foot.

I arrived here yesterday from Bristol, having
made, during the last fortnight, a pretty extended
tour through England and Scotland. You will
remember that we passed our first week in a little
journey through a part of Wales and the West of
England to London.

We entered London in a violent and most disagreeable storm. For the next ten days the weather
was detestable; but I managed to do nearly all I
expected to do, at the British Museum and other
places. I saw many interesting men, and trav-

ersed London in all directions. When P—— and the girls went into Derbyshire, I changed my lodging from the Strand, where I had a room that overlooked the chimneys of London, to Bury Street, St. James's, where I commanded an extensive view of the mouldering face of an old wall, with about two square feet of sunshine. Here I remained a fortnight. The rest of the party made a leisurely journey northward, through Derbyshire, visiting many interesting places on the way during this time.

London is a vast reality, which it requires time and study to get an idea of. Its extent is amazing. You seem to be journeying through an interminable wilderness of houses and streets. I have spent days in walking through them, with no other guide than the Indian has in the primeval forests, traversing many miles by the course of the sun; and surely nothing truer was ever said, than that a great city is a great solitude. Of certain classes of objects I have seen a single specimen: for instance, I went with Dickens, L——, and one or two others, to a low theatre, beyond Smithfield Market, where the poorest classes of operatives seek their amusement at the cost of sixpence. The stage-box, which we took, cost us one and sixpence apiece. Then I went once to the Covent Garden Opera: — the theatre magnificent, and the immense audience made up of the richest and noblest of the land, the performances by Grisi, Mario, and others being on a scale of perfection corresponding to the character of the company.

A few evenings later I dropped into Matthews's Theatre, and found him personating a Yankee, for the amusement of the middle classes; and doing it very well, except that my native ear detected several false idioms, and some confusion between the dialects of the North and South. That, however, made no difference to the English; since they call by the name of Yankee whatever is found between Canada and Mexico, and between the Atlantic and Pacific Oceans. Finally, I went one night to the French Play at St. James's Theatre, — a beautiful house, admirably arranged; where I had great pleasure in seeing M. Regnier, whom I had met at Dickens's, play in " Le Bonhomme Jadis," and in " Le Médecin Malgré lui " of Molière. This is all my theatrical experience; though I hope to see Rachel, who is now playing in London, on my return.

I sent —— a copy of the London Times, containing an account of the " Literary Fund Dinner," where I am put down as one of the speakers. In an evil hour I consented, at the request of the Americans in London, to respond to one of the toasts, having already received an invitation to be present. This was the day before the dinner. I had also an invitation to Sir Thomas Noon Talfourd's for the same evening. The moment I promised to make the speech, my peace of mind left me. I went home ; sat down to call together my scattered thoughts ; wrote out the substance of a speech ; lost the whole day in anxious meditation ; spent two shillings for a shower-bath to brace me up to the task ; got ready just as the carriage came to the door ; and drove lugubriously to the Freemasons' Tavern, where the dinner was to take place.

Mr. D'Israeli was the chairman for the year. I had a great curiosity to hear him, as he is quite the leading orator of the House of Commons. He was detained before a Committee on Bribery, until some time after the appointed hour. Finally, we were seated, and the dinner began ; but a man who has a speech impending has no desire to eat, still less to drink, until his agony is over. When the company had appeased the " sacred rage," the talking began. Mr. D'Israeli was received with great applause ; but, though interesting, his speaking does not approach Mr. Everett's in excellence. He made several short speeches, and one long one. I had written a note to Dickens to say I would try to be at his house between nine and ten o'clock, as I was to go with him to the party at Talfourd's. But time wore on ; several other long speeches — quite as long as Americans make on similar occasions, and not any better — succeeded : ten o'clock came ; the Bishop of O-whee-O (Ohio) was called up to respond to some theological sentiment ; eleven o'clock came, and I sat ruefully awaiting my immolation, inwardly resolved that I would occupy just half a minute and then run. But to my great relief, before they reached the part of the programme where the old Lord S—— and I were placed, there was a general movement among the ladies at the end of the hall to retire. This compelled the chairman to omit all the rest of the speeches, and bring the dinner to a sudden conclusion, so that all the extemporary eloquence I had in my pocket remained unspoken. I had sat on thorns the whole evening; lost my dinner; lost the day; lost the party at Talfourd's; and went speechless and supperless to bed. Was I not a victim, on a most extensive scale? A few days later, Mr. Peabody, the American banker, gave one of his splendid and costly entertainments at Richmond Terrace. Mr. Van Buren, who had arrived in England a few days before, was present. It was really a most superb and *recherché* dinner; with every luxury of earth, sea, and air; and to crown the whole, a concert, in which the best musicians of the Italian Opera — Grisi, Mario, &c. — performed. There were many very distinguished persons present; and as there were to be no speeches except a brief one by the American Minister, and a bit of a reply by Mr. Van Buren, I had no drawback to the pleasure of the evening. We returned to London at two o'clock. Pretty well for practical, sober Yankees.

I believe I mentioned to you a dinner-party at

Dickens's, where I met Lord C—— ; Lord S——
was also there. As this nobleman has become
somewhat distinguished in America on account of
his antislavery zeal, I will try to give you some
idea of him. He is tall, with a serious look ; with
large features, not without beauty. His manner is wholly plain, sincere, and unaffected. Some
things in his public course had not given me a
pleasant impression of him. His influence has
always been opposed to the political enfranchise-
ment of the Jews, for instance. But, on the other
hand, he devotes his time and talents to the poor,
and takes the lead in every measure for the im-
provement and elevation of the working classes.
Through his agency, nearly one hundred thousand
people, who formerly lived in filthy lanes and
crowded cellars, are now comfortably established
in neat "model houses," for which they pay a
moderate rent; and the good work is going on.
He walks about London by night as well as by
day, to see with his own eyes the gigantic mass
of vice and misery with which the city is infested ;
and the condition of the poor in the country is
equally well known to him.

Table-turning and spirit-rapping occupy the
minds of the London people, I might almost say,
more than any other subject. I have not entered
a house without hearing it discussed or seeing
experiments. The handsomest women and the
gravest men are full of wonder at the marvels they

themselves accomplish; and I have had several rather warm debates with ladies and gentlemen who persisted in seeing a mysterious law of nature in what was evidently the work of their own fingers.

At ——'s a circle was formed each night I was there, and the table went round. Nothing could be plainer, in all the cases that I saw, than that the people around the table, after getting somewhat impatient, gave it a push; and when the pushing became strong and general enough to overcome the resistance, then the table went round, *and not before.* But they protested one and all, and believed, that they did nothing, except to hold their hands and *will.* We tried it at Dickens's and at Forster's, with a fixed determination to give the experiment a perfectly fair chance; and the consequence was, in three or four long trials, that neither table, nor hat, nor anything else, moved a hair's breadth.

One day I went with Mrs. Dickens to call upon Rogers. We found him in a very good condition of mind, and ready to converse, though excessively feeble. He is now between ninety and a hundred years old. Mrs. Dickens took me, at his request, over his house, and showed me the works of art. The house is a bijou in its way, and has a most delightful view, from the back window of the drawing-room, into Green Park. It is a combination of the loveliest features of the country, in the very heart of the city. But, after all, the most interesting thing was to see this old man, — the contemporary and friend of Johnson and Burke, — -to hear his anecdotes so wittily told, and to gaze upon his face, so ancient, yet so lively, and into his clear brown eye, as he sat wrapped up in his easy chair, with a black skull-cap on his head. He showed me Mr. Webster's letters to him, one of which was written only six weeks before he died. Before I came away it was arranged that I should breakfast with him, to meet Sir D—— B—— and a few other gentlemen, on the following Monday morning.

I intended to tell you all about this breakfast, but have already used up so much paper that I must postpone it. The evening is now drawing on, and to-morrow I return to London : thence in a day or two to Paris, where P—— and the girls now are. At least they parted from me at Manchester, on Friday, intending to go to Paris yesterday.

I would not leave England without coming here ; and am very glad I did not. Love to all our friends.

V.

I LEFT London this morning, at half past nine
o'clock, for Dover and Calais, having taken a
ticket through to Paris. We travelled through a
delightful country, in all the glory of early summer; the green fields, the blossoming trees, the
rose-bushes, loaded with their glowing honors; the
day exquisite as heart could desire. I felt regret
at leaving friends in London, some of whom I shall
never see again; but I knew that all the time al-
lotted to England was spent, and it was right to
go. The South of England is quite different from
the Midland, the East, West, or North. Its phys-
iognomy is marked and peculiar, but at the same
time thoroughly English; no doubt owing, in
part, to the geological formations, which Agassiz
will explain to you.

We reached the Channel at Folkstone, and,
from that place to Dover, passed between the
" White Cliffs of Albion " and the British Channel. This sight — for the first time seen — called
up many pleasant associations, historical, poetic,
and romantic. Arriving at Dover, we had a
charming passage in a steamboat which was once
a gentleman's yacht, and is now a French gov-

ernment steamer, with a French crew and officers. Going on board I asked a question of a little boy ; " Monsieur, je ne comprends pas," was the answer. Looking up, I saw the tricolor floating in the breeze, and then I knew that I had left the dominions of the English tongue. My first essay in French was to ask the " Capitaine " at what time the steamer would start : to which he replied, " À deux heures et demi, quand les depeches de Londres serout arrivés," and as I understood this perfectly well, I thought it best to stop here, and retreat from the conversation with flying colors.

There were some twenty passengers, — a poor Frenchman who looked as if he were returning to *belle France* to die ; a party of three sisters, rather old-maidish looking, with their brother ; a mother with a very red face that spoke hogsheads of beer, and a gay daughter, in a pink dress with two or three deep flounces, pink cheeks, black eyes, and a handsome figure, which she knew too well ; a short, sturdy, thick-set Englishman, with a cane, who took his place exactly in the centre of the boat, and, planting both feet and cane firmly on the deck, stood there, a living but motionless tripod, from the moment we left Dover till we touched the pier at Calais ; a talkative Englishman, — that rare bird on the earth, with his wife, who went below to avoid sea-sickness ; and myself — engaged for the most part in studying a French manual — made up the number.

I was pleased to get a whiff of the sea-breeze again; pleased to see the Castle of Dover, picturesquely seated on a foreland, and looking out upon the Channel; and especially was I pleased to see the cliffs, so memorable for having given the name of Albion to England, and for having inspired one of the grandest passages in Shakespeare. I gazed long upon the beautiful line of these gleaming heights; but they almost vanished from sight before the shores of France rose dimly on the horizon. The sturdy Englishman took no note of the disappearance of his native land; but there he stood, like the statue of Memnon on the Theban plains, in his adamantine stolidity.

R. S—— had advised me to stop at the Hôtel Dessin; so, when the steamer came to the landing-place, and we walked ashore through the lines of officials with red trousers and swords, I shouted out, "Hôtel Dessin!" whereupon a burly but very civil *commissaire* stepped forward, and with a "Par ici, Monsieur," showed the way to an omnibus which took me to the "Douane."

The Hôtel Dessin, founded by the grandfather of the present proprietor, is the very house where Sterne commenced his "Sentimental Journey"; and one of the chambers is known by his name at the present hour. On leaving the Douane we entered the city gate, drove through some queer-looking streets, and an old square that looked like the Methuselah of squares, into another queer old street; and there stood the *Hôtel*, — plain-looking on the outside. Through the *porte-cochère* we entered a paved courtyard, where I got out of the omnibus, and was received by a polite young gentleman of a waiter, who wished to know if I desired a "chambre à coucher." "Oui, Monsieur." "Par ici, Monsieur": upon which he led me into a quadrangular garden, laid out in old-fashioned, but very pretty style, full of flowers and trees, among the branches of which a thousand birds were singing, and under which seats were placed for the visitors. From this we passed into a hall, the colored windows of which made the light most agreeable, and up a flight of stairs to "numero trente," which was to be my room. A very pleasant one it is: neatly furnished, with two mirrors, a centre-table, side-table, and bureau; and looking out upon the lovely garden, the open window letting in the soft summer air, the perfume of flowers, and the song of the birds.

By the time I had eaten my first French dinner it was nearly evening, and I sallied forth to see the city. First, I went to the old square, and amused myself with watching the cheerful groups of people, — officials with their ensigns of office, women with their neat caps, children, shopkeepers, — all chatting as fast as their tongues could run.

Noticing in one corner of the square a bookseller's shop, I stepped in; and, for the sake of

making a little conversation, I asked if he had
the Paris newspapers.   He handed me one, —
asked me some question, and from that we went
on talking of two or three subjects brought up by
books that I observed on his shelves ; one being
a copy of " La Cave du Père Tom," another a little
book upon " La Danse des Tables," as he called it.
I then bade him " Bon soir," and strolled out to
the ramparts.   From the top of them is a fine
view of the sea and the country, as well as of the
town of Calais.   Having spent about an hour
longer very agreeably in this manner, sometimes
asking questions for the sake of a little exercise in
French, I returned to the hotel.

VI.

PARIS, Sunday, June 12.

AT eight o'clock on Thursday morning the train was to start for Paris; so I had to be up betimes. It was a pretty long journey. The country, for a great part of the way, is flat; and the land not so trim, neat, and carefully cultivated as in England; but the little villages and the farm-houses are much the same in external appearance.

I had bought of my bookseller at Calais a copy of "La Danse des Tables," and one of a play now having a good reception in Paris, called "L'Honneur et l'Argent," — so that I had amusement enough all day. The first-named book is curious, and shows that this fantastic humbug has taken a strong hold of people here. In Germany, still more. They call the spirit-rappers there "Klopf-geister," — *knock-ghosts*, — and the stories circulat-ed are of the intensest nonsense. They carry the moving much farther than we do. They have dis-covered that if, instead of a table, a man is placed in the centre, in a short time the fluid acts upon him, as it does upon tables and hats; and he whirls round in spite of himself, from right to left, as long as the experiment lasts.

I had a very delightful journey, keeping both eyes wide open and listening to the conversation, and I am really pleased to find how well I can get along. We arrived at Paris at five o'clock; but as the passengers were cooped up for some time longer in a room at the custom-house, to have their luggage examined, we did not get fairly into the city until after six.

Driving to the Hôtel Meurice, I found that P—— had left it, and taken rooms in the Rue de Luxemburg, No. 25, where we are all now quietly established.

I have seen but few places yet; but have passed through the state-rooms of the Tuileries, — and magnificent they are, — and the galleries of the Louvre, which are endless. I have walked through all the principal streets of Paris. Yesterday we all went to the Hippodrome, and saw some good riding and driving; among the rest a capital representation of an ancient four-horse chariot race, — only the drivers were women, superbly dressed in Greek costume. To-day L—— and I attended service in the church of Notre Dame de Paris.

Mr. T—— called this afternoon; A—— also: and in a little while in walked M. Ampère. He was very cordial; and inquired after the A——s with great interest. We are all going to hear his lectures, and several other courses, in the Collége de France.

July 6.—To-morrow we set out for Germany and Switzerland, having passed a very agreeable and instructive month in this gay capital. We have liked our apartments much. We found it more comfortable, as well as more economical, to keep house; so we hired a good cook who was recommended to us, and who has proved to be faithful and honest, and have lived as we pleased. We are nearly in the centre of Paris. Our street takes us in two minutes to the delightful gardens of the Tuileries, a few rods from which is the Place de la Concorde,—the most magnificent assemblage of interesting objects;—the Champs Élysées on one side; on the other, the galleries of the Louvre, and the Place de Carrousel. The Place Vendôme, with the glorious column, is in the next street; and the Boulevards are within a stone's throw. The Cathedral of Notre Dame is at a considerable distance, on the island, an ancient part of the city; but the exquisite church of the Madeleine is just round the corner.

Our stay here has been anything but idle;—a French lesson from a very good teacher, who has come every morning, for an hour; then, generally, reading for an hour or two; and the rest of the day spent in seeing the libraries, collections, churches, and public places of the city; or attending lectures at the Collége de France and the Sorbonne. I have heard as many lectures as I could of Ampère's course; and a portion of Philarète

Chasles's, who closed his course with a rhapsody about Miss Harriet Farley, the Editor of the Lowell Offering. These lectures are attended not only by young fellows like me, but by old gentlemen decorated with the ribbon of the Legion of Honor, old ladies, who sometimes bring their sewing, and young ladies, who take notes.

I have been at several of the theatres; not often, yet often enough to understand the character of dramatic art here. Last Saturday, the piece called " Bertrand et Raton " was performed by command of the Emperor, at the Théâtre Français. I had seen it once, but had not seen their Majesties; so we all went, having procured tickets with some difficulty. We had a good box, from which we could see the whole house (and a most brilliant one it was) and the imperial box. Their Majesties came in at the commencement of the principal piece. There was some applause in the pit, but not much in the boxes, except in ours. G——— and I shouted " Vive l'Empereur! " and "Vive l'Impératrice ! " at the top of our voices, and some moustached Frenchmen, in our neighborhood, peeped round to see who those fierce imperialists were. The Emperor looked well; his dress being simple, except the grand order of the Legion of Honor. The Empress is a woman of sweet and gracious beauty. In an age of chivalry, she would be worshipped. She was dressed in pure white, with superb diamond ornaments, flashing from the most beautiful arms and neck in France.

The imperial pair behaved very much like other people ; chatted and laughed together ; applauded the good hits in the piece ; used their opera-glasses to spy out their friends ; and when the play was over, withdrew quietly to go home. At the door of the theatre a large crowd had assembled, and the imperial cortége was saluted again with acclamations as it passed on under a strong guard of mounted troops.

Napoleon is making this city the most splendid in the world. Many streets he is almost entirely rebuilding ; ancient churches he is clearing from the rubbish of ages, and restoring ; old tumble-down houses he is removing. This business has become so important, that a *Bureau des Démolitions* has been established near the Hôtel de Ville, and it has become a common joke to say of such or such a man, " He belongs to the new class in society, — *la classe des démolis.*" The people have no objection to all this : it puts vast sums of money in circulation ; furnishes employment to thousands of workmen ; the " demolished " get heavy damages ; and the expenditure will be more than made up to the country by the increased value of property, and the enhanced splendors of Paris. The army is in the highest state of efficiency. They want to fight, especially with Russia, as an old soldier at the Invalides said to me, " Pour se venger des Cossaques." The Emperor reviews them often in person ; and has gained great popularity by taking the command and manœuvring them himself.

Most of the royalists — at least, the most rational and the best informed among them — support the Emperor, as the least of two evils. I have made the acquaintance of several of the most eminent men belonging to this party here. One, M. D——, who lives apart from politics, and more in the past than the present, gave me a great deal of very interesting information. He is quite a gentleman of the old school, — handsome, grave, almost sad in expression, — with pale face and gray hair, high and white forehead, — with a white cravat at eight o'clock in the morning. His manner is frank, genial, and urbane.

He said at once, "I am a Catholic and a royalist; what are you?"

"I am a Unitarian and a republican."

"Ah," said he, "I cannot conceive a religion without a belief in Jesus Christ."

I said, "We, too, believe in Jesus Christ," and attempted to explain, as well as I could, in my imperfect French, the different shades of belief prevalent among the Unitarians, — that we did not believe Christ to be God, but many of us believed him to be more than man.

"To me," he answered, "Jesus Christ is God. I say these things, not in a proselyting spirit, but to let you see my manner of thinking, — *ma manière de penser.* I accept the dogmas of the Catholic Church as the truth of God."

Speaking of the influence of government on

religion, he pronounced it "fatal," "*funeste.*"
Speaking of books he said, "You must read Bossuet." I told him I had read the "Oraisons Funèbres." "Then read his work on the Errors of Protestantism." "I have read it, and am yet a Protestant."

He told me he thought Reyboul of Nîmes the first poet of the age in France, — that he had written passages as good as any in Racine ; and he recited a tender and exquisite little poem called "L'Ange et l'Enfant," with so much feeling and elegance, that I resolved to get his works.

Another very eminent royalist is the Marquis de la Rochejaquelein, who has just published a book on the present state of France. He is the son of the famous La Rochejaquelein, of Vendean memory, whose history you know ; and he possesses much of his father's spirit and talent. I went to see him with a letter of introduction from M. Defresne. I found him in a handsome apartment, and living in elegant style. He is very stout, tall, and powerful in person, — his features regular, and his whole expression amiable. He was cordial and hearty in his reception of me. Speaking of his own work, on "The Condition of France," he said : "It contains the truth, and this is the reason why nobody has attacked me for it. I had nothing to do with the overthrow of the Republic ; but a republic is not suited to the French people. I support the present government, not from sentiment, but from

reason. I am a royalist; but I see that the Prince
Napoleon has saved the country from anarchy.
His government is not, in itself, the government of
my choice. But if you go to a man, and say to him,
' My dear Sir, your house is badly built, and is out
of repair: the ceiling has fallen in; the walls are
broken; it lets in the cold; it lets in the rain and
the wind, — why don't you leave it ? ' and the poor
man answers, ' All this is very true ; but, under the
present circumstances, it is the best I can get; it is
the only one possible ' ; — what can you say ? "

I told him that I had been much instructed by
his book, but that, in conversation with a lady the
other day, on my remarking that, so far as I could
judge, Louis Napoleon had saved France from a
civil war, her answer was, " I prefer civil war
to the present state of things."

" Ah," said La Rochejaquelein, " there would
have been a civil war; but not in the ordinary
sense of the term. I understand very well what
civil war means between two great parties, — or
where some profound principle is at stake, as in
the Vendean war. But in France, at the time of
the *coup d'état*, there were several parties, and
many subordinate factions. The Socialists were
split up into three or four sections, which, instead
of combining, would have fought one another; and
so of other parties. It would have been a civil war
with many sides; it would have been anarchy and
chaos; and anarchy and chaos would have led in-

evitably to despotism. We have a despotism now, it is true; but its conditions are such that it has no need of cruelty, and it is not cruel. In the other case, the despotism would have been driven into cruelty by the force of circumstances, — by the exasperation of the struggle. I prefer things as they are. But there are many *têtes montées*, who think otherwise. There is Madame ——, from America.   They are *braves gens;* but Madame —— admires Ledru Rollin, Louis Blanc, Mazzini, Kossuth, — *tous ces aventuriers, ces ambitieux*, — who do much harm in the world. I like Madame —— much; she has *beaucoup d'esprit, beaucoup d'intelligence;* she has read much, but knows nothing, absolutely nothing, of France."

When I took leave of him, he said, " I shall come and see you in Cambridge, when we can travel by the electric telegraph, — and we shall come to that at last. But I am too old to go so far in any other way. Ah! it would be a fine thing to go from Paris to Boston in half a minute ! "

One of the pleasantest things that has happened to me here is the making the acquaintance of Jasmin, the poet of Agen. You know something about him. Longfellow translated one of his pieces, — " The Blind Girl of Castel-Cuillè." I wish you would read that translation in connection with what I am going to tell you.

He was a poor boy, apprenticed to a barber at Agen in the South of France ; but he early showed extraordinary poetical talent, composing in his native dialect, the Gascon. This has been a *patois* for the last three or four centuries; but it is in fact the representative of the language of the Troubadours. It is more rhythmical than the French, and is free from its nasal tones, resembling the Italian and Spanish. Jasmin, in the intervals of hair-dressing, wrote in this dialect, and recited his pieces to his countrymen. They were aroused to enthusiasm by this poetical delineation of their daily life, and his fame soon spread far and near. Wherever he went, multitudes gathered around him, and the days of old King René and the Troubadours seemed to have returned. In the course of time, the French scholars and critics found this poetical phenomenon worthy of their attention. A poem of his, called *Françonette*, established his fame. To make a long story short, he has published three volumes of poems under the title of *Las Papillotos*, or " Curl-Papers," without abandoning his original profession of barber. The last volume has been crowned with a prize of five thousand francs by the French Academy, and when I arrived in Paris he was here to make his acknowledgments.

I had been invited to meet him at the *salon* of Madame Blaze de Bury, — a sort of Madame de Staël, — author of a work in French on Austria, Hungary, &c. Well, I went. The company was small, and what they call *choisie*. Jasmin was, of course, the lion, as he has been everywhere in Paris. He talks with immense rapidity, fire, and animation, — is very frank and hearty in his manners, — speaks with freedom of himself and his works, — and is, in all respects, a child of nature, and that nature Southern. He is now about fifty-five years old, with a face of infinite expression, and already marked with deep lines traced by the ardent emotions that have inspired his poetical career. His dark hair and complexion, his flashing eye and varying voice, present an exterior perfectly in harmony with his genius. We had the great and rare pleasure of hearing him recite some of his best pieces ; and what a singular exhibition it was ! It was not acting ; it was not declamation ; but it was a reproduction of the poetical spirit of the pieces, by voice, eye, hand, attitude, and gesture. It was wonderful and perfect. He was possessed and overmastered by the inspiration. Perhaps you remember what I said in my lectures about the old Ionian rhapsodists ; — he is a perfect illustration. In the pathetic passages he wept with uncontrollable feeling ; and I saw the tears flowing down many a cheek.

I had a long conversation with him, and was greatly delighted with his unaffected good sense, as well as with his incomparable vivacity ; and I could perfectly understand the fact, that on many occasions he has been listened to by four or five thousand people, with an indescribable enthusiasm, — that he has filled the theatres of Southern France, when even Rachel had half the boxes empty.

But these exhibitions have not been for himself; they have been for charitable objects.   He has poured wealth into the treasuries of public institutions; he has finished churches that had remained unfinished for centuries; and the cities of the South have vied with one another in bestowing public honors on their poetical benefactor. Two cities have granted him their arms; others have sent him superb seal-rings; others, the freedom of the corporation. The French Academy has decreed that his language is a national language, and that he is a national poet; and the higher literary celebrities of France study and applaud his works. I have sent home some books, and among them is a copy of *Las Papillotos*, in which he has written a few lines, and marked the pieces he recited at Lady Bury's. Since Lady Bury's *soirée* I have seen him many times, and he has come to see us. I have seen on his table the cards of the greatest names in Paris; and the most celebrated *salons* have striven eagerly to secure his presence. His stay here has been a round of the most brilliant triumphs.

A week ago, he with his wife and son breakfasted with us, and I do not know that I ever enjoyed anything more. After breakfast, at my request, he read one of his poems. I was anxious that L—— and H—— should hear him.

The night before last M. and Mme. Jasmin spent the evening here. We invited our fellow-passengers, Mr. and Mrs. I——, and a few others, to come. They remained several hours, and Jasmin not only read one of his best pieces, but sang a song, which is introduced into one of the longer poems, to a popular air of the South. All agreed that the entertainment of the evening was one of the most delightful we had had in Paris.

The bust of Jasmin has been taken recently. Portraits innumerable were already in existence. I was looking at the bust with him one day, and asked him what he thought of it. He took my memorandum-book and wrote, in his language, an epigram, which I translate as follows:

> "Though we 're alike, the likeness is but small:
>   I talk too much; the bust talks not at all."

I forgot to mention, that after breakfast the other morning, little E—— came into the room fresh as a rose. Her bright, animated face, intelligent and sparkling eyes, and unusually fresh coloring delighted the poet. He took her in his arms and kissed her again and again; and seeing my writing-desk open, he sat down and wrote a little poem, marked by great sweetness and beauty. You may be sure that H—— keeps it as a precious memorial.

I could fill up many pages with Jasmin; but time is passing on, and we leave Paris at one o'clock to-day. I sent the other day to —— a copy of the "Journal des Débats," containing M. Mignet's Éloge on Jouffroy. I had the good fortune to hear it, at the annual *séance* of the Institute, to which M. Ampère gave me a ticket of admission. It was delivered in the best style of academic eloquence, and the occasion was one of unusual interest. I have attended also one of the ordinary meetings of the Institute.

A word about Reyboul, the poet. You will find two volumes of his in the parcel of books. Read particularly " L'Ange et l'Enfant"; and you will agree with M. Defresne. Reyboul is a baker. An artist here in Paris told me he went once to Nîmes to see him. Calling on him at ten o'clock, he inquired for M. Reyboul. "Do you wish to see Reyboul the baker, or Reyboul the poet?" "Reyboul the poet." "Be so good, then, as to call again at five o'clock, P. M., and you will find him here." He passed the day as well as he could, and at five called again. Seeing the same person, he said, "Why, I had the honor of seeing you this morning." "Yes, but I was then Reyboul the baker; I am now Reyboul the poet."

VII.

Frankfort-on-the-Main, July 13, 1853.

I WROTE last under the spire of the Strasburg Minster. From Strasburg we went to Baden-Baden, a beautifully situated place, nestled among the mountains, but shamefully perverted to the Devil's worst worship, — gambling. I did not go to see the famous hell; but we all spent the greater part of the day in going up to the old castle, which overlooks the town from the brow of a neighboring hill. It is an immense structure; but the walls have fallen, and trees have grown in their crevices, and have toppled down, lying now across halls and chambers, and intermingling their green with the dark-red ruins around. There are steps along the walls, and bridges or walks around some of the apartments as you ascend from story to story. One old tower is nearly entire, and from its summit the black mountains, the Baden valley, and the distant Rhine are in sight, forming one of the grandest pictures anywhere to be seen. Some one has placed a huge Æolian harp high up in an opening of the wall; and as there is always a fresh breeze, the endless passages, halls, enclosures, and chambers of the old castle are filled with a wailing sound, which one might mistake in the night for the eternal moaning of some lovelorn Ermengarde, who, forced by her father, the iron-hearted Baron Ruprecht, to marry a grisly old count from the Black Forest, though she was in love with the yellow-haired Blondel, — brave as he was graceful, skilled alike in feats of arms and in playing *min-nelieder* on the cithern, — threw herself headlong from the wall, in the vain hope, not only of escaping the hated nuptials, — which she effectually did, — but of ending her sorrows with her life. There now, that sentence contains the germ of a romance, in three volumes. Take it, and add all the rest.

Seriously, it is a wonderful old castle, and is worth a hundred histories to give one an idea of the Middle Ages.

From Baden we went to Heidelberg, where we passed nearly two days. I called on Professor Bähr, — the editor of Herodotus. He took me over the library, showed me the precious collection of old manuscripts, and many other things of the highest interest in a literary point of view.

After this, I clambered up alone to the Castle of Heidelberg, which also is a very interesting bit of mediæval and modern history. The old tun is watched over by the statue of the prince's jester, who used to drink from fifty to a hundred bottles a day. His painted eye rolls with a kind of leering regret toward the empty giant;

and when you knock against the sides of the tun, a
hollow and melancholy sound reverberates through
the cellar, seeming to say, " Vanity of vanities,
— all is vanity !"   The knights, who stand in
niches along the walls, are weather-stained and battered by storms and leaden bullets; and, though
venerable, are gradually crumbling into dust. But
the green ivy, winding over many parts of the
walls, has taken a playful freak to caress one of
the old men of stone, and has formed a verdant
frame, with an arch over his head ; and there he
stands, in a kind of sandstone amazement, looking silently down from his perch of centuries,
apparently thinking himself a good deal better off
than his neighbors.

From Heidelberg we came to Frankfort, where
I am now writing. We arrived last evening, and
you may be sure I was not long in finding my
way to the monument of Goethe, — one of the
noblest works of Schwanthaler, and perhaps the
very noblest tribute ever paid by Art to Poetry.
I saw it first in the lessening light of evening ;
next, under that of the moon ; and again, this
morning, twice, in the full light of day.

I went from the monument, last night, to the
house where Goethe was born. It is an old
mansion, — not in what is now the best street
of Frankfort, — but spacious, rising three or four
stories, each projecting a little over those below.
Oddly enough, Menzel, in his violent attack on

Goethe, accuses him of sympathizing only with the *porcelain* part of the human race ; and now the ground floor of the house where he was born has become a *porcelain shop !* The upper stories are occupied by families, apparently of people in the working-classes, though the general aspect of the house, especially the spacious hall, the broad staircase, and the landings, give evidence of its former patrician and stately character. Goethe's study, where he wrote many of his early pieces, is kept sacred — to sixpences. A drawing of his, some pieces of his handwriting, the bed where he slept, several figures, a portrait, and some other memorials, were shown to us. We entered our names in the visitor's book, paid the slatternly German a few kreutzers, and left the house.

I tried to find where Goethe, the father, was buried, but could not. The stiff old patrician has passed as completely out of the memory, as he has out of the sight, of the city in which he was once a very conspicuous figure. Goethe himself lies buried in Weimar, by the side of the Grand Duke.

We went to see Danneker's Ariadne, in a pavilion in the gardens belonging to Bethmann, the banker. I have seen many engravings of it, but none that gave the slightest idea of the wonderful grace and beauty of the original. It is placed in a room, under a light coming through a colored medium, — the purple light, so often sung by poets, — and the loveliness of the effect is indescribable. None of the praises bestowed upon this work have been exaggerated.

From here we strolled through the delightful gardens of the suburbs; then through some of the narrow streets, and the markets, where the market-women were selling, in provincial German, their vegetables and fruits. The old Cathedral, where the Emperors were crowned, as long as Emperors were, is surrounded by these markets. We went in, — saw the throne and other imperial mementos, — looked at the old pictures, statues, blazons, that hang on the walls, — and then betook ourselves to the *Kaisersaal*, a hall of the Emperors, where they all stand painted by the best masters of the Düsseldorf school, and filling niches in the wall.

3 *

VIII.

DRESDEN, July 22, 1853.

FROM Frankfort we went to Mentz, where we
saw the Cathedral, just as the gloom of evening was coming on. It gave a solemn effect to
the quaint old aisles, crowded with the statues of
mitréd princes who once ruled as military priests
over this beautiful region. I do not know that I
have ever felt a profounder solemnity than in
walking through the cloisters of the older parts of
the Cathedral, paved with tombstones of the ancient abbots, whose carved likenesses, half effaced
by the footsteps of the generations that have succeeded them, still looked up through the shadowy
light of evening, with a stony silence that went to
my heart more than any human speech. As I
was walking, in deep meditation, over these name-
less ecclesiastics, suddenly I came upon the monument of Frauenlob, the Minnesinger. I had
forgotten that he was buried here; and the surprise and pleasure I experienced were like the joy
of an unexpected meeting with an old friend. I
always had a liking for this poet; he was a warm-
hearted, noble old minstrel; true in his devotion
to women, and so much beloved by them that

eight of them bore his body to the grave, and poured over the tomb so much wine that it over-flowed the neighboring cloisters. These facts are duly commemorated on the monument. A statue of Frauenlob has recently been erected near the tomb.

From Mentz we went on board the steamer, to make the voyage down the Rhine. There had been a heavy thunder-storm the night before, and the sky was still overcast. Soon rain came on, with intervals of sunshine, that gave a very singular and striking aspect to the scene.

The rest of the party, fearing a stormy day, and unwilling to lose the beauties of the Rhine scenery, stopped at Bingen, but I continued my journey, being desirous of seeing the city of Bonn and its University. I was not sorry I did; for though there were showers through the day, they only gave an additional variety to the celebrated, but not too celebrated, region of vineyards, castles, crags, and beautiful villages through which this river flows. There were some droll people on board: among them an American, who looked a long time in vain on his map for Cologne; and when a gentleman, better informed, pointed out *Cöln* as the place he was seeking, said, " Wall, now, who would have thought that C-o-l-n spelt Cologne?" Most of the passengers spent their time in eating, drinking, and smoking. Not so an English mother and two sentimental daughters, who were constantly calling to each other with the invariable question, " Is not that very picturesque ? "

I reached Bonn before evening, and immediately went to see Professor Welcker, — one of the best classical scholars in Germany, and one of the most amiable men. I spent the evening very pleasantly in his company. He has visited Greece, and could give me many interesting and valuable details. The next morning I called on the Baron von Rönne, — formerly the Prussian Minister to the United States. He was very kind and courteous ; gave me nearly the whole forenoon, taking me to see all the objects of interest in Bonn, and introducing me to Professor Simrock, whom I was very glad to know, as I had long known his works.

Baron von Rönne told me he had translated Webster's letter to Hülsemann. He admired Webster much, and deplored his death as a calamity to the whole world. I begged him to give me a copy of his translation, which he did. It is an interesting fact for Mr. Webster's biography.

I dined with Professor Welcker, and in the afternoon took the train for Cologne, where I found the rest of the party. There is but little there except the Cathedral, and that is one of the wonders of the world. I was glad there was nothing else to break or disturb the impression of this marvellous old pile, with its massive columns, wonderful colored windows, and grand roof. It is still incomplete, and will be so for many years; but, in its way, it fills the mind with a sense of sublimity that leaves nothing to be desired.

From Cologne we made a long day's journey to Berlin, where we passed two or three days; not without interest, but not so profitably as I expected. I saw Professor Ritter, a fine, healthy, pleasant old gentleman. He spoke with great regard of Mr. Guyot, and was very obliging to me. We spent nearly half a day in the royal palace, the King being absent at Potsdam, his usual summer residence.

There is a collection of queer old things in the upper rooms — or garrets — of the palace : quantities of antique furniture, carvings in ivory, old rusty swords, cocked hats worn by ancient kings and generals. But the oddest thing of all is a wax figure of Frederic the Great, with the clothes, staff, boots, and cocked hat he wore when alive, sitting in an old chair, and looking with a droll expression over the motley assemblage of ricoco by which he is surrounded. He made such an uproar in the world while he was alive, that I could not help wondering he should sit so quietly now; and I half expected to see him jump up with a mighty oath, or kick the old rickety furniture into a thousand pieces. On another side of the same room is a cast taken from him after death, — a thin, dismal-looking face, with the mouth twisted into a horrible contortion by the last agonies; and lying by it, as if to ridicule the presumption of the old King, is a sentence from one of his letters to D'Alembert, — "I will keep a smiling countenance when they bury me." To see this terror of the earth, this mighty warrior, this friend of Voltaire, this would-be model of conqueror, philosopher, king, sitting in wax to be stared at by strangers in his own garret, for a silver groschen apiece, is something of a lesson on the vanity of human greatness.

In the afternoon of the same day we went down to Potsdam, to call on Humboldt, who is always the King's guest, and to see the gardens of Sans-Souci. I sent Agassiz's letter to Humboldt's apartments, with an inquiry whether he would see us then, or would appoint some other hour. He was going out to dine with the King, but would receive us for a few minutes. I never saw a man who was so well represented by the prints; — the likeness is most remarkable. He seemed well and vigorous; asked about Agassiz, spoke of him in affectionate terms, and wished to know why he did not come over to see him.

I told him he would probably come out next summer.

"Ah," said Humboldt, "I shall not be here to welcome him."

I said I trusted he would "live and labor for many years to come."

He shook his head, and said he was too old for

that. We gave him a copy of the "Webster Memorial." He expressed the highest opinion of Mr. Webster, but seemed very indignant at the Fugitive Slave Law, which he appeared to think was a law to reduce all the blacks to slavery.

"Here in Prussia," said he, "every man is free; but in America you make men slaves."

I said there were constitutional relations of the subject, not easily understood abroad; but that no Northern man in the United States was a friend of slavery.

I was tempted to say something about Prussian freedom; — to ask how it happened that I could not enter Prussia without a passport? that on arriving at Berlin I had to send my passport to the police? and how long would the Baron von Humboldt himself be free, if he should profess republican principles, or apply to the conduct of the King, in destroying the constitution, the epithets it deserves? What if he should suddenly say to the King: "Sir, your subjects have been deprived of their rights. They have a right to participate in the affairs of government; and by a stroke of perfidy you have robbed them of it. In your distress you promised constitutional privileges to your people; they confided in you: you have betrayed their confidence. Restore to them what you have wrongfully taken. Make Prussians free. Give them the *habeas corpus.* Take away your armies, who devour the substance of the nation, giving nothing in return, except support to despotism"?

All these thoughts passed through my mind, while Humboldt was — rather rudely I thought, certainly violently — disparaging our country as compared with Prussia. But I reflected that he was not only a very eminent, but a very old man ; and it was not for me to bandy words with him on any subject. So I merely said that I brought the book as a mark of respect to him, thinking it would be gratifying to him to know that his " Cosmos " was one of the last works studied by a person so eminent as Mr. Webster ; — that, of course, there would be different views upon practical questions of humanity, and every man must form his own.

The old gentleman then said : " The book will have the greatest interest for me. I regard Mr. Webster as a most eminent intellect ; and I am *much glorified* that he has occupied himself with my book. But I am deeply concerned about slavery ; and I am sorry Mr. Webster had anything to do with it. *I would not have put my name to it.* Whatever political necessity may require, the individual need not, unless he chooses, connect himself with it." I reminded him that Mr. Webster was not in the Senate when the law was passed ; that " some of its features were not such as Mr. Webster approved, — though there was no doubt that Mr. Webster was in favor of sustaining the Constitution, on this as well as on all other points." He said : " I am glad to hear that ; I supposed he was in the legislature. I am still sorry he said anything in its favor. Perhaps, however, I shall take a different view." The conversation then passed on to other subjects.

The afternoon was rainy, so that we could see only a part of the objects of interest in Potsdam. The superb apartments of the Chateau de Ville — abounding with touching memorials of Queen Louisa, whose beauty and virtues form the brightest page in the history of Prussia — we had the pleasure of thoroughly exploring. We went into the old church, and descended into the plain vault, where Frederic the Great and his father lie, side by side. I placed my hand on his coffin, and a hollow, empty sound came forth. This narrow zinc box, and the wax figure in the Berlin garret, alike say, "*Vanity of vanities.*"

We came from Berlin to Dresden, thinking we might possibly stay here a week or two.

Dresden has one of the two best picture-galleries in the world. We have spent a good deal of time there ; and when I tell you, that in one ,room, and within the range of sight as you sit on one side of it, you have Carlo Dolce's St. Cecilia, Raphael's Madonna di San Sisto, and Correggio's most famous Holy Family, I need add nothing more. I sat there one day until it seemed as if the figures were alive, and I had passed away from earth. I certainly never knew before the power of painting ; and I set down the sight of these most glorious works as an important epoch in my intellectual life. The birthplace of Shakespeare, the living poetry of Jasmin, the Cathedrals of Strasburg and Cologne, the glorious Rhine in its summer robes, the Madonna di San Sisto, form a series of luminous points that seem to suffuse the long journey through which I have passed with a supernatural light.

Another most extraordinary thing at Dresden is the collection of ancient suits of armor. In long lines stand portrait-figures of horses and knights, wearing the coats of steel they wore in life ; lifting their battle-axes, or holding their enormous lances in rest. You think yourself in the presence of the Middle Ages; you expect to see the horses spring forward, and to hear the clang of battle ; and you forget that you are in the nineteenth century, and that these figures are there only to tell us what has been. It is a wonderful scene, which no language can describe, — so vividly does it bring the past and its mighty actors before you. You see the dents in the breastplates, — the breaks in the coats of mail, — the cuts in the helmets; you handle the faded finery of the embroidered robes worn on the battle-field ; you mark the bloody stains; you gaze upon the Black Knights, actually crossing their ponderous lances, which they wielded in a duel for life or death.

IX.

AS it is now somewhat more than a fortnight since I wrote last, I will resume my story where I left off. My last letter was finished at Leipsic, and despatched through the post-office there. In the hurry of travelling, and the constant occupation of the time we spend at the several places, I am obliged to write hastily, and to send off my letters without reading them over; so that if you read any portions of them to other people, pray amend the violations of grammar, and all the faults with which they abound.

Here in Switzerland we are likely to have a breathing-time; so I will give you a little account of two or three practical matters, which, in the din of cities and the pressure of arts, literature, and science, had almost escaped my attention. I dare say you imagine me flourishing in Parisian garments from head to foot. On the contrary, I found on my arrival in England I could supply a considerable quantity of clothing to some of the crew, and when I went to Paris I left one carpet-bag in London. My old gray cap was thought not to be the thing in London; so, in deference to the opinions of others, I bought a new hat; but the London weather soon reduced it to a condition more easily imagined than described, — perhaps it would not be going too far to say that it looked nearly as bad as ——'s best. Further attempts were made (which I firmly resisted) to induce me to get another. I traversed England and Scotland; crossed the Channel; figured a month in France; entered Germany; visited its principal cities, and arrived at Munich with my London hat. It was storm-beaten; it was covered with the dust and cobwebs of ancient steeples and towers; it was knocked in before, behind, and on both sides; it had been battered against the cross-pieces of doors to crypts, and dungeons, and chambers of torture underground, where the light of day never comes; it had been sat on, like a murdered body by a coroner's inquest: but I still wore it; I had an affection for it; "I loved it for the dangers it had passed," and I defied the jeers of the world and the entreaties of friends. At last it ran against some old weapon of the Middle Ages, which had been used in the Crusades to cut off the heads of the unbelievers, — and "what a rent the envious Casca made!" Still, it appeared to me that this ghastly wound might be useful for ventilation; but there are points beyond which — such is the imperfect constitution of our moral nature — it is impossible for the individual to resist

> " the world's dread laugh,
> Which scarce the firm philosopher can scorn."

I bought a new hat in Munich, — city of the arts. The woman of whom I bought it eyed the old one with a quizzical look, and asked if she should send it to my hotel. " Nein," said I, " geben sie ihn einem Armen,"—" No, give it to some poor man," — and so I left it, to run a second honorable career in the service of humanity. My new one still has a strange, uncomfortable feeling. It is heavy, as if made to resist a battle-axe, and I have no doubt it would; for though I have worn it a fortnight, not a dent or break is yet to be seen on its shining surface.

I believe I have not told you anything about cookery yet. It has been a matter of considerable indifference, so many other things have occupied me. But a word or two on that interesting matter will help complete the picture of " the Professor in Europe." In England, I found it much the same as at home. In Paris we lived, by preference, in a very simple manner, ordering but few dishes, and plainly cooked. At the great restaurants, where I dined two or three times, I liked some of the dishes, — particularly two or three of the soups, — and the *turbot à la crême* very much ; all the rest did not please me. When we came into Germany we stopped always at the best hotels. The *table-d'hôte* I tried to like. I did my best to look upon it in what the Germans call a

" world-historical " — i. e. a cosmopolitan — point
of view ; — but all in vain.

They give you a soup, of which grease and
onions are the only distinguishable elements. They
pass round about ten courses of meat, so mixed,
blended, and travestied with seasonings and vegetables that it would puzzle a Philadelphia lawyer
to tell what any of them is made of ; — not one
having the remotest resemblance to the natural
taste of any one of the animals seen in Peter's
vision, and all of them most repulsive to me.

In the midst of the dinner they hand you an
indescribable pudding, sweetmeats, fruits, and
the like. Your potatoes are dressed with car-
away-seeds, and your bread is spiced with the
same. You have green peas and beans stewed in
sugar, and such a stew ! It is a literal fact, that I
have not eaten a dinner since we have been in
Germany. As the dishes have passed round, I
have taken what looked to me most like human
food ; but I could not eat, — and I have, in every
case, fulfilled the rule of Dr. W——, to leave the
table as hungry as I sat down. One does well
enough at breakfast, — one can get good coffee,
and bread and butter ; and once I succeeded in
finding a bit of smoked salmon. The only things
I have eaten with relish are the sandwiches I have
bought at railroad-stations. Alas ! with what a
tender remorse have I recalled the indifference
with which I have eaten a plain, but excellent

dinner every day at home. Boiled chickens with a slice of pork, and potatoes undisguised by oceans of grease, whither are ye fled? Roast mutton, — is it a dream? Beef-steak, — is it only a phantom?

How do you think they get you up a steak here, as we experienced to-day on the summit of Uetliberg? Why, they boiled the beef; then singed it a little; then poured hot water over it, into which they put a piece of butter; then covered it with chopped onion-leaves! I asked the waiter what they called it in German. He said: "Bif-stek. It is an English dish, and the Germans have no name for it." I thought of the poet's awful "deed without a name."

Besides these particulars, there is a universal savor of onion. Even boiled eggs have it. I shall never look at an onion again as long as I live. I assure you, the idea of the superiority of Continental cookery over American is as much a superstition as that of the greater size of Eng-lishmen. Nor is there one of the arrangements of life more agreeable or convenient than our own, and most of them are, to my taste, immeasurably inferior. You have read and heard often about the odd custom the Germans have of sleeping between two beds. It looks droll: but by taking the upper layer, rolling it up and putting the pil-low on the top of it, one can sleep pretty comfort-ably.

After all, perhaps the German way of living is

as rational as any other, and habit alone makes the difference. I see I have occupied considerable space with these details. Do not imagine that I attach the slightest importance to them. I can live anywhere and anyhow, and I have not-experienced the least inconvenience from this utter contradiction to all my tastes and habits. I have only written these things out as a part of my experience, and to show at the same time how well satisfied I am with our American simplicity of life in comparison with the more elaborate style of the continent of Europe.

I have now completed my travels in Germany. In all essential respects, my hopes have been more than equalled. I like the Germans heartily. I like their language and literature; their zeal for learning and science; their good-humor and simplicity, which I have found absolutely universal. Their libraries and collections of art are admirable, and admirably employed.

But there is a deep dissatisfaction, in the minds of the most eminent men, with the state of things in Europe. They have no hope; and where hope has gone out of the heart of the great men of a nation, it is sad for that nation. So far as I have conversed with them, they universally look to our country for the future progress of literature and science. The depth and extent of this feeling, both of despair for Europe and of hope for America, greatly surprised me.

Humboldt is the only man who did not express
it; but he, noble-hearted as he is, is an aristocrat
by birth, by association, by taste; he has always
been the friend, companion, confidant of kings,
and does not sympathize with the aspirations of
the republic of letters here. With this single
exception, I did not converse with one man of
letters or science in Germany who did not envy
the position enjoyed by men of letters and science
in America; who did not freely declare the conviction that America is fast getting the start
of Europe, and will soon outrun her in the
race. And I must say, that, though the treasures
of art and the accumulations of centuries will
always make Europe a school and a storehouse
for American scholars, and a tour in Europe will
always be a source of delight to the man of taste,
of science, or of art, what I have seen and heard
here has convinced me that America is the hope
of the world for literature and science, as well as
for liberty. I thank God for the inexpressible
pleasure and benefit I am drawing from my studies and travels, even for a single year, in the Old
World; but still more do I thank God that he has
cast my lot, my fortunes, my hopes, in the New.
I shall return with a much clearer insight into
the condition of the world; a higher sense of the
greatness of our own position as Americans; and
a stronger hope that we shall not fail to meet the
expectations of mankind, and sustain the responsi-

bilities the Almighty has laid upon us. I began this letter in a lighter mood; but the tone has changed, in spite of me. I shall write immeately from Lucerne; for I have a thousand things to say about dear old Germany. God bless her, in spite of her *table-d'hôte.*

X.

LUCERNE, August 14, 1853.

MY last letter was written from Zurich. In most respects our journey has been very fortunate. In the first place, the seasons have suited us exactly. We were in England at the right time to see the beauty of an English spring, as well as during the busy season of London. June was just the month for Paris, and France ; July and August, for Germany and Switzerland. Then, with the exception of ten days in England, the weather has been most favorable ; and even those ten days were desirable, to show us what an English climate could do, if it tried. It has been about as warm in Germany as we have it in Cambridge ; and this has made it sometimes a little uncomfortable to go about, in the cities, visiting the collections. But, on the whole, we have had but little inconvenience, and have seen the best of everything, without troubling ourselves to see everything.

In England, we had the summit of modern power, with the Middle Ages breaking through the surface, and here and there memorials of Roman civilization. In the collections, we had single specimens of the great painters of the Italian schools, antiques from Greece and Rome, and numerous memorials of the Middle Ages. The marbles in the British Museum, however, surpass all other collections in Europe. In France, we had immense galleries, with still more of the Italian painting, and some of the best of the Spanish school. In Germany, we seemed to plunge deep into the Middle Ages; but here again, together with the works of the early Dutch and German masters, came some of the very best of Raphael and Correggio. In sculpture, there are collections inferior only to that of the British Museum, and some of the greatest works of the modern artists.

So we have passed, as it were, up the stream of time, each movement preparing us for the following with wonderful regularity. Now we have arrived at the great barrier of the Alps, where we rest awhile to breathe the freshness of nature, and to study the eternal wonders of God's creation. Passing over the Alps, we cross, as it were, the mighty boundaries between the modern and the ancient world, — the world of Rome. Nothing can be more admirably timed than this pause among the Alps. Art is wonderful, but Nature is more wonderful. The Alps are the natural boundaries of history as well as of space. On the other side of them is a different world, and a different world of art. We have had foreshadowings of the latter in the pictures of Raphael and Correggio, — the marbles, the Etruscan vases.

I have formed a distinct conception of the German Middle Ages, from the walled towns, the old towers, churches, banners, battle-fields, — from armories where I have seen thousands of suits of " complete steel " preserved as all but living records of the past. The old houses still stand, with armorial bearings, and curious half-effaced pictures on the outer walls. On the arches and sides of cloisters are sculptures and paintings of the most singular character, gradually vanishing from sight or crumbling into dust. You will see here a group of heads, — there perhaps a single eye, which seems to look sadly at you as you pass along, — yonder an arm raised in prayer, — hovering above, scarcely discernible, a Virgin and Child, like the faint figures in a dream. Such eloquent but silent witnesses of the great Past you meet with everywhere; and for me they have a thousand times the interest that the Present, which I sometimes utterly forget, possesses.

On many of the old houses you still read the pious sentences written there by the devout of the Middle Ages. In Schiller's William Tell, Stauffacher's house is described as

> " Painted with many-colored shields of arms
> And words of wisdom, which the wanderer
> Lingers to read, and their deep sense admires."

I never understood precisely what was meant by

this, until I actually saw the very thing. In Bavaria, Wurtemberg, and Switzerland I suppose I have seen hundreds of these quaint and curious embellishments. I copied a single couplet from the painted front of an old house. The picture was on some sacred subject, but too faint to be distinctly made out, except the head of God the Father; and the lines were in old German, pious but stiff. Literally translated, they mean, —

> " Bethink thee, God all things looks on
> That in and out of doors be done."

In the Catholic countries, the figure of the cross is met with at almost every step. In the walls of houses and towers, you see carved crucifixes, and sometimes even painted ones, still carefully preserved. In little devices, small chapels or shrines among the mountains tell the same story. On every rocky projection along the shores of the lakes you see similar memorials of devotion. All this is very striking and curious to a stranger, especially to an American.

We often read about women, compelled to work in the field, like men; and I have heard a good deal of sentimental horror expressed at such a barbarism. Well, I have seen it constantly for a couple of months, and I confess have quite changed my opinion. Such peals of laughter as I have heard from groups of merry maidens resting from their toils at mid-day, under the shadow of

the trees ! such picturesque figures as I have seen
vigorously at work, with their national costumes,
their cheeks brown and healthy, and their eyes
sparkling with animation ! No ! no ! it is a great
deal better than the wretched, consumptive look
of the London seamstress, or the yellow complexion of the dirty factory-girl at Manchester.

At Dresden I saw the Sistine Madonna with
inexpressible delight ; but I saw another sight, not
quite so poetical and ideal, yet still to be looked
upon with interest and pleasure. One day I was
walking through the public square to the picture-
gallery. I happened to notice a woman mowing.
I stopped ; sat down and looked at her for half
an hour. She was apparently two or three and
twenty. Her head was finely formed, and set
firmly on her shoulders. Her hair was neatly
braided round it ; her features were regular ; complexion brown as a berry ; eyes bright blue ; form
vigorous, well rounded, like that of Dorothea in
Goethe's poem. From her ears hung golden ear-
rings. She wore a bright-colored petticoat, reaching a little below the knees ; her legs were bare,
and her feet encased in embroidered shoes. She
was the picture of health, and robust beauty.
She swung the scythe with an inimitable ease and
grace ; and as she did so, there was a placid expression on her pleasant countenance, which spoke of a
good conscience, a contented spirit, and a willing-
ness to do the work which her destiny pointed out.

I examined the swaths; the grass was cut as smooth as velvet; you could not tell where one swath ended and the next began. An English lawn looked no smoother. It was a work of art, high art; and an American farmer might have taken a useful lesson. I wish I could have taken her portrait as she stood before me.

It is singular how certain names grow upon you in Germany and others diminish: at least they have done so with me. Take Luther and Albrecht Dürer. All the world knows the former, and perhaps something of the latter. But I could not bring up my conception of Luther in Germany to the idea I had of him before. I saw his manuscripts, collections of his works, portraits; but his big drinking-cups were after all the most prominent memorials he left behind him. He was a jolly old soul, hearty and honest, I dare say, and banged away at the Pope and the Devil with good will and good effect. But there was nothing high and grand about him. I went to see the place where the Devil is said to have helped him over the walls of Augsburg; but even there, not a gleam of poetry associated itself with his name. The huge drinking-cup seemed to swallow up everything, and the couplet said to be his appeared to tell the whole story;—

> "Who loves not wine, woman, and song,
> Remains a fool all his life long."

In short, his burly face and figure, and the goblets

that testify to his powers, made it absolutely impossible for me to connect any heroic idea with the man.

But how different with Albrecht Dürer! His pictures in the collections at once excited my interest: his portrait completed the work. The marvellous beauty of his face; the sweet, sad expression it always wears; the lofty purity and ideal grace, that seem to transfigure the mortal into an immortal nature, — distinguish him from all other men of those ages. His spirit gained a stronger and stronger hold upon me, every day I was in Germany. I studied every work of his that I could find, and every lineament of his noble countenance is stamped ineffaceably on my memory. At Nuremberg, I traced him from his cradle to his grave. I visited his house; the house of his friend Pirkheimer; and I went twice to the church-yard of St. John, outside the city, to pay my homage at his tomb. I do not know whether his genius and character affect others as they have me; but I would gladly give the time and money for a voyage to Europe, if I knew that I should see nothing else than the works, the portrait, the house, and the grave of Albrecht Dürer.

But I am running before my story. These generalities made me forget that I have not yet told you the course we followed from Leipsic.

We thought ourselves obliged to make a selection, both for want of time to see every important place, and because we found travelling in Germany much more expensive than we had anticipated. So we abandoned Vienna, and did not visit Weimar. We stopped in Leipsic only a few hours,—just long enough to see the outside of the place and the great publishing establishments,—and proceeded to a little town called Altenberg. It is a quiet place, and we had great pleasure in visiting an old castle by the side of a little lake, in which it was reflected. In this old castle Charlemagne once lived.

From Altenberg we went to another nice old town called Hof. In both of these places we saw more of the old-fashioned German life and manners than anywhere else.

Hof is most picturesquely placed on one side of a little river. The opposite side rises in terraces, covered with trees and shady walks, with seats at short distances, where the youths and maidens resort, towards evening, to walk and talk together. We, too, joined the villagers. We crossed the bridge over the beautiful stream, ascended the slope, and, after walking in all directions, sat down on the brow of the hill, charmed with the quiet of the hour and the placid beauty of the scene. The golden light of evening poured into the valley below, and a single star came out from heaven, and looked softly down.

In a few minutes the silence was broken by the plashing of oars, and then a popular German song, sung by young men and women in the boat, rose and filled the air. It was answered by another boat's company at a distance. We remained about an hour, and then slowly returned. As we went along, we passed many a couple either sitting by themselves under the trees or strolling in the winding paths; and many a romance was evidently weaving itself into the web of human destiny. It was as nice a bit of idyllic life as I have anywhere seen, and a perfect illustration of Goethe's Hermann and Dorothea.

Having seen all that was to be seen in Hof, I started at five o'clock for Nuremberg, leaving the rest of the party to follow in the afternoon. I knew it was the most interesting city of the Middle Ages in Germany, and I wanted as much time as possible to see it.

I have already told you about Albrecht Dürer. Another old personage, in whom I have long been interested, is Hans Sachs, — the master-shoemaker and master-singer. He, too, was a native of Nuremberg, and I tracked him out : hunted up his portrait ; visited his house ; and at the old castle saw a copy of the original folio edition of his works, and a pair of boots of his making. Perhaps you have heard the couplet, —

> "Hans Sachs war ein Schue-
> Macher, und Dichter dazu."

> "Hans Sachs was a Shoe-
> Maker, and Poet thereto."

I bought a copy of his works, published in a reduced shape, and by selections, at Nuremberg, and read as many as I could of them on the spot. I sought out his grave, in the same churchyard where Albrecht Dürer lies buried. An old sexton conducted me through the " silent land "; and while we were meditating among the tombs, there came up suddenly a violent wind, almost a hurricane. We took refuge in a little chapel, about five hundred years old, occupied with graves and tombs and portraits of an old Nuremberg family named Holzeschue, or *Wooden-shoes ;* the founder of it having made his fortune by the manufacture of wooden-shoes, in the thirteenth century. His descendants still live in Nuremberg.

It was strange to stand in such a place, and listen to the roaring of the wind and the rattling glass of the windows, surrounded by the dead of so many generations. There were a thousand other interesting associations with Nuremberg; and I found my time fully occupied. But I have no room to go into the details now, nor would they be very interesting, if written out.

From Nuremberg we journeyed on to Munich, where we purposed to stay for some time. We found excellent quarters there, and I had letters that enabled me to see, under the best auspices, everything I desired. We remained a week, and examined at our leisure the various collections of ancient and modern art with which the city is enriched.

You know old King Ludwig had a passion for art, and aspired to make his capital the Athens of the modern world. To a wonderful extent he has succeeded. He called about him all the best artists of Germany, and expended all his resources on sculpture, painting, and architecture. Munich is the city of art. The collections are large, important, most admirably arranged, and liberally opened to strangers. The buildings for them are built expressly for the purpose, and by the ablest architects; and everything is in harmony. The Ægina marbles — next in value to the Elgin collection in the British Museum — are beautifully arranged in one of the halls of the *Glyptothek*, or sculpture-gallery. These were my special object of study; and while I was at Munich I learned them by heart.

We went to the theatre only once, — and then to see Schiller's Don Carlos, capitally played, though its inordinate length was cut down about half.

I formed some very interesting and valuable acquaintance there; particularly Professor Martius, the great botanist; Thiersch, the Professor of Greek; Skhinas (pronounced Skeenas), the Greek Ambassador, and his wife; and the Baron von Maurer, a Bavarian nobleman of great eminence, both in politics and literature.

Professor Thiersch has long stood nearly at the head of the classical scholars in Germany. He was especially interesting to me, because I first gained a radical knowledge of the Greek verb, as long ago as 1822, by studying a work of his which my teacher, Mr. Simeon Putnam, accidentally possessed. He was not at home when I called; but in the course of the afternoon he came to our lodgings, and called on me. He is a gray-headed old gentleman, and always walks with a cane, and accompanied by a dog. He speaks English a very little. He invited me to walk with him to a " Bier-Keller," where he would introduce me to the principal celebrities of Munich. I forget the name of the Keller, but Agassiz will doubtless remember it, as he must have been there many a time. It lies at some distance outside the city, on a hill which is hollowed out for the beer-barrels. The surface is occupied by a house and a garden with trees. Under the trees are arranged plain wooden tables and benches to match. A band of musicians is in attendance, and as the evening comes on, the whole is lighted with candles.

The extensive gardens are filled rapidly by all sorts of people, — students, citizens with their wives and daughters, professors, lawyers, and so on. The Keller furnishes absolutely nothing but Bavarian beer and black bread, for which each person pays six groschen, or about four or five cents. If he wants anything else, he must bring it with him.

Arriving at the place, Professor Thiersch conducted me through the tables, — the occupants of which saluted him with the greatest respect as we passed along, — until he found the one he was in search of. There were sitting Steub, the author of an admirable work on Greece ; Fallmerayer, the author of a great work on the Sclavonian immigrations into Greece ; Müller, the first Orientalist in Germany ; and four or five other gentlemen, whose names are classical in the literature of the age, — sitting on a rough bench, at a table of black and weather-worn plank, each with a pot of beer, and a slice of bread as black as the table.

An eminent jurist, whose opinions are law over half the civilized world, had brought in his pocket a slice of ham, wrapped up in a piece of newspaper, which lay before him, and added something substantial to his entertainment. He cut it up with a jackknife and laid the bits on the black bread. Professor Thiersch called the damsel in attendance, ordered two pots of beer and two slices of black bread, and we joined the learned revels of the company.

I never met a more intelligent, genial, and pleasant circle ; and for the sake of their delightful conversation I readily drank the beer and ate the bread, which without such a seasoning I should have found it impossible to worry down. It was a most curious and characteristic scene, and I have described it partly for Agassiz, with whom I wish you would talk about it. I think he will recognize the fidelity of the picture.

At the end of the evening we returned, and Professor Thiersch invited me to his house. His family were seated at a tea-table in the garden, — his wife, two daughters, and a sister ; and as I had not supped very heartily at the " Bier-Keller," I had no objection to a nice cup of tea and a sandwich. The young ladies were agreeable, and I had a very pleasant time.

Professor Thiersch continued kind and attentive during all my stay in Munich. We all passed an evening at his house with a small party. He has a son, — a young man of talent, already distinguished among the artists of Germany, — who has been two years in Athens, and is now in Munich, intending to return to Athens in September.

One day in the Professor's study, I suddenly came upon a large drawing in crayon. I asked if it was not from a Klephtic poem, — " Charon and the Ghosts." " Yes, it is." " Well," said I, " I translated that poem fifteen years ago." " So did I," said the Professor; and then recited his German version. You remember mine, I dare say. It begins, —

" Why are the mountains shadowed o'er, why stand they darkened grimly ?
Is it a tempest warring there, or rain-storm beating on them ?

"It is no tempest warring there, no rain-storm beating on them,
But Charon sweeping over them, and with him the departed.' "

The composition of the piece shows an admirable talent; the very spirit of the poem is so well given, by the grouping of the figures and the expression. You may judge of its excellence, by my instantly recognizing it; and you may imagine what pleasure this little incident gave me as well as my host.

The Professor told me that when the galleries received their present Greek names, — " Pinakothek," *deposit of pictures;* " Glyptothek," *deposit or collection of statues,* — the invention of these terms was attributed to him, and some dissatisfaction was felt in the city; in short, quite an excitement was got up against him. One day, returning from a walk, he found an inscription placed over his door, containing, in large letters, the word " Nepiothek," *a gallery of fools.* He took it down and sent it to the old King, who nearly went into convulsions with laughter.

I called on M. Skhinas a few days after arriving in Munich with a letter of introduction from Ampère. I found him in very handsome apartments, in the handsomest street (Agassiz will remember it, — Ludwig-strasse) in Munich. He was at home, and I was conducted through six or seven rooms, richly furnished and hung with superb pictures and engravings, to the Ambassador's study. He is a gentleman of about fifty or fifty-five, — stout and strong, with a bold, vigorous cast of countenance, somewhat resembling Dr. Bache. His manners are simple, cordial, and as free as if he had never seen a court or been called " His Excellency." He speaks no English, but German and French with great fluency. So I was thrown upon my foreign forces; but what with French, and here and there a bit of German, eked out with Greek when these failed me, I got on pretty well.

The conversation turned at first on casual subjects, but M. Skhinas is an ardent politician, and so his talk imperceptibly glided into the " Question de l'Orient." He began by saying that the future would be occupied by two colossal figures, Russia and America. Western Europe, in his opinion, was already on the decline. England had been, and still was, a great power, but she had reached her culminating point. Germany was also going down. The power of Russia, already vast, was fearfully increasing. It became us Americans to ponder well how we should wisely employ our power. The English had not been wise in their external policy. Where they ought to have made friends, they had made bitter enemies. The course of Lord Palmerston towards Greece in the affair of the Jew (—— will explain this) was *unsinnig, unglaublich,* senseless, incredible. The Jew was not a British subject, but a subject of Greece, and amenable to her laws. He had long enjoyed the privileges of Greek citizenship, and his claim beside was wholly unfounded. The conduct of Lord Palmerston in blockading the Peiræus to enforce this claim, had made the British name odious to the Christians of the East. It was a strong power bullying a comparatively weak one. The English had, by this act of unjust interference with the laws of another nation, set the example which Russia alone followed. The demands of Russia upon Turkey were a plagiarism upon the English demands on Greece ; and now America had made the great mistake of imitating England and Russia, in the case of Mr. King. " Mr. Marsh's demands," said he, " upon the Greek government were unreasonable, and impossible to be granted. Mr. King had offended against the laws of Greece ; had been tried and condemned by a Greek tribunal. Mr. Marsh required that the judgment of the court should be annulled. But the King cannot annul the judgment of a court. The King is no Sultan ; had we desired to have a Sultan, we should never have taken the trouble of making a revolution ; we should have kept the old Sultan. King Otho is a constitutional monarch, and the Greeks are a free people. The administration of justice is independent. The municipal organizations are admirable. We have parliamentary debates, free speech, and a free press. How can a constitutional monarch annul the judgment of a

court? Should he make the attempt, it would cause
a revolution." This was the substance of what he
said in a conversation of an hour and a half.

So much for the American part in the Oriental
question. As to the general subject, M. Skhinas
showed me a pamphlet he had written, not yet
published, and another written by an eminent
Athenian gentleman. I took them to my room
and read them. They developed views quite new
to me, and such as I have nowhere seen in the
discussions of Western Europe. They both as-
sume the certainty of the approaching dissolution
of the Turkish empire, and then proceed to dis-
cuss the question how that dissolution can be
brought about with the smallest disturbance to
the equilibrium of Europe. Both assert the impossibility of bringing Turkey within the range of
European civilization, or of compelling the Turks
to place the Christian population of European
Turkey on the same footing with the Mussul-
mans. The ineradicable fanaticism of the Turks,
and the incurable vices of their character, make
such an idea hopeless.

What motive induces the great powers of Europe to adopt the policy of protecting and pro-
longing the existence of the Turkish empire?
Surely not love of the Turks; but jealousy of one
another. The apprehension that, if one should
be allowed to aggrandize itself with the spoils of
Turkey, it would disturb the balance of power,

and endanger the security of the rest. But the force of events is greater than diplomatic arrangements. Turkey cannot long be kept up; and the only safe solution of the Eastern question will be to push the Sultan back into Asia, where he properly belongs, to add to the present kingdom of Greece the European provinces of Turkey, and to establish a new Greco-Byzantine empire, with the capital at Constantinople. This would make a power of about fifteen millions; not large enough to excite the alarm of Europe, but sufficiently large to make itself respected.

All this is very curious, and explains the fact that the Greeks have not sympathized with the efforts of France and England, while on the other hand they have not joined the Russians. They want Constantinople themselves, and they mean to have it, if they can get it; and for my part, I heartily wish they may succeed. The friendship of Western Europe for Turkey is a contradiction to the past, and has nothing to rest upon but present policy. I believe the interests of European civilization would be promoted by restoring Constantinople to the Greeks. It was theirs, from five or six centuries before Christ, down to 1452; and they ought to have it now. Whether the Great Powers will permit so good an arrangement is another and much more doubtful matter.

In the course of the evening I received a pleasant note from M. Skhinas, inviting me to dine with a few friends, which I gladly accepted.

Well, I dressed up in my best (no great affair that, you will say) and went at four o'clock, — a wonderfully late hour for Germany, where they usually dine at half past twelve. The company consisted of M. von Maurer, Professor Thiersch and his son, two military gentlemen, and myself. It was a very elegant dinner, and the conversation, though I lost part of it, very interesting. It was almost wholly on Oriental affairs. In the height of the tide, old Professor Thiersch filled his glass with champagne and proposed " L'avenir de la Grèce." " Avec Constantinople," added another, by way of amendment. The company sprang to their feet, — I, of course, with the rest, — clanged glasses together, and drank a most zealous bumper in honor of the Greco-Byzantine empire — that is to come.

This M. von Maurer, of whom I have spoken, was the leading member of the Regency in Greece while King Otho was a minor; organized the government entirely; made the code for the administration of justice; and on his return to Bavaria, wrote a most able work on Greece in three volumes. Since then he has been President of the Council, and Secretary for Foreign Affairs, and is now the leading orator in the Bavarian House of Peers. He is a noble-looking person, and his bearing is as frank and unaffected as it is highbred. I had known his name before, and something of his connection with Greece; and I was well pleased with such an opportunity of seeing him more nearly. The next day M. Skhinas proposed to take me to call on him. I readily consented, and had an hour's conversation, speaking in bad French, but with the pleasant assurance that his was as bad as mine.

He made many inquiries about the American Constitution, and you would have laughed heartily to hear me expounding the relations between the Federal government and the States, in such French as was never heard before, to a Bavarian minister. He was curious to know all about President Pierce, and I helped him to as much knowledge as I could muster. In return, he gave me a good deal of information about the government of Bavaria, which surprised me.

But as you must be getting tired of all this, I will return to Madame Skhinas. She invited me to take tea with her the next evening, promising to show me the court costume of a Greek lady. I went accordingly, and found her sitting alone in the drawing-room, arrayed in the magnificent dress of gold and silk, with golden head-dress, which makes the Oriental beauty so superb. I cannot undertake to describe the dress; but it may serve to show the simple and unaffected manners of this high-born woman, whose position in the diplomatic and fashionable world is as distinguished as her birth, to tell you that she explained the parts of the costume, and on what occasions it was worn, merely for my information, and with all the good-humor of a laughing girl. She looked, in my eyes, much like a princess in the Arabian Nights, and the whole tone of her conversation had a tinge of Orientalism, singularly contrasting with our Western European style of expression and thought.

M. Skhinas came in by and by, and we had another long talk about the Eastern Question and the Greek Church. He has a profound conviction that the Greeks have preserved the traditions of the primitive Church ; and, while admitting the rights of all other Christian communions, he thinks the Greek Church justified in claiming, historically, to represent the Church as established by the Apostles, from which it is directly descended. He spoke again of Mr. King and the demands of Mr. Marsh ; and then reverted to his favorite idea of a Greco-Byzantine empire. All this was very interesting, and much of it quite new to me. I was glad to be possessed of these views before going to Greece.

The next day was the last of our stay in Munich. I went to see a few things I had not before visited, — among the rest to call on Madame Bavaria, a lady about one hundred feet high. We ascended into her head, and from between the locks of her hair had the first fair view of the Alps.

I called on M. von Liebig, and have seldom been more pleased than with him. He has a noble countenance, — frank, beautiful, and highly animated.

Towards evening I went, with much regret, to take leave of M. and Madame Skhinas. I found them just walking out to enjoy the cool of the evening. We walked for some time through the most agreeable parts of the city. They urged me to dine with them the following day, promising to have an early dinner; but, though much tempted, I felt obliged to decline, as the time appropriated to Munich had expired. I really felt sad to quit these excellent and most intelligent people; but I hope I may somewhere meet them again.

From Munich we went to Augsburg, where we spent a day in visiting the objects of interest, — the home of Queen Hortense, and a very interesting gallery of old pictures, containing, besides some invaluable paintings of the early Augsburg schools, several works of Dürer, Murillo, and Titian, and a very extraordinary portrait by Leonardo da Vinci, recently discovered.

From Augsburg we went to Ulm, by *Postwagen*. We walked around the city walls and on the principal promenades, but found little to detain us. So the next day we took the train for Friedrichshafen, and thence crossed the Lake of Constance, to Constance, which, though not in Switzerland, is just on its border.

Here I had a deeply interesting time in investigating the history of John Huss, the martyr, who was burned in 1315. But I cannot now write you about it in detail. I will merely say, that I traced out every place where he was imprisoned in the city; examined the contemporary archives, most obligingly opened to my inspection by the Burgomaster; followed him into the Cathedral, where he received the sentence of condemnation; then went with the procession through the streets of the city, to the neighboring field, where he was tied to the stake and burned. I assure you, while I was doing this, the sad scene drove the present from my thoughts, and I saw the Emperor Sigismund, the prelates, bishops, and cardinals of the council, the executioners, the whole awful spectacle, more vividly than I saw the people who were moving about me.

XI.

Thun, August 23, 1853.

WHEN I wrote my last letter I was already in Switzerland, and had seen something of the Swiss; but had more things to tell you about Germany than I could crowd into a dozen sheets. We had begun to see the outposts of Switzerland, in Bavaria; and the attraction of the Alps hurried us on to Constance, the border town. Here, as I wrote you, I found ample subjects of the most interesting nature, in the history of the place, especially the martyrdom of Huss and Jerome of Prague.

Having finished all that I desired to do there, we left Constance for Zürich, passing through Zug, and by the Lake of Zug, one of those exquisite mountain lakes so numerous in Switzerland. The scenery all the way, was beautiful. At Zürich we saw all that was to be seen, — not a great deal; but among other things, the Zeughaus, as they call it, or collection of ancient and mediæval arms, some of them curious and valuable as memorials of the early wars of Switzerland against the Burgundians. Many complete suits of armor from the old battle-fields were there, —

spears, battle-axes, and a peculiarly heavy lance, with a heavy head set all over with spikes, and called a *morning star*, — a singular name for such a bloody and destructive instrument.

The place is not much visited ; nobody else was there with us. I always try to vivify an idea, by embodying it in some manner. I had often tried to imagine how a knight of the Middle Ages would feel buckled up in his " complete steel," on a hot day. Being a middle-aged man myself, and the day being very hot, I asked permission of the keeper to try the experiment of equipping my-self in one of those old Burgundian panoplies. He willingly complied with the request, looking, however, a little amused and surprised. I selected one of the two largest in the collection, and, the keeper acting as squire, I was soon encased from head to foot, — like the ghost of Hamlet's father, " armed *cap - à - pié*." I could, however, just squeeze myself into it ; it pinched in many places ; and as this belonged to one of the stoutest knights of the Burgundian host, it is very evident that the notion of the greater size of the warriors of the Middle Ages as compared with our own, is, like that of the greater size of Englishmen as compared with Americans, a mere superstition. I had the most difficulty in getting the helmet on ; but at last pushed my head into it, buckled it se-curely, took off my spectacles, and drew the visor down. Next, I seized a huge battle-axe, and then marched across the hall, while G—— and the girls were sitting down and laughing. I could walk well enough, except that I seemed to be a little stiff in the joints; there was also a slight difficulty in breathing through the visor, and a little hardness of hearing through the iron side-pieces. I could not see much, except directly in front, and there only in spots. Add to this, the heat was excessive, and the weight of the armor was rather more than one wants in a summer day. The battle-axe was something of a load, too, about as much as Satan's spear in Milton, taller than " the mast of some great ammiral." With these exceptions, the armor was comfortable enough; and I think our ancestors must have had a cosey time, after they got used to it. I walked about in it for several minutes, swinging the axe in the most formidable manner, and could have borne it a good while longer. But having satisfied my wish to embody an idea, I requested my squire to help me out of the harness, and I must confess I breathed more freely. It was easier walking, seeing, hearing, talking; I could wear my spectacles, which I could not under the visor; and, upon the whole, I congratulated myself on having been born in the present age, rather than in the time of Charles the Bold of Burgundy.

From Zürich we went to Lucerne, — again through a lovely country, with the Alps constantly rising upon our view. We decided to remain here for some days, look about us, and prepare for a vigorous attack on the Alps. We had already made a sort of preliminary survey, by ascending the Uetliberg, — a very considerable mountain in itself, but not much, compared with the higher Alps, to which it performs the part of sentinel.

We stayed a week at Lucerne, reading, wandering about the beautiful valleys in the neighborhood, studying the mountains, and getting ready for a march among the Alps. Lucerne is considered by many the most beautifully situated place in Europe. I think there is no doubt that Lake Lucerne is the finest of the Swiss lakes. Our rooms looked directly down upon it, and over to Mount Pilatus on one side, and the Righi on the other. Mount Pilatus is seldom ascended; the Righi often, on account of the splendid panorama of lakes and mountains one enjoys from its summit. There are curious legends accounting for the name, *Pilatus;* but as they are told in the guide-books, I will not take up the space to repeat them. The top is often wrapped in clouds, all day long; and omens of the weather are drawn from this circumstance. A German couplet says:

> " If Mount Pilatus wear a cap, then is the weather fair,
> But if he bear a sword aloft, be sure that rain is there," —

the sword being one of the sharp peaks, piercing the sky in clear weather, but betokening the approach of a storm.

Towards the end of our week, we set out for Righi, by way of Kussnacht and Goldau. We drove along the lovely shores; crossed over to Lake Zug; passed the Chapel of Tell; drove through the village of Arth and its smiling valley to Goldau, which, you remember, was overwhelmed by an enormous landslide, burying the town and its inhabitants a hundred feet deep in earth and stones, — one of the most awful catastrophes that ever overwhelmed a community. I had seen the ruins of palaces and castles; but here was a mountain in ruins. The valley lay dreary and desolate still; only a few houses, a small inn, and a church stand over the grave of the village. In the centre the falling mass piled itself up almost into a mountain. I walked to the top, and looked around on the wide waste wrought there nearly half a century ago; and while I stood alone on the sad pile, a raven croaked in the air over my head, and made the gloom of the solitude still more gloomy.

From this spot we ascended the Righi, I on a horse, and G—— on foot. The ascent is by no means so difficult as that of Mount Washington, though the mountain is considerably higher. Clouds were flitting about the summit, but the successive views we enjoyed were magnificent. All the accessories which enhance the poetry of an Alpine journey were there. Pilgrims, slowly winding their way up to a mountain shrine, saying their prayers as they toiled along; by the way-side rude paintings of the stations of our Lord's progress to the Hill of Calvary; here and there groups of travellers like ourselves; herds of cows, grazing on the green slopes that rose from the mountain stream, whose bed we were following; the tinkling of the cow-bells on every side; the *yodling* of the herdsmen, as they responded to one another from hillside to hillside; the châlets dotting the green pastures; men descending with loads of cheeses, and the utensils employed in making them, on their backs; a woman carrying a basket of chickens up to the inn, to supply the wants of the wayfarer; Capuchin monks trudging up the steep path, and showing the way to half a dozen black-coated priests from the regions below (I mean *the earth*); goats hanging from the rocks, as Virgil describes them, and scarcely deigning to look down on the clumsy bipeds; birds sailing aloft in flocks around the distant summits, — all these excited our interest during the fatiguing march.

When we reached the summit, we had only about fifteen minutes of good weather; yet that was enough to give us an astonishing prospect, of unsurpassed beauty, variety, and extent. Then a thick cloud gathered around the mountain's head, and shut out the magnificent vision as completely as if every feature had been obliterated from the face of the earth. But, as we descended, we soon came below the cloud, and again enjoyed a series of views like those we had in going up. We returned to Goldau ; took another look at its solitude and desolation ; entered the little church where the names of the victims are recorded ; then drove home under the heavy shadows of the Righi, while the opposite chain was lighted up by the full moon.

The next day we set out to cross St. Gothard, the Furca, and the Grimsel. We took the steamer down the lake, to Fluelen. The afternoon was indescribably beautiful, and the wonderful and massive shores stood out from the mirror-clear water, producing the most sublime effect.

I do not know that I ever had a more interesting voyage. We watched the rocky walls, and their extraordinary forms, with unflagging attention ; and, as there were several Bostonians on board, the conversation often reverted to Agassiz and his lectures. We tried to picture to ourselves the forces which had upheaved these giant masses, and twisted the solid strata into every kind of course ; but when one of the party said, " Imagination falters, — we want Agassiz," — all assented. I would have given a great deal to hear a lecture from him, as we swept by those wonderful barriers.

We stopped that night at Altorf, and visited all the spots connected with the legends of Tell. Whether the story be true or not, it has sunk into the hearts of the people, and all its incidents

5 *

are constantly presented to them in paintings, statues, and poetry. All over this part of Switzerland there are houses, the fronts of which are adorned with pictures of Tell, Winkelried, Fürst, the death of Gessler, the apple scene, the sworn league at Rütli, and so on; and in the villages one constantly sees the boys shooting at marks with crossbows.

All this is very captivating as we enter Switzerland; but there are other things of a widely different character that force themselves on the traveller's attention. I was not prepared for the misery and degradation of so large a part of the people. Dirt, the goitre, cretinism, beggary, falsehood, cringing impudence, stand by the wayside, and make the heart sick. I was half inclined to turn back from the Alps, and not attempt the passage. Old men, young men, boys, children scarcely able to speak, women of all ages, surrounded us and persisted in their demands, with a shamelessness that shut up all feeling of compassion, exhibiting, not only the diseases from which they were, in some cases, actually suffering, but pretended diseases, and artificial sores. We saw one old man hide his hat, and then he came up to us bareheaded, with a piteous story that he had nothing to shelter his aged locks from the storm. A stout boy was shooting at a mark with a crossbow, after every shot begging for money, telling us his name was William Tell. *Schenken sie etwas,* — " Give me something,"— seemed to ring in our ears at every turn, and from morning till night.

I was totally unprepared for this in Switzerland; I expected it in Italy. What would the old heroes of Sempach and Morat have said, could they have seen, in prophetic vision, their descendants lying and begging of the passing traveller, running after carriages, thrusting their hands in at the windows, and exhausting the patience of the most merciful? I do not believe this state of things exists in the retired parts of Switzerland. It seems to me most probable that the inns and highways, by which the travelling world is constantly pouring its currents through the country, must have attracted the lazy, worthless, and dishonest offscourings of the population. Murray's guide-book, however, asserts that the whole population of Switzerland is corrupt. It would be as rational to infer the universal corruption of the English nation, from the enormous system of pocket-picking practised on strangers at the universities, in the churches, at noblemen's castles, at the Queen's palace, and in her stables, to say nothing of cabmen and other cheats on a smaller scale.

But this is a digression from the Alps. The road up St. Gothard is a wonderful piece of engi-. neering, mounting apparently inaccessible heights by a series of terraces or *tourniquets*, so that carriages are very easily driven up. The Reuss flows down, and the sound of the water is heard the whole distance, though the river is sometimes so deep below the road that one can scarcely see it. Then the rocky walls rise steep and bare on either side, seeming to rest on the deep foundations of the earth, and to support the sky on their summits.

I walked a considerable part of the way to enjoy the wonderful scene more completely. It was a good day's journey to the Hospitenthal, or valley of the Hospice, on the height of the pass. This valley is a beautiful spot, green and lovely itself, though at so immense a height, and surrounded by snow-capped pinnacles. We spent the night here.

The next morning we started for the Furca Pass, and the Grimsel; but no more carriage roads. I was strongly tempted to walk the whole distance, from the Hospitenthal to Meyringen; but reflected that I was twenty years older than I was twenty years ago, and much heavier than when I was much lighter, — so I finally decided to compromise the matter by taking one horse for myself and our courier. The rest of the party had each a horse, and two men were employed to take Edie the whole distance, some fifty miles, in a chair.

Now, if I were animated by the proper traveller's spirit, I should rise into the sublime, in my description of the appalling dangers from which we miraculously escaped. I should make each particular hair stand on end by telling you what dizzy heights we scaled by paths scarce a foot in width, along the edges of perpendicular precipices, ten thousand feet or more in depth. I should freeze your blood with horror by depicting the mountainous masses of rock just tottering to their fall, by which we had to pass. I should make you shudder to think of the mighty glaciers we crossed, and the yawning crevasses, a thousand feet deep, over which we were obliged to jump. I should thrill you with the thunder of the descending avalanche, that came within a hair's breadth of burying us five hundred feet deep in snow. I should — But enough of these awful adventures, that trip so freely from the pens of summer tourists.

In plain prose, and rigid truth, the whole journey was exciting in the highest degree. The path *does* wind along the edge of tremendous precipices, and above it the rocky mountain-sides *do* rise sheer and awful up to heaven. Sometimes the path descends so steeply that it seems impossible to go down without breaking your neck ; again it seems to go straight up into the air, and the wonder is, how any four-footed beast can possibly climb it, without rolling over backwards. If you look up, you half believe the mountain is coming down upon you ; if you look down, you are struck by the exceeding probability that you may reach the bottom a great deal sooner than you intend. With all this, you have an abiding confidence in your sure-footed and faithful beast, and you know that he will carry you safely through.

I walked about half the whole distance; but it so happened that I rode over the worst parts of the way. I felt astonished, delighted, and constantly amazed by the grandeur of the gigantic scenery; and only once did I feel in the least startled with any sense of danger. In one place, in the steep side of an enormous rock a way is scooped out, just deep enough for a horse to pass, and high enough for the rider, if he stoops. The side of the road towards the abyss is guarded by a wooden railing. Near this spot a beggar-girl had placed herself; and as my horse entered this rather critical passage, she came up and spoke in the peculiar, inarticulate whine they all employ, standing between the horse and the rocky side. The horse shied an instant, pressed my leg against the slender railing, and I looked over into what really seemed a fathomless abyss. There was no actual danger, for the horse knew his footing exactly; but the appearance of danger set my blood in motion for a moment, and made my pulse beat at a pretty rapid rate. Agassiz will remember this spot.

But I am getting before my story. We dined at the Furca Pass, and then continued our course, making for the Grimsel. We passed several small glaciers on the right and left, and soon came in sight of the beautiful glacier of the Rhone, — the first real glacier I had seen. I was glad to find that our path led across a considerable portion of

it; and as I was walking here, I had a good opportunity to notice all its peculiarities. Before
reaching its extremity the road left it and ran
along the mountain-side.

We crossed the Rhone by a bridge about five
minutes' walk below the end of the glacier. I
counted seven streams issuing from it, and uniting
below; three larger than the rest, and perhaps
one main stream, which should be considered the
Rhone. I was interested to notice the great mass
of stones, mud, and rubbish which it had brought
down, and carefully laid across the valley. We
had the glacier in sight for some time, as we
clambered up the mountains on the right bank
of the Rhone; but as the river was not going our
way, we reluctantly parted company, soon after
he got released from his icy prison-house.

Towards evening we came into the classical
dominion of Agassiz, — the valley of the Aar, and
the Grimsel. I assure you my heart beat with
unusual pleasure, as my eye rested on these
scenes, so familiar to me, and yet so strange; and
I eagerly watched every characteristic feature, as
we slowly picked our way down the mountainous
bank of the Aar, to the little inn, — the Grimsel.

I was doomed to a considerable disappointment;
for when I inquired for the old host, who knew
Agassiz so well, he was no longer there. A new
man entertains the passing traveller; and, what is
worse, a new king — another Erl-king — has seized

the vacant throne of ice; the palace of Agassiz has been swept away by the resistless course of the frozen stream, as remorseless and destructive as the stream of Time ; and though the memory of Agassiz freshly lives among these mountains and these realms of snow and ice, it is the memory of an illustrious but departed dynasty, — a sort of Rhamses the Great, whose gigantic figure awes the existing race, but sways it no longer.

The end of the glacier is some miles up the valley, from the inn. We had seen it from one of the heights over which we passed, but I longed to get a nearer view. It wanted yet an hour or two of dark, and I set out alone, up the valley of the Aar, to meet the descending glacier. It was a wild scene, and the walk was much longer than I anticipated. However, on I went, passing over immense piles of earth and rock that here and there half filled the valley, and turning corners, round each of which I thought to meet my old and frozen friend. At last I just came in sight of his broad front, as the darkness spread its wings over the valley, and I dared not go nearer. I turned to retrace my steps, and then the wild grandeur of the place came over me with triple force.

The stars took their places, one by one ; but the deep shadows along the sides of the valley darkened into an awful blackness ; the huge and jagged rocks sprang up into a thousand weird and fantastic shapes ; the streams that dashed down the headlong heights seemed to multiply and strengthen their tumultuous voices, as if they clamored to fill the ear of Night; while from the bed of the valley the Aar sent forth a low but mighty undertone, distinctly and continuously heard amid the shouts of the lesser rival waters. The intensity of the solitude was indescribable; and, with all these sounds crowded upon the strained sense of hearing, a strange, appalling silence brooded over the deserted road of the ancient glacier.

It was not so easy as I had supposed to find my way, but my head is steady and my foot is careful. I got out of the path more than once, but was not confused, and groped my way back again; and so by slow degrees regained the inn at half past nine o'clock, profoundly impressed with the sublimity of a solitary walk up the gigantic foot-path trodden some millions of years ago by the ice-king, to keep an appointment by night with a glacier, and fully resolved never to seek another interview with so lonely and majestic a personage, under exactly the same circumstances. The ghost of Hamlet's father was a pleasant old gentleman compared to this; and yet I am glad to have had precisely this experience of the Alps.

The next morning we resumed our march. Our procession made a very respectable figure, — five horses, two guides, our courier, and Edie with her bearers. There were two English parties crossing at nearly the same time. They stopped over night at the Grimsel, and started, one before and the other after us, in the morning.

We had a delightful continuation of our journey. At a place called Handeck, we saw the splendid fall of the Aar, and the play of the rainbows in the foam. The height of the fall is considerably greater than that of Niagara; but the volume of water is so much less, and the surrounding features — the woods, rocks, and chasms — so totally different, that no comparison ought to be made. Each has its own beauty and grandeur, by which it must stand or *fall*.

In traversing these regions, I recalled Agassiz's writings and lectures with infinite pleasure. In my lonely walk up the Aar, I looked for the scratches and grooves made by the old glaciers, on the bottom of the valley, where the rock was exposed, and still more along the sides, up to the range of granite needles which stand along the heights. And as we descended the valley of the Aar, we noticed the smoothed surface of the lateral rocks, with the fine lines traced in a direction nearly parallel to the axis of the river.

The most remarkable portions are the projecting masses of rock at the places where the river makes a turn, which stand out like the round towers at the corners of ancient castles, smooth as if chiselled by the mason, and rising many hundreds of feet above the present bed of the river. If this was the work of an ancient glacier, one can see perfectly well how the tightened pressure of the immense mass, turning the corner, crowding from above and drawing from below, should have wrought the surface, at these particular points, into a polish which has better resisted the wear and tear of time and weather than the other spaces, where no curve is made. At some distance below the Grimsel there is, on the left of the river, an immense and sloping mass of rock, over the lower part of whose surface the path runs, protected by a fence, which is supported by wooden stakes driven into the rock. All over this the grinding process of the glacier is very distinct. In some spots the surface has been picked, like a millstone, by time; but even here, over the tops of the still remaining points, the grooves are traceable, all running in the same direction.

These appearances diminish as we descend the valley of the Aar, and quite disappear before arriving at Guttannen, the sides of the mountains being completely broken, except in a single place, where there is another of those natural round towers, standing as if to defend the mountain fortress from the assaults of Time the Destroyer.

This is the region of enormous land-slides, blocking up the valley, and narrowing the bed of the river; of breaks in the rocky masses, rent by awful convulsions of nature; of huge ravines, hollowed out by snow, ice, and water; of great enclosed valleys, once the beds of lakes, and now smiling fields of grain and grass, the descents to which are wonderfully steep and wild.

These were the general features of our journey over this remarkable portion of the Alps. At St. Gothard and the Furca, the principal chains of mountains in Switzerland meet; and within the compass of a few miles the rivers of Switzerland, Germany, Italy, and France take their rise, flowing to all the points of the compass. Here is the heart of the Alps, — that enormous granite heart from which the veins and arteries diverge; that heart, rocky-hard and icy-cold, from which, however, circulate the joy and freshness and fertility of the surrounding lands, — from which the fields of Switzerland, the plains of Lombardy, the vineyards of the Rhine, draw their life and gather in the gifts which gladden the heart of man and make his face to shine.

During the Saturday and Sunday, when we were slowly passing from the Hospitenthal to the valley of the Meyringen, I was haunted with the thought that we were moving through a cathedral of the Almighty's building. The enormous aisles were the ravines and ancient glacier-beds His wisdom had designed. The walls were the solid mountains He had built. The clustered columns were the rocky piles which the old glaciers, His workmen, had hewn and chiselled out. The spires were the granite pinnacles, so tall, so slender, so exquisitely traced, which His hand had set up on the gigantic parapets and walls. The painted ceiling was the blue arch of Heaven, which He had spanned from side to side. The lighted tapers were the sun, the moon, and the stars, which His breath had kindled. The pictures were the green slopes, the dark forests, the white snow,—emblem of purity,—the glancing ice, the many-tinted flowers, whose slender forms and fragile beauty contrast so strangely with the austere sublimities around them, and whose fragrance is the incense of Heaven. The music was the wind roaring from the mountain gorge ; the organ-tones of the river, pouring through its channel, worn by many thousand years, and never suspending its impressive monotone; with the sharper variations of the smaller streams, playing through their rocky pipes, and the crash of the distant avalanche. And what was the fitting worship for such a temple of God ? Silence and awe.

Goethe was right when he said, that speech is impertinence in the great presence of Nature. The thoughts capable of expression are mean and insignificant; and man, the babbler, can only stand abashed and overpowered by the sense of the Infinite, which these tremendous works of God in the realms of Nature awaken.

We had lovely weather during the entire journey, and nothing happened to mar its pleasures in the least. We arrived at Meyringen safe and sound, before Sunday night; and a few moments after we were safely housed we had a beautiful shower, and heavy thunder on the distant mountain-tops. As we approached the vale we were again assailed by beggars. At the turnings of the road young girls stationed themselves, and as we passed, saluted us with the Ranz des Vaches. You know I never could resist the influence of music; so, though I had made a firm resolve never to give a sixpence to a beggar, I could not help throwing down a few pieces to the first pretty groups we encountered, in their Sunday dresses and broad straw hats. But they came a little too frequently; so, like Ulysses, I compelled myself to resist their siren voices, shut my purse remorselessly, and went on my way. The next attack we had was made by boys standing on their heads, the moment they saw us approaching, and then running up for money as if they had performed a meritorious action. This it was comparatively easy to resist.

We spent the night at Meyringen, and the next morning went on to Brienz. We crossed the Lake of Brienz to Interlachen, passing by the beautiful falls of the Giessbach.

Interlachen is a charming spot between the Lake of Brienz and the Lake of Thun. It is the resort of swarms of summer tourists, and resembles in this respect Newport and Saratoga. The Queen of Holland was there during our visit; but as we had sent our court dresses forward to Thun, we did not call on her Majesty. I trust she did not consider herself slighted by the omission. The grounds are cool, refreshing, planted with noble trees, under which we walked, and watched the gay figures that flaunted by. There is a deal of affectation among these summer tourists, men and women, here as well as at home. Girls, in lacka-daisical mountain-dresses, with the large iron-pointed *alpenstock*, as if they meant to climb the Jungfrau and Mont Blanc; with broad Swiss hats, as if they really meant to live in the Alpine pastures, (all worn with a jaunty, conscious air of being irresistibly attractive,) make a queer contrast to the sincerity and simplicity of the Alpine nature.

The next morning early we hired a boat, and were rowed down the lake to the falls of Giessbach, where we breakfasted. We climbed up the side of the mountain to see the succession of cascades which together form what is called the Giessbach, — a very lovely spot, the silver waters framed in the green foliage, and grassy lawns giving an air of freshness and repose to the scene.

Returning in the same way to Interlachen, we took the afternoon boat for Thun, — another town delightfully placed on the shore of the lake. It was singular to feel the hot sun of midsummer, and see the vineyards with clustering grapes on one side of the lake, while rising high on the opposite shore stood the eternal snows of the Eiger, Mönch, and Jungfrau. I watched these mountains, especially the last, with great interest. I looked at it carefully through G——'s telescope, and tried to picture Agassiz crawling up the icy margin of the topmost peak. One person has been killed within a year in trying to make the ascent.

From Thun we took a carriage to Berne, where we stayed all night. There I saw Mr. Fay, our resident Minister, who gave me much information about the state of Switzerland, which at this moment is very critical.

The bear is the armorial *bearing* of Berne; in recognition of which they keep four live bears in an immense stone enclosure, at the public charge. We paid our respects to these embodied majesties of the mighty state, and treated them to bits of bread. I went so far as to expend thirty centimes in three loaves, for the pleasure of feeding these creatures. It was amusing to see how well *they* had been taught to beg. One — the biggest of the four — when spoken to, would stand on his hind legs, turn his head with a sentimental look, and pass his paw, in the most affecting manner, over his black snout, — saying as plainly as bear could say it, *Schenken sie etwas*, — and we gave him bread.

From Berne we went to Freyburg, where we passed the night; and from Freyburg to Morat, near the famous battle-ground of Charles the Bold, celebrated in Weber's old ballad, beginning

" The tidings flew from land to land."

From Morat, yesterday afternoon, to Neuchatel, where I close this letter, having promised in my last to write you only brief epistles. It is now Saturday, the 27th of August. My room looks down on the lake, over to the whole range of the Bernese Alps, and within a stone's throw of Agassiz's former house. I have seen his portrait, in the little reading-room of the Hôtel des Alpes, where we are. Kindest love to all.

6

XII.

AT Neuchatel I saw several of the Professors,
— among the rest, a fine, handsome, animated young man, M. Vouga, who, I believe, has
the place that Agassiz formerly held, and was educated by him. He called on me, with M. Prince,
the Greek Professor. I met by accident Professor
Berthoud; but the Misses Berthoud, to whom
Agassiz gave me a letter, were in the country. I,
passed a very pleasant evening with the Rev. M.
Godet, and some of these gentlemen. They were
curious to know all about Agassiz and Guyot, and
made many inquiries respecting our system of education. They seemed surprised at what I told
them, and unanimously agreed that, in one.funda-
mental point, — the four years of college study
preceding the special or professional studies, — our
system is infinitely preferable to theirs. They
used the strongest expressions of regret that with
them the young men commenced their special
studies so early; condemning the practice as a
great obstacle in the way of a truly liberal education. This surprised me; but I think their view
a just one.

I liked the Neuchatel people much. The place,

too, is very charmingly situated, with the finest conceivable prospects. We were not able to ascend any of the neighboring heights, on account of the clouds and rain.

From Neuchatel we went to Lausanne, — I in the diligence, and the rest of the party in a carriage. A Swiss-Frenchman and myself alone occupied the *coupé*. He was very talkative, asking a million of questions, such as, " Is the Fall of Niagara on the Mississippi ? " " Do girls receive any education in America ? " " Is New York in Massachusetts, where they have the Maine liquor-law ? " " Are there any apples and pears in America ? " " Do people have to get passports when they travel in America ? " " Can the President go to war ? " " Is there any university in America ? " " Are there any educated doctors ? " I expounded all these subjects as well as my limited French would allow, with a good deal of amusement to myself. It was, at all events, a capital exercise in speaking French.

At Lausanne we stopped at " Hotel Gibbon," which occupies part of Gibbon's garden, where he finished his History. I went, of course, to see his house, still standing; and it was interesting to read the name " Curchod " on one of the signs.

The next day we came down to Geneva, by land, along the northern shore of the lake. The weather was delightful. The scenery along that shore is soft and beautiful ; the lake itself of a most remarkable azure, and tranquil as the sky.

XIII.

BRIEG, September 6.

I DID not expect to write again until we reached Milan; but being detained at this place by a heavy rain, I am well pleased to have the opportunity. One thing is very certain, — travelling is not playing. I do not think my time was ever so fully occupied, as since I have been on the Continent. In England, I gave myself up more to the spirit of holiday; but the moment I touched the shore of France, I began to work; and ever since, the only trouble has been to find hours enough for what it seemed to me indispensable to do. Since we entered Switzerland, — contrary to my anticipation, — I have been as busy as I was in Germany. But there is so much to excite one's interest here, that it is impossible to rest. In all my travels I have chosen to combine study with sight and place seeing, rather than to spend all the time in running about; and in consequence I have been obliged to omit some places and things which most travellers make it a point to see, for the sake of seeing others more carefully, and of having time for other subjects.

As soon as we entered Switzerland I read the

Swiss constitution carefully through, in order to form some idea of the present government; and, as opportunities offered, I have inquired into its operation. It is modelled on our own constitution, with some great, and very unwise, modifications.

There are, in the present condition of Swiss society, elements that threaten the stability of the government. There is the fiercest hostility, breaking out occasionally into acts of violence, between the religious sects, — between the Catholics and Protestants. There is a strong Cantonal pride that submits itself unwillingly to the central administration. There is a powerful aristocracy, — particularly in Berne, — who bear a deadly hatred to the government, and would gladly see it overthrown. Add to all this the detestable doctrines of the radical party, — worse here than anywhere else, — and the open hostility of the surrounding despotisms, and you see at once in what a critical position the Swiss Confederacy at this moment stands.

Since I have been in the country I have read the greater part of Zschokke's History of Switzerland, in connection with the famous battle scenes which I have visited. You can imagine what interest the scenes themselves have lent to the description.

Another subject has occupied me a good deal. I have given you, in one of my letters, an outside view of Alpine pastoral life. It has made a very pleasing impression on me ; and I was delighted to find this life reproduced in the popular poetry. There are several local dialects in Switzerland, — in the German part, modifications of the German language. I have made a collection of the songs, some of which give the most faithful pictures of Alpine life, and have a charming natural beauty. I had the good fortune to travel in a diligence with a man who understood these dialects ; and as I was occupied with one of my volumes, he helped me to many passages which the German language was not sufficient to explain. I intended, also, to make a collection of the Ranz des Vaches, and perhaps I shall still be able to do it. At all events, this combination of poetry with common life has been a constant pleasure to me, during our rambles among the Alps.

At Geneva, we had several violent thunderstorms. I wish you would turn to Childe Harold, and read his description of Lake Leman in a calm and in a storm. We saw them both to perfection. But the rainy weather there not only kept us from pursuing our journey among the Alps, but so broke up the roads and bridges as to interfere with our plans in other respects. We sent L—— and H—— to Martigny, while G—— and I went to Chamouni, to pay our respects to Mont Blanc. The streams had been swollen by the rains, and several bridges were swept away, so that we had to go in a small carriage. We set out early in the morning. The journey lay through a lovely region at first; gradually it grew more rough and wild. Everywhere were marks of the violence of the storm, and in some places our progress was slow. We passed through the grandest ravines, with gigantic walls of rock, rising almost perpendicularly; and night overtook us long before we reached Chamouni. But suddenly, as we were crossing a bridge at Villeneuve, the clouds broke away from the distant summit of Mont Blanc, and the snowy mass shone with dazzling lustre in the rays of the sun. As evening drew on, the whole range of the mountain was disclosed, and that peculiar rosy tint called " the glow of the Alps " spread over it, — certainly the most magnificent spectacle I ever beheld. We stopped in a little village to rest the horses. I sat down on the trunk of a fallen tree, and watched the changes of the gorgeous vision, until the sun, which had long disappeared from the valley where we were, finally withdrew his last rays from those heaven-kissing heights, and the purple and rose and pink faded away into the cold white of snow under the light of the stars.

We had to walk for a considerable distance. A walk by night among the Alps is very solemn. In one place the bridge over a roaring stream from the mountain had been carried off, and the road was completely broken up. An old woman came out from a neighboring châlet, with a lamp about as large as a glowworm, and helped us over on a single log, — rather a narrow footpath for the night. The carriage was dragged through the stream with difficulty, and broken. However, we reached Chamouni safely, and passed the night there. The next day we had a superb view of Mont Blanc in the morning light. We had no time to go up to the Mer de Glace, and, besides, the weather was very uncertain; so we took mules and rode through the mountains to Martigny.

Our course lay through the region of glaciers. We passed five large ones, — directly by the end of two of them, — through the valley of the Arve. The path wound through valleys, up the sides of mountains, through wonderful gorges, over passes, up to the Tête Noire ; then to Forclaz, from which the glorious mountains of the Bernese Oberland and the valley of the Rhone came into view. It was a second Sunday among the Alps, in God's own temple, with the sights and voices of Nature's solemn worship all around us.

We met the rest of the party at Martigny, and thence pursued our journey for two days along the valley of the Rhone.

Isella, September 7.

We have just crossed the Simplon. The day has been partly rainy ; but as we came up on the Swiss side, the clouds — ocean-like in extent— sometimes rolled away, and opened distant views, deep down into the valleys, and up to the snowy pinnacles. We dined at the Hospice, with the Pères Hospitaliers, and came down to this place this afternoon. The descent on the Italian side is the most wonderful and majestic piece of Alpine scenery we have yet passed through. The mass and height and forms of the rocks are beyond the power of language to describe. The waterfalls that come down their sides seem to drop from the clouds, and the sound of the Doveria, rushing between the walls of its deep and narrow channel, is the voice of many waters. Its solemn monotone fills the valley in which we now are, and its foaming surface is visible from my windows.

6 * I

XIV.

Milan, September 10, 1853.

MY last letter was finished at the foot of the Alps. We are now fairly in beautiful Italy, and in one of its loveliest and richest cities.

We left Isella the day before yesterday, travelling along the valley of the Doveria, the mountains gradually lowering on either side, then breaking into isolated masses, and at last fairly descending to the plain. The weather was beautiful, and we were soon made conscious of the Italian sky. The day before, I wore my thickest winter coat; we encountered a snow-storm, and at the Hospice of the Simplon we crowded around a wood-fire, that sent up a cheery blaze into the capacious chimney. In twenty-four hours, at Domo d' Ossola, we felt the summer heat again; we had reached the land of the lizard, hundreds of which lay basking in the sun, — the grape, clusters of which, just ripening, overhung the road, — the castanea, which threw its delightful shadow across the way, — the fig, pleasant to the thought, but insipid to the taste, — and the lemon, as Goethe and Byron sing. The contrast was wonderful, —

Northern and Southern nature;—the language, too, passing suddenly from German to Italian; the looks of the people, so much more animated; the houses gayer and more airy; the frescos on the exterior and the pictures in the little roadside chapels displaying a more poetical sense, and a deeper and more universal feeling of art. Here I plucked my first Italian grape, and bought my first Italian book. It was a holiday, and the whole population were in their gala dresses, strolling idly about the streets, and over the country.

Beyond Domo d' Ossola the plain is bounded by gently sloping, but high hills; villages, country-houses, churches, with their campaniles or belfry-towers, dot their green sides with a charming variety of human interests; and the sound of the distant church-bells came down into the valley, with a thousand delightful associations. The wind played softly around us, and the deep, deep blue — the first we had seen of the sky of Italy — bent over us. So we journeyed on, the pleasure of the day interrupted only by an occasional beggar, coming up to the carriage with his piteous look, and whining tale of poverty and woe. But even these were different from the shameless rascals who persecute you in Switzerland. They are neither so impudent nor so persevering; and they do not curse you, as the others do, if you refuse to give them money.

We dined on the lovely shore of Lago Maggiore; and after dinner drove along that beautiful sheet, lying as tranquil under the canopy of heaven as if it were reposing in slumber. The shades of evening succeeded the colors of sunset; and the moon — I had not yet seen it, though it was several days old — silvered the smooth surface of the lake. Slowly and quietly we passed the Isola Bella and the Borromean Islands, rising like a dream of beauty out of the bosom of the water. I cannot express the glory of these scenes, nor the strange contrast they presented to the wild and solemn grandeur of the Alps, which we had so lately felt. It seemed impossible that we could have passed so swiftly from one to the other.

We stopped at Arona, a small town on the west of the lake, for the night. Early in the morning we resumed the journey. At Isella our passports had been called for, and our luggage slightly examined, as we passed into Piedmont. Now, we had the more formidable barrier of Austria to go through; and from the stories I had heard, I fully expected that half, at least, of my books would be seized. But, though almost everything was examined, nothing was objected to. I was careful to show them all; but told them they were books I had picked up in travelling, and were only for purposes of instruction and amusement. As they were mostly in German and in the dialects of Switzerland, none of which were apparently understood by the officials, after looking at them gravely for a moment, they passed them without a word of comment. G—— had three or four bunches of cigars; rather more, they thought, than *one* person ought to have; so they very good-naturedly assumed that I was a smoker, and handed over one half to me, and the cigars all passed without further question. I have nowhere found the slightest disposition to annoy or detain us unnecessarily. The whole system of passports and custom-houses is a nuisance; but we have found the officials, everywhere, polite and obliging.

Our journey lay through the broad rich plains of Lombardy. For the first time we saw the noble white oxen, celebrated in Virgil's time, and beautiful animals they are. We passed numerous plantations of mulberry-trees, cultivated for the silkworm, and extensive fields of Indian corn, which had a home-like look. Towards evening we began to pass handsome country-seats, shaded avenues, and other indications of a great city. By and by the splendid " Arch of Peace," — one of the finest monuments in Italy, — greeted our sight. Here again our passports were examined, and in a few moments we were rolling over the paved streets of Milan.

We took lodgings at the Hôtel de Ville, on the Corso, and within sight of the Cathedral. Our rooms are really beautiful. " I dreamt that I dwelt in marble halls " has ceased to be a dream; the floors are tessellated marble, and the ceilings are tastefully adorned with frescos. The furniture is elegant, and the table incomparably better than the best in Germany and Switzerland; and here we shall remain three or four days.

I ran out immediately to see the Cathedral. It has been nearly five hundred years in building; and a series of the greatest architects in the world have, during that period, in regular succession, presided over the work. The greatest sculptors, from Michael Angelo down, have chiselled the three or four thousand statues that people its niches, fill its canopies, and stand on its pinnacles. I saw it first at twilight. Its marble tracery seemed to fill the sky. The loveliest star of evening was slowly gliding among the Christian heroes and saints whose marble forms were drawn upon the heavens, to which they seemed to belong more than to earth. The figures in the niches along the sides of the Cathedral were thrown into shadow, and peered dimly out into the coming night. I walked slowly around this assemblage of wonders, and was compelled to admit that all I had yet seen of the splendor of Christian temples fell below this one most magnificent act of devotion, still unfinished, though already five hundred years in performing.

This morning, as soon as I was dressed, I went again to the Cathedral. The sun was streaming through the eastern colored windows, and filling the vast spaces of the interior with a subdued, but

rich and splendid light; and hundreds of worshippers were kneeling and repeating their prayers, in
different parts of the church. Whether you look
up to the lofty and wonderfully curved ceiling,
down the lengthening aisles, across the transept,—
whether you dwell upon the clustered columns, or
fretted vault, or painted windows of the apsis,—
your senses are enchanted and your mind is filled
by the vastness of the conception, the matchless
beauty of the details, and the wealth of genius with
which they have been executed. The Alps are
unique, in their way. It is absurd to compare
our mountains with them. You feel in the imme-
diate presence of the Almighty as you traverse
their mighty passes, or cross their mountain aisles,
and look up to the pinnacled heights that bound
them. The sight of the glacier, and the com-
mingling roar of rivers and water-falls, impress
you with evidences of majestic power, such as no
human work ever produces. But of all things I
have ever seen, the effect of the Milan Cathedral
comes nearest to that of one of the great works
of God.

In the course of the forenoon we all went there
together. A service was performing, and we
heard a part of the Gregorian Mass. One hundred and eighty priests are attached to the Cathedral; perhaps fifty were present. The chanting
had a somewhat monotonous, but very solemn and
unearthly sound.

We ascended the Cathedral with a guide ; first to the roofs, among the pinnacles, where the eye wanders over an immese garden of marble plants and flowers, with which the balustrades of the flying buttresses are richly ornamented. A guide is as much needed here as among the Alps. Next we went up to the roofs of the transepts, and were on a level with the statues on the pinnacles, — a goodly company. Here we saw, each by itself, in a compartment of the roof, Michael Angelo's Adam and Eve. Then we ascended the principal tower, and looked down upon the statues as upon inhabitants of the earth. Here we were among the gilded stars, with which some of the highest are surmounted. Up, up we went, by a narrow staircase, winding among the open tracery, looking too fragile to support itself, and piercing the air, until the dizzying effect of height is lost in its immensity.

The city lay far, far below us ; the streets were narrow paths ; men like ants, and carriages moving dots. Northeast and north the horizon was bounded by the mighty barrier of the Alps, whose snowy heights glistened in the distance ; east, south, and west the eye ranged over a wide and magnificent prospect of plains, villages, and cities ; and over all hung the sky of Italy. What more was wanting ?

After an hour or two spent high up in the air, we descended to the subterranean spaces. Here

we saw the chapel and tomb of San Carlo Bor-
romeo, rich with silver and gold and precious
stones. Here the saint himself lies in his coffin
of rock crystal, mounted with wrought silver, and
cased in a silver frame, carved elaborately by one
of the first masters of Italy. Here for three centuries he has lain. For five francs the silver case
is opened, and we are allowed to see the mum-
mied lineaments, black and grim, of one who was
in life generous and brave and great. Innumerable precious stones — emeralds, topazes, diamonds,
sapphires, and rubies — shed their splendor over
the ghastliness of death.

XV.

VENICE, September 18.

WE arrived to-day at Venice. From the balcony of my room I look out upon the peaceful waters. There is a full moon, shining down upon canal and lagoon, — tracing with matchless beauty the ship with all her rigging, and the light gondola, beneath the silvery surface. Just opposite I see the Isola San Giorgio, and the sweep of waters over which passed the bridal pomp of the Doge, when the stately Bucentaur bore him to the Lido to wed the Adriatic. On my right stands, on his lofty column, the winged Lion of Saint Mark. Beyond the mouth of the Grand Canal rises in the transfigured air the dome of Santa Maria della Salute. It is now midnight; and beneath my windows the hum of voices and the tramp of feet are beginning to die away, while the waves of the Adriatic plash gently against the shore, as if the deserted bride had come to seek and win back her too long absent lover. I mourn for thee, Adria. The Northern barbarian has stolen into the place where thy Doges dwelt, in palaces of marble and gold. Thy mourning and thy wooing are in vain. Thy splendid love is a dream of the past. Well, before I quite lose my senses, let me tell you our various adventures since I wrote last.

We spent a whole week at Milan, resting, like Hannibal's soldiers, after crossing the Alps. Every day, and often twice or three times a day, I went to the Cathedral, which drew me by a fascination I did not care to resist. I went there morning, noon, and evening; and listened to the Ambrosian ritual with an interest and a. pleasure I never expected to feel in a Catholic service. On Sunday we attended High Mass, and heard the best sermon I have listened to since I left home. It was in Italian, and I lost some portions of it; but so excellent was the good father's enunciation, that I followed him gen   lly with ease.

Another great pleasu.. has been to read Manzoni's *Promessi Sposi*, the scene of which, you know, is laid in Milan and the neighborhood. I used to think it rather a dull book; but the descriptions are so true, and the objects introduced are so interesting, after having seen the things themselves, that I made the work a sort of guide-book. The characters, too, are such as one meets with every day in the streets of Milan.

You know the great theatre of La Scala is there; and you know, too, that every musical aspirant must pass the ordeal of Milanese criticism before his reputation is established. It so happened that the theatre was reopened for the season on the last night of our stay there. The opera was *Il Trovatore.* It is a story of a noble infant stolen by a gypsy, who had a grudge against his father; most unreasonably, since the only injury he had ever done her was merely to cause her to be condemned to death by burning, for having attempted to practise the evil eye. The old gypsy stole the boy, intending to put *him* into the fire which she had herself escaped. By mistake she threw her own child into the flames, and did not find it out till he was nearly consumed. Then she resolves to bring up the stolen child as her own, and to seek her revenge in another way. The instinct of noble blood leads the youth to deeds of arms and the chivalrous accomplishments of the Troubadours. Leonora — a noble lady — falls in love with him. The Count, the brother of the lost child, falls in love with Leonora. They have several rencounters. The Count, finding his love despised, forms a plot to carry the lady off. The Troubadour, of course, pops in, just in time to prevent its execution; — a duel; — Leonora borne off in triumph by her lover. Meantime, the old gypsy is arrested, and, being questioned, is proved to be the old lady who burnt the baby; thrown into prison; condemned a second time to be burnt. Lover and Leonora are just on the point of marrying, when the news is brought him of the extreme peril in which his respected mother stands. Away he rushes, saying to the astonished bride, " I was a son before I loved you; and in spite of your tears, I must go." He calls a band of followers, and runs to the rescue; is defeated; is himself cast into prison; and both mother and son await their execution. Leonora hears what has happened; goes to the Count, and implores him to spare her lover. The Count says, " The more you love him, the more I want to kill him." Leonora, in despair, proposes to give her hand to the Count. The Count, overjoyed, asks " whether he can believe his own ears." Apparently thinking he can, he turns to give orders for the lover's release. Leonora takes poison behind his back; goes directly to the prison, and tells her lover he is free. The lover, astonished, looks at her; suspects something; swears she is a traitor. The poison begins to work; he looks again, suddenly catches the idea, and then swears she is an angel, and berates himself for having said such hard things of her. At this moment the Count enters; and, seeing Leonora dying, exclaims, " What, take poison for him? Executioner, away with him!" The executioner obeys. The old gypsy says, " Now I am avenged, — he was your brother." The Count exclaims, "And I still live?" — and the curtain drops without any answer whatever to the Count's question.

I had no idea it would take up so much of my paper to give a sketch of the pathetic plot of this famous opera, which was awaiting the judgment of the critics of Milan — and my own. We secured a box near the stage, so that we might see and hear well. It is a magnificent theatre; the audience large, discriminating, and tremendously critical. The curtain rose, with immense expectation. Some applause, and some hissing. By and by, there was a fine passage so vehemently applauded, that the singer came forward three times to acknowledge it. But as the piece went on, the applause lessened, the hissing increased; and the curtain dropped before the opera was completed. We came home and consoled ourselves with a broiled chicken and a glass of wine.

It was curious indeed to witness the rigor with which the Milanese punish the slightest fault, — or what they choose to consider such, — in any performer, no matter how eminent; but to quiet people like ourselves the hissing was an intolerable nuisance.

The next morning we set out for Lodi, and visited the bridge where Napoleon made his terrible pass; — then went on to Crema, where we spent the night, in a veritable old-fashioned Italian inn, — rooms big and bare as a barn, beds as broad as the plains of Lombardy, and charges as high as the dishonest host could persuade us to pay.

The next day we went to Brescia, where we saw some fine pictures in a private collection; others in the churches; but, most interesting of all, the remains of an old Roman temple, with numerous sculptures of Greek workmanship, and a bronze winged Victory, almost perfectly preserved, and most exquisite. From Brescia we went on, striking the southern end of. Lago di Garda, a lovely lake, with finely moulded hills on the north, sloping softly to the south, until they lose themselves in the Lombard and Venetian plains. The weather was perfect, and the peculiar haze — like a veil of the most delicate and scarcely perceptible pink — hung over the distant landscape, under the blue sky, and beyond the blue waters.

We stopped an hour on the borders of the lake, and then continued our journey. At Peschiera, a strongly fortified town on the confines of Lombardy and Venice, we dined on an ancient chicken, coeval with the Roman temple ; then, turning from the Lago di Garda, took the road for Verona. The country became more picturesque ; the vines were festooned from tree to tree ; we saw the wine-press, and the men treading out the grapes.

We entered Verona under the light of an Italian sunset, — purple, orange, golden, — flooding the earth, transfiguring the walls, habitations, and spires of the city, and mantling the hills with a transparent purple mist. We thought of Catullus, the first of Roman lyric poets, who was born there ; we thought of Romeo and Juliet, who are buried there ; and we imagined ourselves to be the " Two Gentlemen of Verona." We lodged in a good hotel, and, being a little fatigued, retired early. We were up early the next morning, and visited the old Roman Amphitheatre, — a superb structure in admirable preservation, — where Vespasian exhibited a great gladiatorial show in honor of his wife, a Veronese lady.

As we returned, and I was in the passage to my room, I heard my name suddenly called : and who should it be but Mrs. C——? She has been travelling in the North of Italy, with a servant; happened to stop at the same hotel, and was just leaving her room to go *to* the Amphitheatre, as I was entering mine *from* it. This accidental meeting (Mrs. C—— recognized my gold spectacles from a side view merely) was a most agreeable incident. We had but a moment's conversation, however, and then parted, to meet again next week in Florence.

At eleven o'clock we took the railway for Venice. The journey was very pleasant, and in three hours the train was thundering over the magnificent bridge, — two miles and three quarters long, — that crosses the Lagoon, and brings you into Venice. We were detained a little while at the station to have our luggage examined ; and then, calling a gondola, were swiftly rowed down the great canal, lined with palaces of historical renown, in sight of the Rialto ; then turned into a side canal, swept under the Bridge of Sighs, between the Ducal Palace and the Prison, out into the water in front of the Piazza San Marco, with the Palace, the Winged Lion, the Basilica, domes, spires, pinnacles, and statues innumerable, seeming to fill the air and look down upon us. We passed on by ships and gondolas, and, turning into another canal, were at the steps of Albergo Reale Danaeli, once a palace of the Mocenighi, and now a very splendid establishment. The staircases are wide ; the steps of white marble ; the rooms adorned with pictures and statues ; the ceilings frescoed, and the floors tessellated. A marble bust of Minerva stands in the corner of the room where I am ; and a frescoed angel, in the centre of the ceiling, is kind enough to hold the chandelier. Nymphs and goddesses, flowers and columns, urns and vases, are painted on the walls, and two huge mirrors reflect this goodly company and myself, as I sit here — otherwise alone, for my fellow-travellers have gone to bed — writing.

After dinner we took a gondola, with a couple of gondoliers, to see a little of this marvellous place. Venice is like no other city. It is a gorgeous dream. It is oriental and mediæval, and altogether indescribably wonderful. We were rowed out by the opposite island of Giudecca, through the canal of the same name. The sun had just gone down, and the evening star, scarcely perceptible in the splendid colors of the west, appeared just above the horizon. The ships, the dome of

St. Mark, the Winged Lion, the Campanile, were drawn darkly on the golden ground of the sky. Thousands of gondolas were hurrying to and fro. We rowed into the Lagoon; passing churches on the left, the Campo di Marte on the right, and the great railroad bridge just before us. The Grand Canal winds through the whole city; it is the *great street*, on which the most splendid palaces stand.

We passed through the entire length of this Grand Canal, and as we emerged into the open waters on the other side of the city, the full moon had just risen, and was illuminating every object in the transcendent scene. Crowds of people were walking in the Piazza San Marco; the gorgeous oriental front of the Basilica shone wonderfully, with its gilded mosaics; the marble statues which crowd the upper walls of the Royal Palace stood out in bold relief against the sky; military music filled the Piazza, and the Venetian songs of the gondoliers came up from the canals and the Lagoon.

Later in the evening, since I have been writing, a barge with twelve lights shot out in front of St. Mark, presenting the appearance of a fiery serpent, as the lights waved to and fro with the motion of the boat. It was a society of twelve, who cultivate Venetian music, and sing all the Venetian songs. I watched the motion, and listened to the sounds, from my balcony; and, singularly enough, they rowed at last up to the corner of the canal just below me, and, stopping, sang half a dozen songs. If I had been a beautiful woman of nineteen or twenty, instead of an old Professor whose portrait frightens his friends at home, there would have been something decidedly romantic in this little episode of a midnight serenade in Venice. However, the singing had a most agreeable effect, in the splendid night, with so many objects of un-paralleled interest in sight, under the glorious beauty of a full Venetian moon. At the close I applauded, and the fiery serpent wound his way silently across the Lagoon.

XVI.

PADUA, September 20, 1853.

I PUT a letter in the post-office at Venice this morning, containing a hurried account of our first evening in that city of enchantment. I write now at Padua, having left Venice this afternoon. Yesterday, we took a *valet de place*, as we had but little time, and traversed the city, in a gondola, in all directions. We visited the principal churches, where the best pictures of the Venetian school are found; the Academy of the Fine Arts, the glory of which is Titian's Assumption, and the Palazzo Manfrini, containing the finest private collection of pictures, by Raffaelle, Correggio, Caracci, Guido Reni, Bambi, Pietro Perugino, Carlo Dolce, and other old masters, in all Venice. This is a noble palace, and its owner, one of the most eminent patricians here, throws it open twice a week to the public. It so happened that we could not stay in Venice for the regular day, and I was obliged to do what I have done before, — to send in my card, and ask permission to see the collection. Otherwise I must have left Venice without seeing some of the best pictures in the world. So I sent my card, as " Professore della Letteratúra Greca nell' Università di Cambridge, America," explaining that I was under the necessity of leaving Venice the next day. We were most courteously admitted, and saw at our leisure, uninterrupted by a crowd of visitors, the precious treasures, — all the rooms being most kindly, thrown open to our inspection. I have enjoyed nothing more entirely since I left home, than the quiet hours spent among the master-works collected in this splendid palace. We went afterward to another remarkable collection of Tintoretto's masterpieces, then to the Ducal Palace.

The most gorgeous scenes of modern history cluster around this magnificent residence of the Doges. We saw under the roof those most cruel prison-cells, the close and stifling rooms called the Piombi, or leads; below, the Doge's residence, the Senate-chamber, the rooms of the Council of Ten and the Secret Council of Three, with secret stair-cases, by which prisoners were brought for examination by tortures; still lower, the dungeons in which state-prisoners were confined, — small, dark, dismal, with just a ray of light from a passage shut in by stone-walls of amazing thickness. Here was the place of execution, whenever reasons of state forbade the public display. Here was the narrow door through which the strangled body was taken, placed on a boat, and borne away to a little burying-ground for criminals. Here still stand the frames of the beds on which they lay. We went through these dark passages, and into these narrow and hopeless cells, with a guide and a candle; and the imagination of Dante himself could scarcely picture a more infernal scene.

From these dungeons we passed over the " Bridge of Sighs," which crosses a canal to another gloomy-looking structure, still used, as it was in the days of the Republic, for a prison. The bridge is covered and dark, with apertures cut through the stone-walls at the sides. I was not sorry when we emerged from these horrible places, — horrible in themselves, and still more so from the frightful deeds which history has associated with them. You cannot imagine a more tremendous contrast than they present to the gay and splendid outer world of Venice. All we read of heaven and hell gives but a feeble idea compared with the feeling we experience in coming out of these terrible places and ghastly memories, into the cheerful light and busy life and gorgeous art that crowd the Piazza of San Marco.

The last place we visited was the church of San Marco. Here all the treasures of the East and the West are concentrated. The floor, covering acres, is of tessellated marbles and lapis-lazuli; the walls and ceilings, both of the exterior arcades and the interior, are entirely covered with mosaics, on a golden ground, representing an endless diversity of subjects; columns brought from the Holy Land

and from Greece, and statues captured from sub-
jugated nations, are built into this amazing structure. Over the entrance stand the four bronze
horses, carried from Rome by one of the emperors of Constantinople; brought from Constantinople by one of the Venetian Doges; captured
and taken to Paris by Napoleon; restored to Venice at the peace of 1815, and now likely to deco-
rate St. Mark's until Venice sinks into the sea.
Under the great altar is enshrined the heart of
St. Mark (I did not see the heart, but I saw the
shrine, and was assured that it contained the
heart), the patron saint of the Republic. The
most extraordinary thing, however, is the present
condition of the floor. Venice, you know, is built
on piles. These have settled in some places, particularly under the foundation of St. Mark's. You
seem to be walking over petrified waves of many
colors. In some places the pavement is more than
a foot higher than in others, and you must step
carefully, or you will fall. A sensitive person
might be made sea-sick by these undulations of
form and color.

I was bewildered by this extraordinary assemblage of ages, styles, countries, and materials.
It was like a dream, in which the mind passes
through time and space with inconceivable rapidity. On my first visit, I did not attempt to
form a clear conception of so heterogeneous —
though not inharmonious — a combination of di-

verse objects.   I allowed them to make their own impressions, and left the impressions to be arranged and cleared up by subsequent visits.

In the evening we went out again on the Lagoon.   It was a still and splendid repetition of the Venetian sunset we had already seen, — a phenomenon of Italian nature which justifies and explains the coloring of Titian.

XVII.

MODENA, September 24, 1853.

ON Wednesday afternoon, having completed the time we had allowed ourselves for Venice, we came by railway as far as learned Padua, the birthplace of Livy, the seat of a great University, and the place where Portia, in " The Merchant of Venice," pretended to have studied the law.   We had a couple of hours before evening to go round and see so renowned a city, and then the fancy struck us to complete the tour by the evening light.   We first visited the famous church of San Antonio, full of splendid bronzes, sculptures, and paintings.   Then we went to the Botanical Garden, one of the best in Europe, and I cannot describe to you the delicious impression the objects of Nature made upon me, after having dwelt among the creations of art alone.   The Garden is admirably laid out and well kept, and is a charming assemblage of odoriferous plants, from every clime, superb trees, forest and fruit, and flowers of exquisite colors.   The pine rose green and erect ; the fir, the elm, the oak, the nut tree lifted their verdurous branches up into the golden sky of summer, while fountains played their pleasant music

7 *

and filled the air with coolness. It was another Italian evening, and the domes and campaniles of the city shone in the glorious hues of the hour. The Garden is in the city, and these fair objects are all around it.

Here I saw the palm-tree which Goethe studied so carefully, and which, by suggesting to him the first idea of his theory of the metamorphosis of plants, has become illustrious in the history of science. I stood long before this beautiful tree, and fancied it was not unconscious of the interest and admiration it excited.

My admiration of Goethe's genius has grown upon me almost daily here. I have found his descriptions of the Alps no less precise than poetical. His science gives accuracy to his poetry, and his poetical spirit gives glow and animation to his science. His letters on Italy are incomparably better than anything else I have read on the same topics; not entering much into details, but extracting the finest essence and aroma of this classic land.

From the Botanical Garden we went to the palace of a Paduan nobleman, and saw by candlelight his splendid saloons, and curious works of art; among the rest, a group of sculpture wrought from a single piece of marble, and consisting of sixty-six figures, representing the last judgment of the wicked.

Next we visited the great hall, one of the largest

in the world, where are the bust of Livy, an un-
doubted antique, a statue of him by some modern
sculptor, his tomb, which they say contains his
ashes, and a big wooden horse, as large as the
horse of Troy, formerly dragged through the city
on festivals. The walls are decorated with frescos, which, however, we saw imperfectly by the
candle-light.

We then took our way to a famous *café*, built
of marble, partly of an ancient temple, where we
took ices (the Italian ices are the best in the
world) and listened to the performances of a minstrel — young, pretty, and modest-looking — on
the guitar. I was desirous to hear a song or two,
(naturally, you know, having such musical friends,)
and, approaching, I asked her in choice Italian if
she would not sing. She nodded, and in a moment struck into a song that rolled through the
marble halls, and made the chatting crowds of
loungers hold their tongues, and listen in rapt attention. She went on from song to song — it was
in an open piazza — for half an hour; when, drop-
ping a piece of silver on the table where she stood,
we walked away and returned to our lodgings;
passing by the tomb of Antenor (uncle of the
pious Æneas of Virgil), the founder of the city.
There is no doubt his bones are there, (though it is
very doubtful if he ever lived,) for the guides assure you they were found near an ancient church.
Early in the morning we visited an old Roman

arena, and the chapel of Giotto, the interior of which is wholly covered with frescos of his painting, and at half past seven took the railway for Vicenza.

Our object in stopping at Vicenza was chiefly to see the great works in architecture of Palladio, who was born and died here. They are in a bad condition, generally. The house he built for himself is the dirtiest spot in Italy. We ascended the staircase, but were glad to get back again into the street. One old palace of his building has a fine front, but the interior shows marks of decay and ruin. A splendid old picture of Paul Veronese is fast fading from the neglected wall. Palladio built a theatre, on the plan of the ancient Grecian. Here my expectations were more than gratified. It is a beautiful structure, adorned with sculptures, and in all respects a classical edifice. In 1846 they played the Œdipus of Sophocles here in an Italian translation, before the Scientific Association, who were invited from Venice to see it, and a brilliant assemblage of Italian beauty. I spent a delightful hour or two in studying the plan of this theatre, and reading the translation of Sophocles, a copy of which I bought there.

We took a carriage and drove to the cemetery, where is the superb monument of Palladio, and many others, with beautiful sculptures by the finest artists in Italy. Next we went to a villa in the neighborhood of the city, also built by

Palladio, and then took the railway for Verona. Our object in stopping here again was to visit some of the churches, and the tomb of the gentle Juliet. We took a carriage at the station, and drove about. The most curious monument here is the tomb of the Scaligeri, the ancient rulers of this famous city, who, not content with setting themselves over the city during their lifetime, built these lofty mausoleums, and had their bodies placed in elaborate marble coffins, high up in the open air, where they have lain for many centuries. The Cathedral has some works of art of great merit. As to the tomb of Juliet, it is a stone trough, once used as a washing-tub, in a very dirty building of one of the wings of an old convent, and in the very outskirts of the city. I could not help laughing at such a burlesque of sentiment. There is not the least evidence that this old tub was ever seen by Juliet; and yet scarcely a day passes that it is not visited by pious strangers, who ring for admission, sigh over its brim, pay their *zwanziger* and walk away, feeling that they have only performed their duty to romance and Shakespeare.

That duty religiously over, we again took the railway for Mantua, the birthplace of Virgil, where we arrived early in the evening, thinking all the time of Bucolics, Georgics, and Æneids. But Mantua is a low, swampy, unhealthy place, — an excellent place to emigrate from. I applauded Virgil's good sense in packing up his trunk and

going to Rome; and we determined to imitate his
illustrious example. So, early in the morning, we
set off in our carriage, and, taking a hasty glance
over the place, drove out of its southern gate, and
pursued our way toward Modena. But here I
must pause, as we are just going over to the palace of the Duke.

XVIII.

BOLOGNA, September 24.

A T Modena we went to the palace of the Duke, and a very nice palace it is, as the Englishman says. One could manage to live in it with tolerable comfort. It is not so stately nor so gorgeous as many palaces we have seen; but it has some fine pictures and beautiful statuary, and is a much more cheerful-looking establishment than palaces usually are.

From the palace we went to the famous old cathedral, much admired by some, but possessing in my eyes neither beauty nor taste; and as to the pictures, I did not see one that I would give a sixpence for.

But the Campanile has an interesting association with literary history. If you look into the book of the Poets of Europe — under the head of Italian Poets — you will find, I think, some passages from the poem of Trissino called the "Secchia Rapita," or the Rape of the Bucket. In a war between Modena and Bologna, the forces of the former seized an old bucket in Bologna, and bore it off in triumph. This stupendous event occurred in 1225, about a year after the great Campanile was built.　Twenty or thirty steps up from the foundation of this there is a dungeon-like room, approached by heavy iron doors, three in number, and three iron keys of ponderous size unlock them, and a mighty bolt, besides the lock, is drawn outside the door.　From the centre of this room hangs, suspended by an iron chain, and has hung for six hundred and twenty-eight years the 15th of November, that same old, iron-bound bucket, that once hung over a public fountain in Bologna.　The chain passes through a ring in the ceiling, and is attached by a padlock to a staple in the wall, the key of which is kept by the Podestà of the city.

L—— and I got a sight of this old bucket, for two zwanzigers, — about thirty-six cents, — one paid to a man for giving notice at the seat of government, that certain signors from foreign parts desired to see the bucket, and the other paid to the official gentleman who in due form brought the keys and opened the three locks.　I could just reach the bottom of the bucket, as it hung from the ceiling, by standing on tiptoe.　I punched it with a paper-cutter I happened to have in my pocket, and found it so decayed that the ivory blade passed quite through at the side.　There it has hung, as I have said, for more than six centuries :

> "E non è cavalier, che di là passi,
>   Nè pellegrin di cónto, il qual non voglia
>   Veder si degna e gloriosa spoglia."

There is no cavalier who that way passes,
Nor wanderer of note, who doth not wish
To see such noble and illustrious spoils.

Nota bene, I punched the bucket with an ivory paper-knife at ten o'clock in the morning of September 24, 1853. I am thus particular, because Trissino tells us that it was hung up there at three o'clock at night, after Manfredi, the clergy, and Monsignore had made a long prayer to the saint, that is, Saint Geminianus, the patron of Modena.

This poem is famous in Italian literature, and has had no little influence on the English. The title of Pope's " Rape of the Lock " was borrowed from it.

We resumed our journey and reached this city of sausages about three o'clock. The country about it is more varied and cultivated than is usual in the North of Italy ; and the heights of the Apennines, in sight nearly all the way 'from Modena, relieved the monotony. We have seen but little here, except long chains of sausages at the shop windows. It is said no dog dares show his face in Bologna. We met a very small puppy in the streets, but he was not yet sufficiently grown to be profitable. We shall probably start to-morrow morning for Florence.

Let me now go back to dreamy Venice. The last day we were there, I took a gondola and was rowed over the Lagoon to the island of San La-

K

zaro, to visit the Armenian Convent. It was another of those perfect Venetian days, seen only here and in the pictures of Titian. A soft breeze, just enough to stir the air, flitted over the water, along the surface of which it gently moved, not breaking, but just bending the glassy expanse. I could not help feeling all the luxury of the time, the place, and the motion, as I reclined on the cushioned seats of the gliding bark, and surveyed the magical scene around me, and the glorious sky above. The gondola shot past the entrance of the arsenal, near which are two marble lions, brought by one of the Doges from Athens, — noble sculptures, belonging to the best days of Athenian art, and now decorating an Austrian garrison.

When we were fairly out of hearing from the shore, I entered into conversation with the gondoliers. They spoke in whispers, though we were a mile at least from any human being; but what they said showed the wretched condition of the people, whom they described as miserably poor. "In former times," said the eldest of the two, "Venice was rich and powerful. The commerce of the world came here, when Doges ruled. Gold was abundant, and every man had enough. But now there is no commerce. We are under Austria, and have no liberty. We are poor and miserable. Men like me earn but two zwanzigers a day, and the prices of provisions are high. Sometimes I receive a *buona mano* (present) from gentlemen who employ me; but my wages are only two zwanzigers a day."

As we passed by an island on which the hospital stands, the younger gondolier stooped down and whispered: " I was in that hospital three months. In the revolution of 1848 I received a musket-ball in my shoulder, and was sent over here to be cured."

They knew I was American, or they would not have dared, even on the water, to speak of such things, — so rigid is the Austrian police.

About three quarters of an hour brought me to the landing of the Armenian Convent. You remember what Byron says of this community. I was most kindly received by one of the monks, who took me over the whole establishment, showed me the manuscripts, the library, the printing-office, the garden, and gave me ample information on their language, history, literature, and religion, — much of it very curious, and to me entirely new. Their language has no relation, as a language, with either the Greek or the Latin ; but it has this singular connection with the former, that translations of some of the Greek writers exist in the Armenian, while the originals have been lost since the translations were made. These have been published by the good monks, with retranslations. Their ritual dates as early as the fourth century, near which time their nation was converted to the Christian faith. It is, therefore, one of the oldest in the Christian world, and their translation of the Scriptures is very ancient, much older than the earliest entire translation in the Latin. At my request, my excellent guide repeated the Pater Noster in the Armenian, to give me a specimen of the language. It sounded soft and harmonious. Politically they are under the Turkish government, having no connection with Venice or Austria; and their relations are almost wholly with the East.

I examined the books they have translated or written and printed there. They make a considerable library. They have translated Homer, Virgil, and other ancient writers, and some modern ones. I bought a grammar, a collection of popular songs (with a literal English version), and a copy of the ritual, as memorials of the visit; and after a forenoon spent in a quiet, but most interesting and instructive manner, in this retreat of Oriental learning and antique piety, I came away.

I should have mentioned that I saw in their chapel a singular painting of the Virgin, by a converted Turk, — the only Turkish picture I ever heard of. It has a very peculiar, pensive beauty, wholly unlike any Italian Madonna of any school. A Turk's conception of such a Christian subject may, I think, be put down among the curiosities of art.

Returning, I went to the Royal Library, in the Ducal Palace, to see a famous copy of Homer, —

the whole Iliad on parchment, and dating in the tenth or eleventh century. It is very beautiful, and one of the most important manuscripts in the world. Some of the leaves are illustrated, — there is a picture of Helen, of Achilles, and so on ; but they are in the worst style of Byzantine art, — clothed in Byzantine costumes, which are anything but heroic. Achilles looks like a dunce, and Helen has none of those charms

"For nine long years that kept the world in arms."

I went through every part of St. Mark's Church again ; and, lastly, ascended the great tower, to combine all I had seen into a single, general view, and I can tell you I never saw such a sight. To look down on the domes and palaces of Venice, — to let the eye rove over the Lagoon, the islands, the Lido, and the distant Adriatic, — to take in the villages, plains, cities — north, west, and south — in one magnificent panorama, lighted by the sun of Italy, — is enough to make an epoch in one's life.

I do not find that I get exhausted with the interesting objects I see almost every day; on the contrary, I need the twenty-four hours of every day to see them and reflect on what I have seen. Then comes the evil necessity of eating and sleeping, to waste these precious moments. It is now growing late, and we shall start early, — so I must say good night.

XIX.

FLORENCE, October 1, 1853.

MY last letter was written all along the way, and posted immediately on my arrival in Florence. I trust it is safely on its way to England, and will reach you in good time.

From Bologna we commenced our journey over the Apennines. The mountains looked friendly, and the mountain air was refreshing; but the Apennines do not, in the smallest degree, compare with the Alps. Their shapes are pleasing, and the valleys, green and well cultivated almost to the highest points, are beautiful.

I took a long walk, as I had so often done in the Alps. I was alone, and enjoyed greatly the quiet of the scene and hour. The weather was delicious. On the summit the views were extensive in all directions, and charming. I lay down on the grass, and rested in the shade, until the carriage, reinforced by a yoke of oxen, came up.

As I lay, meditating and looking up into the deep sky, a young Italian, who had been gathering grapes from a sunny slope just opposite, came up and gave me a large bunch, apologizing for their inferior quality, as they grew at such a height.   He was as inquisitive as a Yankee, and I answered all his questions.   He seemed astonished at my having come such a measureless distance to see Italy.   In turn I questioned him; but his ideas were limited to the farms of the Apennines, with some notion of the distant city of Bologna, at least fifteen miles off.   The toiling oxen at length came in sight, and I resumed my place in the carriage.

We passed the night in a village that we reached in the afternoon.   The inn where we stayed was an old-fashioned Italian *locánda*, — rude in the last degree.   The rooms had no locks, and only one had a latch.   G—— attempted to drive a nail in the wall, to fasten his door with a string; but he broke off a foot or two of the wall, which was nothing but plaster.   The beds were so high, that I had to climb into mine over a chair.   They were hard and ridgy like the Apennines, and peopled with a wild population of chamois, commonly called *fleas*.   From these enemies of the human race I have not suffered; they do not like me, — they have no taste for Greek Professors.

We set out early in the morning, having no great temptation to lie late in bed.   It had rained heavily in the night, and the storm còntinued through the forenoon, at times coming down with great violence; and it was a pretty wild scene, among the Apennines, — one I was glad to witness.   But early in the afternoon, as we approached the descent into Tuscany, the weather cleared away, — the sun broke out, and opened a prospect of marvellous beauty.

For the last dozen miles before entering Florence, the road passes through a region diversified by hills whose slopes are covered with trailing vines, and dotted with white villas. This continues until the Val d' Arno, in which Florence lies embosomed, comes in sight. The whole view makes a very agreeable impression; and you enter the city — having passed the custom-house and surrendered your passport — with the expectation of finding everything to please the eye and gratify the taste.

The custom-house officer said it was necessary to open our luggage. "Absolutely necessary?" I asked. "Yes, sir, absolutely." The courier was ordered to see what virtue there was in zwan-zigers (about eighteen cents each), and we found that the absolute necessity of examining our luggage, to make sure that we had no prohibited articles, and no instruments for the overthrow of the Grand Duke's government, was measured by exactly two of these silver pieces. Having received these, the gentleman in the cocked hat and sword made a comprehensive survey by putting his head into the window and taking it out again, then nodded to the vetturino that all was right, and on we drove to the Albergo Reale di Gran Brettagna, on the Lung' Arno.

Well, Florence is a beautiful city. It contains
the Medicean Venus, "the statue that enchants
the world"; the Madonna della Seggiola of Raffaelle; some of the principal works of Michael
Angelo; the Campanile of Giotto; Titian's Venuses; the monuments, in Santa Croce, of Dante,
Alfieri, Galileo, Filicalia; streets, arcades, and
bridges bordered with exquisite statues; and the
Baptistery, with the bronze gates, which Michael
Angelo said were worthy to be the gates of Paradise.

I shall not have time to give you an account
of all I have seen; but I have visited the principal
objects, and have sat hours and hours in the Tri-
bune, — the apartment in the Palazzo dei Uffizi
which contains the Venus de' Medici, the Apollino,
a selection of Raffaelle's pictures, two Venuses of
Titian, and masterpieces by several other artists.
The room is beautifully lighted, and the first time
I entered it the sunlight was falling over the left
shoulder of Venus, and illuminating her face as
she looked towards it. There are in other rooms
numerous antiques of the highest order of beauty;
foremost among them Niobe and her children, in a
large saloon specially arranged for this unequalled
group.

I found the heads of the principal philosophers
and poets of Greece and Rome. The one which
struck me most singularly was that of Socrates.
I could not doubt that it was a perfect portrait,

although in expression, and in some of the details of the features, it differed from several others I had seen.

The gallery of the Pitti Palace — the residence of the Grand Duke — is one of the most admirable in the world. It contains, with many other remarkable pictures, the Madonna della Seggiola, which, for sweetness and beauty of expression, seems to me to transcend all other pictures I have seen, and for softness and harmony of coloring to go beyond all human powers of execution. The first sight of it makes an epoch in one's life.

You have heard of the portrait of Dante, in a fresco picture, discovered some years ago by our countryman, Mr. Wilde. I have been to see it. It is on the walls of an old chapel, in a building once occupied by the Podestà of Florence, and now a prison. The interior was painted by Giotto, the friend of Dante; but in the course of time the chapel fell into neglect, and the pictures were covered with a coating of whitewash, or paint. Since Mr. Wilde's discovery, several others have been brought to light. The portrait represents Dante at the age of thirty-six. It is a most interesting monument of the past.

The house of Michael Angelo is still kept up. The present occupant is the Conte di Buonarotti, a lineal descendant of the great artist, and a most estimable man. He is the Grand Duke's Minister of Public Instruction. The house has never been out of the family. I visited it, and saw the chairs, tables, sword, and numerous other relics of Michael Angelo, which are preserved with precious care. There are pen-and-ink drawings, paintings, and sculptures of his, just as he left them, and all characteristic of his stupendous genius.

XX.

ROME, October 6, 1853.

I HAVE been two days in Rome.   G—— and I left Florence in a diligence, last Monday (it is now Thursday), having placed the rest of our troupe in the Casa Guidi with the .——s.

The last day of the very interesting week I stayed in Florence, I took a carriage and drove all around the city to get a general view of the whole, having already visited the most interesting places in detail.   I drove to see the house where Benvenuto Cellini was born; that where Alfieri lived, and other houses connected with the illustrious men who have made the name of Florence immortal. I drove by Greenough's former studio, now changing, in the hands of an Englishman, into a dwelling-house.   Its tasteful structure was characteristic of the genius of its former tenant, and gave me a sad pleasure as I gazed upon it, and thought of the warm heart that once beat there, and the busy brain that once toiled there, — now in the silence and darkness of death.

I looked at the ancient palaces with the feeling, incessantly forced upon one in these old European cities, of the shadowy, evanescent life of man, and of the wonders he yet leaves behind him, when God has breathed into him the breath of genius. These statues, works of Cellini and Angelo; the pictures in yonder palaces, the loveliest creations of Raffaelle, Titian, Perugino, — what a wonderful sense of the greatness of the human mind they inspire!

We were up early on our way to Rome, by Sienna. From Florence we went to this latter city by a railway, which gave us time to drive through Sienna, and visit the Cathedral and the Academy of the Fine Arts. The Cathedral has some splendid works, and the Academy some paintings, interesting in the history of art, but not otherwise of much merit. Having accomplished thus much of sight-seeing, we took our places in the diligence and were fairly off for Rome.

The excessive heats of summer have laid nearly all Italy bare; and I am not sorry to see the beautiful undulations of its surface without the drapery which clothes them in spring and early summer. The road, for a considerable part of the way, was rough and over mountains; but there was not a mile that was not gratifying to the sight, or to the imagination, or to the memory.

All night we travelled, stopping only to sup at a little inn among the Apennines, where we ate everything the house contained, except the butter, which was too strong for us. A journey over the rough roads of Central Italy is not exactly favorable to sleep. Some of my companions closed their eyes and pretended to doze. I did the same; but the jolting vehicle made all such pretences hypocrisy, and killed every little nap before it had time to seal up the weary eyes. Slowly the night wore away; the silence interrupted only by the demands of the postboys at the changing of the horses for *qualche cósa per il postiglióne*, which they have no right to ask, and we no power to refuse.

By and by the east began to light up; the rosy fingers of Aurora pointed the way for the chariot of the sun (pardon this bit of Homeric description), and the drowsy travellers rubbed their eyes and pretended to awake, — first my Bohemian neighbor, next a blue-eyed Roman lady, my *vis-à-vis*, and at last a Neapolitan gentleman, who sat by her side. G—— was in another part of the diligence called the *banquetto*, — a kind of chaise perched on the top of the whole establishment.

The lady took a bottle of wine out of a little bag, drank herself, and offered some to me, which I declined. The gentleman took a cold chicken out of another bag, which he did not offer to share with anybody, and which, therefore, nobody declined. The Bohemian took some peaches out of an unfathomable pocket, and gave me one. The lady then handed about some little cakes of chocolate, which we ate, supplying in fancy the cream and hot water. Bits of brown bread and thin slices of Bologna sausage came next, — whence I could not exactly comprehend; so that, by the time the sun was up, we were in good condition and *en grande toilette* for the day. At meal times the passengers from all departments of the dili-gence — i. e. the *banquette*, the *coupé*, the *in-terior* — met on common ground, and had a good deal of amusement. So we got on very sociably together, and by and by, as if by common con-sent, all other topics were lost in the absorbing thought that here we were, just coming in sight of Rome.

The bare and desolate mountains, the Lake of Bolsena, on whose shores the malaria allows no human being to live; the autumn-tinted foliage on the few trees we saw here and there; the out-spread plains; the Campagna di Roma, which be-gan to come in sight; the great Roman oxen, just like those which Cincinnatus drove; the distant and scarcely visible blue line of the Mediterranean Sea, — prepared the mind gradually, by their va-rious and melancholy beauty, for the sight of " the Niobe of Nations."

At four o'clock, — the westering sun pouring a flood of golden light over the earth, and the bounding hills veiled in a delicate mist, — the dome of St. Peter's rose, gigantic and sublime, into the silent air, and the palaces, spires, obelisks of Rome, one after another, stood out against the sky. Yonder is the Quirinal Mount, and the palace of the Pope. Near it stand the colossal marble horses, with the great forms of Castor and Pollux subduing their impetuous strength, — the work of Praxiteles and Phidias. There is Trajan's Column, with the history of his victories winding round it, to the summit. Yonder dark line, filling the southern horizon, is the outer wall of the Colosseum. Nearer stands the Capitol, surrounded by the Senator's Palace and colossal equestrian statues. On the other side, sweeping down the opposite slope, are the columns, walls, and bases of the temples and palaces which surrounded the ancient Roman Forum ; the Arch of Septimus Severus ; the Column of Phocas ; the Temple of Saturn : there winds the sacred way, over which Horace walked ; on yonder height are the ruins of the Palace of the Cæsars ; and here is the spot where Cicero addressed the Roman people, while Rome was yet free.

The first hour after the sight of Rome greets you is perhaps the most memorable in the life of an educated man. It is impossible to describe it ; it is impossible to convey an idea of the beauty of the picture Rome presents, seated on her seven hills, and surrounded by the exquisite mountain ranges of Soracte, Albano, and the Apennines on one side, and the broad plain and the distant sea on the other.

Goethe truly remarks, that Rome is the centre of the history of the world ; that if we study history anywhere else, it is from without, inward; if we are at Rome, we look out from within.

It is indeed so. But after all, when one has lost a night's sleep, Universal History, Rome, the Forum, Cæsar, Cicero, give place to the claims of the drowsy god. I went to bed, and tried to read; but, my eyes closing with a snap, and absolutely refusing to open, I blew out my candle, and slept as soundly as the Scipios at the Ostian gate, — without a dream of Christian or Pagan, ancient or modern, Rome; oblivious of Pope, Cardinal, Jupiter, Apollo, the Muses, the Colosseum, and the Vatican; until the morning light, peeping into my windows, and through my bed-curtains, told me that it was time to get up, and that I was indeed in the centre of the civilized world, and in the very heart of History. How brightly the sun shone over this great "city of the soul"! How gloriously rises the dome of St. Peter's! How the Egyptian obelisks pierce the air and point to the sky! What did I do on these two glorious days? Be patient, and you shall hear. Love to all. I shall write soon to L——.

XXI.

On Board the Bosphorus, October 14, 1853.

ONCE more I am at sea. I mailed a letter
for you yesterday* at Naples; and immediately afterward G—— and I embarked on board
the French steamer, for Constantinople. It adds
but a few days to our intended voyage, and the
present moment is one of profound interest in the
East. The probability seems to be that war will
soon break out between Turkey and Russia, and
this may be the last year of Turkish sovereignty
over the ancient Byzantium. We shall remain
there but a few days, and then return to Athens,
where G—— will stay about ten days, and I shall
establish myself for the winter. We left the Constantinople part of our journey undetermined until
the last moment; then, finding from the best information that all was safe, made up our minds to see
the City of the Crescent.

You cannot imagine the beauty of the scene, as
we passed out of the Bay of Naples, — the semi-
circle of hills, on whose slope the city is built;
Herculaneum, Vesuvius, Pompeii, Posilippo, in

* This letter, which contained the journal of the author's sojourn in Rome, was never received.

the glorious light of an October afternoon; Capri, just out of the harbor, veiled in the soft purple atmosphere; the sea calm, unbroken even by a ripple. But when the sun went down behind the hills, there came a flood of molten gold over land and sea, such as I never saw before, and surrounded us and every object far and near, so that the ship and sea and neighboring shores seemed transfigured.

CONSTANTINOPLE, October 20, 1853.

I DARE say this date will surprise you, as well as the long interval between this and that above. Well, history (which is philosophy teaching by example) will explain.

We went in the Bosphorus as far as Malta, — passing through the Sicilian straits, the ancient Scylla and Charybdis. As we approached, I was curious to see how far Homer's description was borne out by the present state of this famous passage. I took up the Odyssey, went to the forward part of the ship, as Ulysses did, and watched, as he did, for Scylla. He had a sword; I had the Odyssey opened to the passage. The monster did not seize my companions; but while I was standing and carefully comparing the words written three thousand years ago with the facts of the present moment, a huge wave dashed over the prow of the ship and drenched me from head to foot. The strength of Scylla is lessened, but not destroyed. I was astonished at the truth of the description, leaving out a few embellishments. There was the rock of Scylla, running out into the water on the left, and there was the sand of Charybdis on the right, and there was the violent current and whirlpool ; but I am bound, as a conscientious traveller, to state that I do not believe the story of the ship having gone down into the whirlpool, and after six hours' detention being tossed up again, — Ulysses meanwhile hanging "like a bat" on the branches of a great fig-tree that stretched over the waters. There is not a bit of a fig-tree there.

Getting through the strait, we lost sight of land before long, and struck off in a direct course for Malta, leaving Syracuse, Ætna, and the southern cape of Italy far behind. Another fine afternoon and glorious evening on the blue Mediterranean ; another early rising to see the sun, with Malta in the distant horizon. At seven o'clock we entered the harbor, — the most extraordinary station in the world. The island is a high rock, covered on the side of the sea with the palaces of the old knights, and the public buildings of the government.

As the steamer would not leave until the afternoon, we went ashore and set about seeing the island. It is one incessant up-hill and down-hill. The cathedral is a gorgeous old church, full of mosaic floors, pictures, superb tombs of the old knights, statues, gilding, silver, and gold. The Governor's palace — once the residence of the Grand Master — is a splendid and spacious establishment, with paintings, Gobelin' tapestries, long corridors, and immense saloons.

The sirocco wind was blowing hot from the sands of Africa, and the reflection of the burning sun from stone pavements, and walls of houses, and rocky hillsides, helped the sirocco to melt every particle of strength out of our limbs. It is well to experience a little of everything. The sirocco gives you a new idea. I thought I had been suffocated before; but all I had ever felt of heat was cool and refreshing compared with this. We bore it like heroes, and saw all we cared to see in this famous island.

Happening to meet the British Admiralty agent, he told us that Her Majesty's steamer Caradoc was in port, would start for Constantinople in the afternoon with important despatches, and would get there three days earlier than the French boat. He would arrange a passage for us if we liked, though the ship was not intended to carry passengers, but only the diplomatic correspondence.

We gladly accepted his obliging offer, and in the afternoon were rowed on board. We found there the Queen's messenger, the daughter of Admiral Dundas (commander of the fleet), and two or three naval officers, going up to join their ships at the Dardanelles. The ship, therefore, was no common affair; it was expected with immense interest, and its arrival might decide the fate of Europe and Asia. We shared in the common feeling, and were in the position of two flies on two coach-wheels. We did not raise a great dust to be sure, but we did raise a prodigious foam.

On, on, on over the blue waves. The day passes; another splendid night. The night passes; another glorious sunrise. Yonder at our left peers from the morning mist the land of Laconia, the ancient Tænarum; far before us the southern point of Attica, Sunium with the columns of its ancient temple standing; nearer, Cerigo, — the island of Cythera, famous for the temple of Venus and the birth of Helen; on our right, another of the Grecian isles. On we go between the two islands, and the mainland stretches away and loses itself in the distance. ·We pass between Sunium and Zea (the old Ceos where Simonides was born), with a dozen more of the isles of Greece within the horizon, desolate, but beautiful in their desolation; we pass through the passage between Eubœa and Andros, and watch the shores until night descends, and once more we are dashing through the open sea, straight for Tenedos and the kingdom of Priam.

Early the next morning I am on deck again. I ask the man at the helm where we are. " Tenedos is in sight; and here is the shore of Asia." Ah! thought I, he has doubtless read Virgil; he has stolen the poet's very words, " *Est in conspectu Tenedos.*" Looking around me, I recognize familiar objects. There rises Mount Ida; yonder is Gargara; farther north is the site of "windy Troy."

Rapidly we near Besika Bay, across which stretch the lines of the confederate fleets of France and England. There lies the flag-ship of Admiral Dundas, and, a little farther, floats the tricolor of Admiral Hammelin, — the Agamemnon and Menelaus of the united armaments. We create a tremendous excitement in the fleet. Boats from one ship and then from another put off to get the news from us, and boxes and parcels from home. We hear in turn that the fleets are about to move up the Dardanelles, and that something is going to happen.

We wait two or three hours, and then away we go head foremost into the Hellespont, to carry our despatches up to Lord Stratford de Redcliffe, the British Minister. We learn that the Sultan has declared war, hostilities to commence on a certain day, unless the Russians withdraw their forces in the mean time. We steam along the Trojan shore. There, where a boat's crew are taking in water, opens the mouth of the Scamander. On the right rises the tomb of Achilles, and at the other extremity of the shore, the mound of Ajax. Between these lay the Grecian fleet and the line of tents four thousand years ago. On, on we go, to Sestos and Abydos, famous for the loves of Hero and Leander.

Evening comes on, and the moon again favors us with her light. We cannot go to bed; for Constantinople is to come in sight at midnight. We have left the Homeric track, and are now close upon both the European and Asiatic shores. At midnight, " Constantinople " is shouted out. We see, in the moonlight, the seraglio point with its glittering domes; minarets shooting up, slender and crescent-topped, into the sky; trees of the Sultan's gardens lying black against the west; here and there scattered lights over the hills on which the city stands. The " Golden Horn ", suddenly opens, and we see opposite to us the quarters of Tophana, Galata, and Pera; the shores lined with arsenals; the Sultan's palaces and harems; the heights crowned with domes and diplomatic residences.

Away we go, in a dream, — an Arabian night, full of sparkling waters, crescents, kiosks, minarets, seraglios, and cypress-shaded burying-grounds: for the Minister is not in Istamboul, and we must not stop until we find him. We plunge into the Bosphorus, and make with all speed for Therapia, a dozen miles up, and close to the entrance of the Black Sea; Istamboul fades away, and I — go to bed.

We wake in the morning to find ourselves lying at anchor, with the Turkish fleet on one side, and the Egyptian on the other. The sun has not risen, but it is already a busy scene among the ships. We call a *caïque*, and are rowed ashore by an old Turk, to Therapia, — the place where the amiable Medea scattered poison, when she was pursuing Jason, but now so healthy that all the foreign ministers choose it for their residence in preference to Constantinople. And here ends our cruise on board Her Majesty's steamer Caradoc.

XXII.

CONSTANTINOPLE, October 23.

I HAVE now passed almost a week in these regions, but have not time to give you any full account of the thousand interesting things I have seen and heard. I have twice seen the Sultan; have heard a lecture in Turkish, by Professor Colonel Tahir Bey, on Trigonometry; have taken a Turkish bath; have smoked two pipes with the Patriarch of Constantinople, and one with the Patriarch of Jerusalem. I have passed six times the whole length of the Bosphorus: once, sitting in Turkish fashion (vastly picturesque and Oriental, but causing many aches in the legs), on the bottom of a caïque, rowing close under the Sultan's palace, at sunset, and hearing soft music from some imprisoned Fatima. I have been over every quarter of Constantinople; have travelled in the steamboat with an old Turk and his harem, — about a dozen wives and as many slaves, — who were going to Constantinople for a frolic; have been jostled in the bazaar by Turkish ladies, shopping as zealously as if they were Christians; ducked in a steamer with a company of Ulema (Doctors of Law); and — the rest next time.

XXIII.

TROY, October 25, 1853.

I SUPPOSE you hardly expected to get a letter from me, written at Priam's capital. I am not *exactly* in the old king's capital; for the villanous Greeks the other day sacked the town, under the orders of the chiefs, Agamemnon and Menelaus, so completely that a stranger finds no house of entertainment standing, — in fact, no house of any sort.

We are, therefore, compelled to keep on board, and at this moment we are moving along the Trojan shore, between Tenedos and the mainland, with all the points of the Homeric Troy as distinct as possible, on our left, — the plain, the promontories, the long stretch of beach, on which the "thousand-shipped fleet," as Æschylus calls it, was drawn up; in the background the Trojan and Phrygian hills, Ida, Gargara, and the height once occupied by "lofty Troy": but Troy is no more, and nature alone remains unchanged.

I cannot doubt that Homer saw this spot. I have this morning been reading the Iliad, face to face with the scenes of the immortal tale. The features of the landscape are only incidentally brought into the description, and not formally or minutely painted; but every epithet applied to them by Homer is as true to-day as it was three thousand years ago. I do not see how any one can traverse these seas and not believe in Troy, and the personal existence of Homer. It would do the learned critics of Germany no harm to come here, and look about them a little, before they decide that Troy is a fable and Homer a myth.

As I look on the shore I see the "foaming sea," and as I turn my eyes in the opposite direction, they rest on the "wine-faced deep," — which phrases Homer has put into a single verse; and, as there is a pretty strong wind blowing, I hear the roar of the loud-resounding sea ($\pi o \lambda v \phi \lambda o i \sigma \beta o i o$ $\theta a \lambda a \sigma \sigma \eta s$) exactly as Homer heard it, and imprisoned the sound in the most sonorous line ever written by a poet.

We have the originals from which Homer drew, except the populations that made up this rich and powerful kingdom; but it is easy for the imagination to repeople these spots with the heroic figures that live forever in the Iliad. I seem to see, as we sweep along, the forms of Achilles, Patroclus, Diomedes; I hear the neighing of horses, the rattling of chariot-wheels, and the clang of arms. On yonder height rise again the buried walls of Troy, with the regal palaces they once enclosed. There is the Scean gate, and just with-

in stand Hector and Andromache, holding that
pathetic conversation which has moved the heart
of thirty centuries. Farther on reappears the
tower, where the old councillors sat in debate,
and Helen approaches them, radiant with a
beauty which warms the blood in their ancient
veins, and I hear them say:

> "No wonder such celestial charms
> For nine long years have kept the world in arms."

SMYRNA, October 26.

TROY, and all its visionary scenes, vanished from
my sight soon after I had finished the preceding
sentences. On we went, along the coast of Asia
Minor, past many a famous shore and sunny isle.
The wind became strong and the sea violent,
bringing up many a passage in the Iliad, where
the sound of the verse gives the very echo of the
anger of the sea. We had not many days on
the Atlantic of more tumultuous agitation of the
water, and tossing of the ship, than yesterday
and last night.

We entered the pass between Mytilene (the
ancient Lesbos) and the Asiatic coast a little before sunset ; and, many superb sunsets as I have
seen in Italy, I never saw anything more glorious
than the splendors that lingered long on the Lesbian hills, after the sun went down. The clouds
had cleared away, and the range of mountains
was veiled in purple, over which the sky was

flushed with burnished gold, and the evening star shone forth with unusual magnificence. Sappho's fragments have more than one exquisite description, which shows that she had enjoyed the same superlative beauty. You know Lesbos was her birthplace, and you may be sure I thought of her as we dashed along her island home. We stopped at the town of Mytilene for an hour or two; but as she was not there, I did not go ashore.

This morning we awoke in the harbor of Smyrna, — one of the seven birthplaces of Homer. Going ashore, we procured a guide, and rambled about the town in all directions. The river Meles, near which Homer is said to have been born, runs near the town. On both banks are burying-grounds, with tall cypresses, and tombstones surmounted by sculptured turbans. At the bridge is the great gathering-place for the camels, and the central point of the commerce of Asia Minor. We found hundreds of camels there, either loading for a new journey, or just arrived from the interior, and it was one of the most curious sights I have yet seen. We met several caravans also, in the streets, and wending their way through the bazaars, and could not help admiring the patient and intelligent look of these animals, though each caravan was led by a very small donkey.

When we had finished our survey of the glittering temptations displayed in the bazaars, we hired donkeys for a ride into the neighborhood, up a mountain on the top of which are the ruins of an old castle, built by the Genoese. From these tumbling walls we had a most superb prospect of the whole city of Smyrna, the harbor, the Lesbian hills, and the valley of the Meles, far away into the interior, with the beautiful mountain ranges that shut it in.

Here, recently, have been many robberies and some murders ; but they have now got the leader of the banditti in prison, and he is to be sent up to Constantinople, with the pleasant prospect of losing his head. We spent an hour or two more in the bazaar, where I bought for you one of those famous storm-petrel coats, which you admire so much. I hope I shall succeed in bringing it home ; but it may be seized at some custom-house as a dangerous and revolutionary garment. I shall do my best, however.

Smyrna is a very amusing town. The variety of languages, dresses, colors ; the horses, donkeys, camels, dromedaries ; the bazaars with their endless variety of merchandise, — diversify the spectacle with infinite matter of entertainment. We passed through, not only the European or Frankish quarter, but the Armenian and Turkish, so that we really saw the *outside*, at least, of everything ; and having seen this, we came on board the steamer, which renews her voyage this afternoon.

Now let me go back to Constantinople and the

Turks. We were very fortunate in our visit there. In the first place, the weather was good, — even beautiful, except part of one day. As I told you in a letter which you will probably never get, we passed Constantinople and went up to Therapia, just at the entrance into the Black Sea. Most of the foreign ministers live there, our own among the rest. We stopped at the house where he has apartments, and saw him immediately. I saw, also, at Therapia, many people, — English, French, Turks, and others, more or less connected with the Turkish service, — from whom I picked up a good deal of information. If you have looked into the newspapers, you must have seen the " Eastern question " more discussed than any other for the last six months.

There is something very queer in the political complications which have made the Christian powers of the West the supporters of the crumbling empire of the Mahometans. The explanation is to be sought in the desire to preserve the balance of power in Europe, and in their fear of Russia. Whether they can postpone the catastrophe long, is a very doubtful question ; and whether the interests of humanity and civilization will be promoted by sustaining a government founded on principles entirely hostile to both, is another very serious question which the statesmen of Europe must put to themselves sooner or later.

So long as the Turkish religion remains what it

is, — an imposture, — so long will any real progress of the nation be impossible. The Koran is at once their law and their gospel; and the Koran sanctions practices which Christianity and sound reason condemn as detestable, and which experience proves to be ruinous in the end.

Polygamy is approved by the Koran, and is universal among the rich classes. The best men in Turkey — the men who have a European reputation, like Reschid Pacha, the Minister of Foreign Affairs — have harems of wives and slaves, no one can tell how many. The Sultan has innumerable wives, and increases their number every year. It is a common practice of the great pachas to send him, on every occasion of a great festival, a present of a handsome young woman, whom they have bought of her parents for this purpose; and there is nothing disreputable to them, or to the girl, in this; on the contrary, it is a high and enviable honor to her. And the Sultan can pay no greater compliment to the proudest dignitary of his empire, than to make him a present of one of his wives.

I was assured by a Greek physician, who has a large practice among all the nationalities of Constantinople, that infanticide is fearfully prevalent.

Female children are articles of commerce. They are purchased by dealers, when young, and carefully brought up, for sale. These, however, are not *slaves*, but *wives*. They are taught to dance, and to play on some musical instrument, but nothing more, and their health is carefully attended to. The price of a wife — say from eighteen to twenty years of age — varies from twenty to fifty thousand piasters, that is, from a thousand to twenty-five hundred dollars, according to her personal attractions and the supply of the market.

The Turks ·are essentially an indolent people. To sit cross-legged on a carpet, and smoke the chibouque all day long, is their highest conception of felicity. Generally speaking, they do not drink wine ; but brandy is not prohibited by the Koran, and they do not deem it a sin to indulge in it. They consume vast quantities of *rakee*, a kind of gin or whiskey, which was not known in the time of Mahomet, and therefore is not prohibited by the Koran.

But the great curse of the race is the vicious organization of society, as I have briefly indicated above; and this is deeply rooted in their law and their religion. It can be cured only by the utter overthrow of both; and the fanaticism of the Turk, still as violent as ever in the body of the nation, makes any change in this respect hopeless.

Meantime, other nations are advancing in culture, population, and power, while the population of Turkey is rapidly diminishing, and her power is nearly wasted away. Her vicious administration fetters labor, and makes it unproductive.

England, especially Lord Palmerston, applauds her as a *free-trader;* but Lord Palmerston forgot to mention, when passing a glowing eulogium on her enlightened policy, that, while English goods, for the benefit of England, are admitted almost free of duty, Turkish products cannot be *exported* without paying twelve per cent. The consequence is, that corn, for example, can be brought from foreign countries cheaper than the Turks can raise it, while no Turkish product of nature or of human industry can be sent to a foreign market so as to remunerate the producer. It has inevitably resulted, that the Turks are miserably poor, and are becoming more so every day.

These are some of the features in the picture of Turkey, as they have appeared to me in the rapid glance I have taken. On the other hand, the Turks have interested me in many respects.

The father of the present Sultan commenced a series of reforms, the aim of which was to place Turkey more in harmony with the spirit of the age and of Christian civilization : not that he had any great respect for Christianity. His successor, Abdul Medjid, has wisely carried them on. They relate chiefly to the army. The European costume and drill have wholly taken the place of the old Turkish dress and tactics. I have seen large bodies of cavalry and infantry, including artillery, and, to my eye, they appear as well, except some want of exactness in manœuvring, as any of the armies in Europe. They are larger and better-looking men than the French soldiers. The changes made by the Sultan, in these respects, are undoubtedly great improvements.

I was amused to hear of one consequence of the adoption of pantaloons, in the place of the former Turkish trousers. When I saw the Sultan going to the mosque the other day, I noticed that the troops did not prostrate themselves, as I supposed was their custom; and as a Mussulman cannot show any respect by raising the hat, they stood stock still, and bolt upright, while their sovereign was riding through the lines. I inquired the meaning of this want of reverence, and was told that the custom of prostration had been abandoned, from the fear of tearing their pantaloons, ever since the Turkish trousers had ceased to be worn. The old conservative Turks, who thought the Ottoman dominion at an end when the Oriental trousers went out, may have been right; no one can foretell the consequences of omitting a mark of reverence in a government so founded on external homage. The Ottoman supremacy may have resided in the nether garment, — it may have been a petticoat government after all.

They have done something in education. I visited, as I told you, the military college, which strangers seldom have an opportunity of seeing; and I was surprised by what I saw. It is an extensive and admirably organized establishment, with about twenty professors, most of whom have been educated in Western Europe. About one hundred young Turks are in training there. The sons of Omer Pacha sit side by side with the sons of the indigent, on terms of perfect equality. They have a good library, mostly of French works on science; a tolerable collection of minerals; a chemical laboratory and a philosophical apparatus; an excellent telescope; models of machines, &c. Their lecture-rooms are better arranged and lighted, and more elegant, than any I ever saw in America or Europe. Their annual examinations are invariably attended by the Sultan, — an honor paid to science by no other European sovereign. The students' rooms are kept in excellent condition, and their morals and health are anxiously cared for. The Professors have published many text-books in Turkish, for the use of the College. They have a printing-press, which I saw in operation, and they have printed, not only books, but several excellent Turkish maps. I bought a Turkish Algebra, which I think of sending to P——, and a map of Constantinople.

Professor Tahir Bey, to whom I was introduced by an Armenian Professor in the medical college, (one of the few Turks who speak English,) gave me all the explanations I asked, and politely allowed me to be present at his lecture on Trigonometry. I accepted the invitation with many thanks, and few things have interested me more deeply. The room was admirably arranged. The audience consisted of about ninety or one hundred young men, sitting on benches, each with his note-book before him. The Professor illustrated his subject on the blackboard, and I never saw a more attentive or intelligent class. He was fluent in speech, and ready in drawing his diagrams. Of course I could not understand a single word he said, and was able to follow his lecture only by following the work on the blackboard. But I saw that he understood what he was about, and that he was really and ably teaching these youths the same sciences which young men at their age are studying in our American colleges.

I had no time to visit the medical college, which I regret. There is a marine school also, which, I believe, is well conducted; and there are numerous private schools for the children of all classes. But the military schools absorb the attention of the government, and in the institution I saw I had an opportunity of witnessing the best the Turks have yet done.

It is a common notion that the women lead a very retired life, in the seclusion of the harem. Nothing can be more erroneous. In passing up and down the Bosphorus, nearly half the passengers were Turkish women. Three times, a whole harem, consisting of fifteen or twenty women, partly wives, partly slaves, came on board, from the palace of some rich old Turk, under the care of a black guard, with a terrific sword by his side, to go down to Constantinople on a frolic; or perhaps to go shopping in the bazaars. They were dressed in various colors, — green, blue, mouse-colored, pink. The veil, or *yashmah*, was drawn over the forehead, and the lower part of the face, up to the middle of the nose, leaving only a space for a pair of very black eyes to flash out. I never could help laughing at the figure the negresses made under this disguise.

I took some pains to watch these people, and twice I happened to be in the same part of the boat where they sat. They laughed and chatted with one another, and sometimes with the men standing around them, as merrily as so many Christians. Now and then, if the face was pretty — and there were many pretty faces — the *yashmah* would be gradually withdrawn, and I had the opportunity of observing quite at my leisure. In each harem there were two or three Circassian ladies of the most exquisite beauty. These were probably the thirty-thousand-piaster wives. But there was no variety in their expression. Some of the women are immensely fat, and they roll along, bundled up in their robes, in the most ludicrous manner. One of the most laughable sights I ever saw was an old Turkish lady, with a pair of spectacles stuck on her nose, and exactly filling the aperture of the *yashmah*, while she was eagerly cheapening a piece of silk. The common women run about, looking like bundles of dirty linen going to the wash of their own accord; others, a little higher up the social scale, look like bundles of linen coming home from the wash. It is very amusing to see the little girls of ten or twelve years. How any of them keep their clothes on I cannot imagine.

When the Sultan went to the mosque, the windows of the houses along the streets, though protected by *jalousies*, were filled with black eyes peeping curiously out; and a very fat Turkish lady, with about a thousand yards of Brousa silk wound round her, stopped her carriage just where we were standing, and waited to see His Highness pass. Nearly opposite the palace is a low, broad wall, the top of which was crowded with green, pink, yellow, and mouse-colored bundles containing women, with negresses in attendance.

In the afternoon of the same day (Friday, the Turkish Sabbath) we took a caïque, and rowed over to the "Sweet Waters" on the Asiatic side of the Bosphorus. This is a favorite resort, being a little valley, with a stream, and trees overshadowing it. Here we found a large number of Turkish ladies with their attendants, reclining on carpets, bolstered up by luxurious cushions, and sipping their coffee or sherbet, while their lords were amusing themselves in another part of the ground. Some of these again were beautiful, but of the same order with those I have already mentioned, and scarcely to be distinguished from one another. We met there a company of Gypsies, — very merry and very saucy.

Do you know what an *araba* is? I will explain. An araba is the height of fashion and luxury, and employed only in the very best society. It is a clumsy carriage, like a very old-fashioned family coach, drawn by a yoke of the white oxen of Asia. The inside is covered with a thick bed, and the sides lined with cushions. Here lies buried the Turkish beauty, on her way to sip her coffee at the Sweet Waters. Certainly nothing is more redolent of lazy enjoyment than a Circassian dame rolling about in the araba, as her oxen, driven by a couple of turbaned Turks, or an Ethiopian slave, slowly drag the ancient machine along the road. So much for Turkish ladies.

One day, while I was staying at Therapia, I went down to Constantinople, and, returning to the boat, was overtaken by a tremendous rain. I got thoroughly drenched, and hurried down into the cabin, which was filled to overflowing with Ulema, or Doctors of Law. Being an Alim myself, I thought I might, without impropriety, remain in such worshipful company. By and by, they took out their long pipes, and very gravely began to smoke. I consoled myself with the reflection that they would smoke me dry, and save me from the rheumatism, if they turned me into bacon. The waves were running high, and the boat was pitching at a great rate. The windows of the cabin were open, and one wave bigger than the rest poured in a monstrous deluge over the turbans and robes of the cross-legged doctors, and put out their pipes. Such a scampering of Ulema, such a tearing up stairs of doctors learned in the law, you never beheld. I thought I should go into convulsions. I really believe they thought they were all drowned. At any rate but three or four ventured back into the cabin, though the deck was crowded with passengers, and a young Englishman and I had the room almost wholly to ourselves.

At Constantinople we remained four days, and in that time visited every quarter of the city. We went twice through the bazaars, and I regretted not being rich enough to send silks and carpets home to all my friends. G—— made some pur-chases. I contented myself with buying a few bottles of otto of roses, and looking wistfully at the rest. There were slippers, pearl and golden ; there were silks from Brousa, and rugs from Per-sia ; there were — O dear me ! — a most distract-ing variety of Oriental splendors, which made me feel too sensibly the miserable hiatus in my purse. Hundreds of Turkish women — bundles rather, shuffling about in yellow slippers — were making their purchases of solemn-looking Turks, turbaned and sitting cross-legged on their counters. The variety and oddity of the scene were highly entertaining. I sat down in one of the shops, where I bought some trifle. Coffee was ordered, and I sipped it, as I leisurely surveyed the comical groups around me. When I rose to go, I offered to pay for the coffee, but they told me it was the custom of the place to offer coffee to all who came to buy of them, — a very civil custom, I thought, and worthy of imitation elsewhere.

On the last day of our sojourn at Constantinople we joined a party to visit the seraglio and the mosques. It is a pretty costly affair, — the fees to different official personages, and to the several custodians, amounting to about forty dollars, — so that the custom is to send round to the different hotels, and make up as large a party as possible, to lessen the expense to each. As it was, it cost us four dollars apiece.

We went entirely through the seraglio, — its gardens cooled by marble fountains and filled with flowers, its carpeted rooms and latticed passages. We saw the chambers of the Sultanas, and the gate through which those who had been guilty of offending the Sultan were taken out, sewed up in bags, and pitched into the Bosphorus. We saw the library, consisting of manuscripts carefully locked up, so that nobody can read them; and the ancient throne-room, where the Sultan used to sit in state, and receive the prostrations of his pachas and mighty men. We went to the church of St. Helen, now converted into a Turkish armory, and, finally, to the great mosque of St. Sophia.

Before visiting the last, however, we stepped into a Turkish restaurant, and, taking our places cross-legged on the carpet, ordered *kibaubs*, coffee, *pilaf*, and *chibouques*. I took only a cup of coffee, and as my legs began to ache soon, I resumed the Frankish position, sitting as well as I could.

St. Sophia, you know, was originally a Christian church, the most splendid in the East during the reign of the Byzantine emperors. It is now the centre of Moslem worship, — a kind of Mahometan cathedral. Many people were at their devotions, some singing, some saying their prayers, and some with their faces touching the floor. Among the rest, in one corner of the mosque, were several of the ladies of the Sultan's harem. We looked at them with considerable curiosity. They were dressed in costly silks, but distinguished in no other way that I could see from the other ladies, who were worshipping in different parts of the immense mosque. The roof of the dome and of the side-arches is superbly adorned with mosaics, but in other respects St. Sophia does not compare with some of the great Christian cathedrals.

Constantinople, or Byzantium, as it was then called, was an important place in the age of Demosthenes ; again, after the division of the Roman empire, it became the splendid rival of Rome, and in the history of the Crusades it played a conspicuous part. But it is surprising how few remains exist, to testify to its ancient greatness. Two obelisks in the Hippodrome, a beautiful sculptured sarcophagus, a few mutilated busts, a part of Constantine's aqueduct, with St. Sophia, and St. Helen, are almost all that survives from the early time; and not one of these goes back to the age of Demosthenes. All the rest is Turkish, or modern European, dating since 1456.

The descendants of the original Greek inhabitants have always lived in a quarter of the city called the Phanaro. Here is the present residence of the Greek Patriarch. As I had a good opportunity to call on this dignitary, I was glad to avail myself of it. Dr. Stamatiades — the person I have already mentioned — took me to the palace, a very plain structure, looking out upon the Golden Horn; and we were received in a long saloon, three sides of which were lined with the sofa or divan, covered with carpets.

His Sanctity was seated on the right as we entered, cross-legged, exactly like a Turk. He received us very politely, placed us on the divan, (I did not attempt to cross my legs,) clapped his hands, and, servants appearing, ordered sweetmeats, chibouques, and coffee. First came a grave and clerical-looking figure, with sweetmeats, whereof I duly partook. Next came two other equally grave-looking gentlemen, with two enormously long pipes, and two brazen dishes. The brazen dishes were set in the middle of the room; the bowls of the pipes were placed in the brazen dishes, and the ends of the pipe-stems were placed in our hands. It would not do to decline, for it was a great honor; so great, that no inferior dignitary can smoke in the presence of the Patriarch. The Archbishop of Nicomedia, a venerable, white-bearded old gentleman, came in while we were there. After making his obeisance he skipped up on the carpet, coiled his legs under him, bowed again to the Patriarch, and then to us. Coffee was ordered for him, but no pipe, while a second pipe was brought with most respectful ceremonies to the Doctor and me. I smoked with the gravity of a Turk, but with some inward misgivings as to what would become of me.

We stayed about half an hour. The Patriarch asked me what was the state of my country. I said, "Happy and prosperous." "May God grant it shall ever remain so," was the courteous and Christian reply. He asked a great many questions, which I answered as well as I could; and when I rose to go, I said in Greek, "I greatly thank your All-Holiness for the honor of this reception." He took my hand, and said that it would give him great pleasure if I would often repeat my visit. I bowed, and he bowed, each with hand upon his heart; and so I took leave, probably forever, of the kind and venerable Patriarch. .

At the palace of the Patriarch of Jerusalem just the same ceremony was gone through with, — sweetmeats, coffee, pipes. I smoked again, — the third pipe in a single afternoon, — determined not to fall behind the most ceremonious Oriental in these social duties.

I was sorry I had not time to see the Greek society here, as I might easily have done, through the kindness of these gentlemen; but time pressed, and Greece herself was beckoning in the distance. So on Monday afternoon we went on board the Austrian steamer, in a heavy sea; and when she left the Golden Horn the sun was just setting, under a cloud, but still glorious, — an emblem, it seemed to me, of the storm about to break over the setting sun of the devoted city. I had a presentiment that I should never see Constantinople again; or, if I did, that it would be under other rulers, and that the crescent would erelong be driven back to Asia, whence it came exactly four hundred years ago.

The Sultan is a melancholy-looking man. His face wears the fixed and sad expression of one who is conscious that his doom is drawing nigh; and there is a vague feeling among his subjects that he will be the last of his race to sit on the throne of Istamboul. This feeling is strengthened by the fact that he has only fifteen children, while his father had more than a hundred. So small a family is looked upon by the Turks as an evil omen for their sovereign. I fancied, as I gazed upon his sorrowful countenance, that I read a similar foreboding there. The Sultan is a gentle sovereign, averse to bloodshed. He would not surrender the Hungarian refugees, and he would gladly avoid the horrors of war.

The great man here is not the Sultan, nor Reschid Pacha, but Lord Stratford. The able answers to the Russian diplomatists, by which the Turkish Cabinet has surprised the world, have been substantially the work of Lord Stratford, and the whole foreign policy of Turkey has been shaped by this very distinguished nobleman. So, at least, I have been informed by good authority at Constantinople, and I have no doubt of the fact. But this very fact weakens my faith in the possibility of Turkey's maintaining her independence. She will not always have a Lord Stratford to rely upon, nor an English alliance to back the policy he recommends; and though Russia may be foiled for the moment, she will repeat the trial, until Constantinople adds another jewel to the crown of the Czar, — unless the new Greco-Byzantine empire solve the Eastern question, with the consent of the Western powers, before the Russian has another chance.

XXIV.

ATHENS, October 30, 1853.

I HAVE at length reached the city which has been the aim and end of my long travels, and still longer studies, — "illustrious Athens, the prop of Greece." I can scarcely believe that I am here, — that I have been here two whole days. I am glad I did not come before, — glad that I have approached so gradually, — that I have seen the modern culture of England and France, the mediæval of Germany, the mediæval and Roman in Italy, the seat of Byzantine Greek at Constantinople, the earliest Ionian on the coast and islands of Asia Minor; and now my eyes behold the crowning flower of ancient genius and art, in the sublime remains of Athens.

From Smyrna we had a rough passage, through the Ægean Islands, to Syra. At Syra we were theoretically in quarantine, but remained on board the ship all day. Tell J—— I sent the package for Mr. E—— on shore, not being allowed to go myself, because, coming from Asia, I was presumed to be infected with the plague. In the afternoon Mr. E—— rowed off to the ship, but could not come on board, because it was presumed that he

N

would catch the plague of me, and so endanger the lives of his Majesty's subjects in Syra. We talked, however, a long time; I leaning over the side of the ship, and he standing up in the boat. We could not shake hands; for that would have sent him to the lazaretto for twenty-four hours, as a plague-stricken person. He inquired eagerly about J——, and all her father's family, and listened with the greatest interest to all I could tell him. I promised to visit him in Syra, if I could possibly find the time. At length he returned, with many hearty adieus.

At ten o'clock in the evening the steamer was again under way. I never passed a more tremendous night. The wind howled and screamed through the cordage, the waves roared, the ship pitched and tossed on the agitated waters; the timbers creaked and groaned, as if they were in mortal agony; the furniture of the cabin danced about from side to side, knocking at the doors of the state-rooms, and banging against the tables, as if the foul fiends had got into every leg; and we, the unhappy passengers, who tried in vain to sleep, were unmercifully beaten against the side of the ship, and the outside of the berths in which we were uncomfortably stretched. My ribs still ache with collisions between them and the ribs of the vessel. When all is quiet, the Mediterranean looks so blue and gentle you would suppose an angry murmur impossible; but when the Boreas of Homer, or the Zephyrus, lashes the billows, then is the same blue Mediterranean an ungovernable vixen, — screaming, scolding, buffeting everybody that stands in her way. One of our guns was dismounted, and one of the officers had his finger crushed, and fainted with the pain. It was a wild night.

When I went through the form of getting up in the morning, — pretending to open my eyes, which had not been closed all night, — I found we had doubled the promontory of Sunium, and were dashing along the western coast of Attica. The sun was just rising over the hills, clear and brilliant, as if he had never known a cloud. Hymettus was in the distance, loftier than I expected to find it; Pentelicus soon gleamed in sight; on our left lay Ægina; before us Salamis, and the strait where the great defeat of the Persians took place.

The plain of Athens gradually opened, with Parnes and Cithæron on the north. The Acropolis, at first but a speck in the centre, rapidly grew upon our sight, as we approached it. Then the Parthenon, in its ruined but glorious beauty, stood against the sunlit sky, and the monument of Philopappus on the Museion hill. The craggy brow of the Areopagus next met our view. Now we were skimming along the Phaleric harbor. In a moment more Munychia lay before us. Next, rounding a point, we swiftly entered the Peiræus, and in a few minutes were anchored where the ancient war-galleys — the fleets so often mentioned by Demosthenes — were wont to ride, before they started for Thermopylæ, or Byzantium, or Sicily.

But our twenty-four hours of quarantine, which began at Syra, were not yet over. We were still, for an hour or two, theoretically infected with the plague. An old doctor, looking like a battered bust of Hippocrates, came alongside to inspect us. We were mustered on deck; he nodded, and we retired. At length the moment of release arrived. We scrambled down to a boat which Miltiades had already engaged for us; rowed ashore, stepped into a hack — O contradiction to all classical experience! — and were driven by a coachman over the Peiraic road, between the ruins of the walls of Themistocles, up to the city of Athens. We passed the olive-groves of Plato's Academy; dashed up to the Temple of Theseus, dismounted and went through it; climbed the Areopagus, where Orestes was tried and Paul preached; looked over the Forum to the Pnyx, and the Bema whence Demosthenes harangued the Athenians; climbed up to the Propylæa; mounted the marble staircase leading into the Acropolis; went through and round the Parthenon; examined the piles of sculptured marbles still remaining on the ground; admired the Erechtheium; looked round upon the matchless panorama of marble mountains that encircle the plain; descended, stopping at the newly found temple of the Wingless Victory on the way; walked along the southern slope, surveying the ruins of the Odeion and the site of the Dionysiac Theatre; jumped into our degenerate hack and drove to the still standing columns that form a part of the gigantic Temple of Olympian Zeus; passed under the Arch of Hadrian; drove to the Temple of the Winds in the street of Æolos; then, to bring the journey to a quite modern termination, dropped my luggage at the Hotel d'Angleterre.

Here I took leave of G——, who, instead of passing a week or two in Greece, as was at first proposed, grew impatient to rejoin his family in Florence, and therefore resolved to content himself with this flying visit to Athens, and to proceed to Ancona by the same steamship, which would leave the Peiræus at four o'clock, — unconsciously justifying the words of Ulysses in the second Iliad :

> " For he who from his wife a single month remains
> Impatient grows on board the many-benchèd ship,
> Tossed by the winter's storms, and the tumultuous seas."

So here I was, quite alone, planted in the midst of Athens. After resting a little from our classical scramble, I dressed, took a guide, and went out with some of my letters of introduction. Mr. King was out, Mr. Finlay was at dinner; Sir Richard Church was in, and I had a pleasant halfhour's chat with this hero of the revolution, and present senator. With him I found Mariani, one of the Triumvirate of the late Roman Republic, — a very large and quite distinguished-looking man.

Next, I went to see Mr. Hill, the father, almost, of modern Athens. He received me very pleasantly, and, after talking awhile, walked out with me. As we passed the King's palace, the carriage was at the door, and it was evident that their Majesties were going to drive or ride, — for there were saddle-horses, too. So we waited to see them. In a short time the Queen appeared, got into the carriage with one of her women, and drove away. She has a gracious and agreeable look, but did not seem to me to be very handsome. The King came in a few moments, dressed in the Greek costume, and, mounting his horse, galloped by, bowing politely to me and the other loafers, who stood, hat in hand, to see his Majesty pass.

We went next to see Mr. Arnold, an American missionary stationed here. At his house we found several gentlemen, arranging an excursion to Marathon for the next day. They invited me to join it, and I gladly consented.

We also called on Mr. Wyse, the British Ambassador here. Mr. Winthrop gave me a letter to this gentleman, and I wish you would take an early occasion to see him, and say how much I am indebted to him for this kindness. Mr. Wyse is one of the most accomplished men I have ever

met, — a scholar, an artist, an experienced states-
man, and everywhere regarded as a man of in-
flexible integrity.

I spent the evening at Mr. Hill's, having accepted an invitation to dine on Sunday (to-day)
with Mr. Wyse. It was very curious to hear the
Greek spoken as the language of society. A
Greek lady was making an evening visit there;
and Mr. Hill's adopted daughter, called Elizabeth
of Crete, is a young Greek lady, who not only
speaks the modern Greek with elegance, as her
mother tongue, but knows the ancient Greek better than most European Professors, and reads Homer and Sophocles just as we read Shakespeare
and Milton. She speaks English, too, though with
something of a foreign accent. Her family was
killed by the Turks, her property destroyed, and
she left an orphan and penniless. She was first
placed in a missionary school, and then taken into
Mr. Hill's family, living entirely as one of them.
She repeated several Cretan ballads that have
never been published, and read other pieces from
Fauriel, with singular taste and beauty.

I have not got over the strange impression it
makes to hear the Greek familiarly spoken; — to
hear a well-bred lady using the language I had
been studying these thirty years, with the facility
I have in using English. I say *the Greek;* for
the language spoken now by educated people here
is substantially Greek. It is absurd to speak of
the Greek as a dead language.

This very day, I went up to the Areopagus. At first the place was utterly deserted. Not a human being was there, nor in the Agora, once so full of busy life, nor in the Pnyx, where the whole population used to assemble to hear their orators; nor at the Propylæa, once thronged by stately processions. I was absorbed by the thoughts such objects could not fail to inspire, and by the infinite contrast between the past and the present. I thought of Paul preaching to the philosophers, on the spot where I was sitting, silent and alone; of Demosthenes thrilling the assembled Athenians with the loftiest sentiments of patriotism, as he stood on the rocky platform on the opposite hill; of Socrates, discoursing to his weeping friends on the immortality of the soul, in the dungeon almost within a stone's throw, — so near that I could see the mortises in the living rock where the beams of the wooden front were inserted. I was running over the thoughts of the great Apostle, and of the scarcely less great heathens, whose names are forever linked to these spots; and as I mused, a ragged but bright-looking boy came up, and spoke to me. I entered into conversation with him. He told me, in excellent Greek, that he came from Chalcis, beyond the mountains; his father died two years ago; his mother was still alive. I asked what he was doing in Athens. He waited and did errands in a coffee-house. Wishing to try him a little further,

I pointed to the Temple of Theseus, and asked him what it was. He answered, in as good Greek as Xenophon would have used, "The Temple of Theseus." I pointed to the dungeon of Socrates. Said he, "The prison of Socrates." "Who was Socrates?" said I. "The ancient philosopher," was the instant reply. This again was odd, though of course perfectly natural, that this little Chalcidian ragamuffin should converse in Greek with so much greater facility than I could, using only a single word that was not classical—and that was *coffee-house*—in the course of fifteen or twenty minutes.

I went yesterday to Marathon. We drove in a carriage to Cephissia, near which, you remember, Plato had a farm which he left by will to his son. Here we breakfasted on coffee and boiled eggs, and for the first time I used the knife and spoon that —— gave me, to the great admiration of my companions. Thence we rode on horseback round Pentelicus, and over the high mountains that shut in the plain of Marathon. It was a very fatiguing ride, the road being steep, and as rough as any mule-path among the Alps. But the views all the way are magnificent; and when, after four hours' riding, the plain, the sea, Eubœa on the opposite side, and the mound beneath which lie buried the Athenians who fell in that most memorable battle, burst upon our sight, we could not restrain an exclamation of wonder and delight. I

10

had not been at all prepared for the perfect and splendid beauty of the place ; and when you add to this the historical associations, you must not wonder if I find it hard to express the full measure of gratification I experienced in that great moment.

We galloped all over the plain, which is six miles long and two miles wide. We ascended the mound, and, lying down on its summit, read the description of the battle in Herodotus, with every feature of the scene distinctly before us; then we galloped along the shore of the " much-resounding sea," and, having satisfied our curiosity, returned through the little village of Marathon, by another and less difficult road, to Cephissia, — where we took more coffee, — then went home in our carriage, having before us a glorious Athenian sunset, bathing in golden light the heights of Pentelicus, Hymettus, Lycabettus, and the distant hill of Eleusis. Thus ended the first entire day in Greece.

To-day I went, as I have already said, to hear St. Paul on the Areopagus, Demosthenes on the Bema, Socrates in prison, and Dr. Hill in the English chapel. This evening I dined with a small party at the British Minister's, and had a delightful and instructive time.

XXV.

ATHENS, November 6, 1853.

LET me now tell you more fully than in my last letter how I spent my first Sunday in Athens. In the forenoon I heard Dr. King, the American missionary, preach to a small assembly of Greeks, in his own house, in Greek, an excellent sermon, to every word of which I could cordially assent. Then I took a copy of the Greek New Testament, and, walking round the Acropolis by the street of the Tripods and along the upper ranges of the Dionysiac Theatre, passed the Odeion of Herodes Atticus, and the Propylæa, down into the valley on the north of the Acropolis, and up the stone steps to the Areopagus. I read the admirable discourse of St. Paul, standing as he did, "in the midst of Mars Hill." I read it five times, from beginning to end, — twice aloud, in presence of the same natural features of the scene that lay before his eyes, and many of the grandest objects of art that he saw, ruinous, but still sublime. The discourse in the Acts is evidently only a sketch of the sermon as it was delivered, but I think it embraces all the main points. Standing there, on an elevated rock, " in the midst of Mars Hill," silent, with the Acropolis before me, covered with fragments of idols and ruins of " temples made with hands," — the seats of the Areopagites around me scarcely traceable and crumbling with age and the weather, and no one to occupy them, except the fancied forms of the Epicureans and Stoics who encountered St. Paul, — I could well understand the noble eloquence with which the Apostle spoke to his curious hearers of the " God that made the world and all things therein," who is " Lord of heaven and earth, and dwelleth not in temples made with hands."

These words are even more striking now than they were when St. Paul uttered them. Then these glorious temples stood entire, and the statues that peopled or surrounded them seemed like an assembly of gods ; now the gods are prostrate, or carried away to adorn the museums of distant lands. Heads, arms, legs, mutilated bodies, majestic and beautiful indeed, but thrown down from their high places, and broken in pieces, or laboriously put together by the antiquary, are all that remain, around the ruinous and time-stained columns, which stand so mournfully on the spot which they once made the central point of Grecian worship. Surely, the Apostle's words sound more solemn after eighteen centuries have wrought so tremendous an argument for their truth. If any temples built by human hands deserved to be the dwelling-place of God, it was the temples on the Acropolis; and what are they now? Wonderfully do those old columns, friezes, and architraves stand out against an Attic evening sky; wonderfully do they reflect the rays of the sun, as he comes up in his morning splendor, over the ridges of Hymettus. But God is in the setting and the rising sun; He is enthroned on the blue arch of the sky; He looks down from yonder crescent moon, that hangs over the Acropolis; His breath is the soft air which sweeps over those beautiful mountains and these spreading plains: but surely He dwelleth not in the mouldering temples, made by human hands, however cunning. St. Paul, having so powerfully declared this truth, passes on with admirable tact, and brief but effective eloquence, to the brotherhood of men, and the future judgment of the world by the Saviour, and closes most impressively with the resurrection of tho dead.

From his first allusion to the unknown God, he kept as close as possible to the range of Grecian thought. For Greeks had conceived, in their better moments, of the unity of God and his spiritual nature; one of their poets — quoted happily by St. Paul — had declared that men were the children of God; the doctrine of repentance had dawned upon the souls of Socrates and Plato, and a future judgment was distinctly believed and taught in their schools: but when he spoke of the resurrection of the dead, he, suddenly overleaped the boundaries of Grecian thought, and left his hearers in amazement, gaining, however, some proselytes, " among the which was Dionysius the Areopagite, and a woman named Damaris, and others with them."

After an hour or two on the Areopagus, I walked across the deserted hollow to the prison of Socrates. Here I sat down on a rocky seat, and read the two dialogues — the Criton and Phædon of Plato — the scene of which is placed here. They contain, I have no doubt, the substance of the conversations of Socrates with his disciples, during the last two days of his life, and are remarkable for the truly Christian character of the moral and even the religious doctrines taught by that incomparable man. It must have been within a few feet of the place where I sat that these conversations were held.

I have already given you a general idea of this prison. The existing rooms, or dungeons, are excavated in the rock, exactly east of the entrance to the Acropolis. On the outer face of the rock are still remaining the holes into which the joists of the wooden part of the building were inserted. One of the rooms is square, another is circular, with an opening at the top. As I sat, I looked directly over to the front of the Parthenon and the Propylæa; on my left lay the Pnyx and the stand from which Demosthenes spoke; farther on, in

the same direction, I just saw the corner of the
Temple of Theseus, the best preserved temple in
Athens; to the right lay the silent plain of the
waterless Ilissus. The sun shone brilliantly down
on the Acropolis, bringing out the exquisite propor-
tions of the Parthenon more distinctly than I had
yet seen them. Beyond, rose the lofty height of
Lycabettus, and clouds were resting, as usual, on
the range of Parnes. A few fleecy vapors were
sailing across the distant sky and casting their
shadows down upon the furrowed sides of Pentelicus and Hymettus.

The hum of the city on the other side of the
Acropolis scarcely reached me in the prison. Far
and near, solitude and silence reigned, except the
buzzing of a bee echoing through the stony rooms,
the tinkling of the sheep-bells from the neighboring slopes of the Museion Hill, and now and then
the voice of a shepherd, who, with crook in hand,
directed the course of his flock.

From time to time, a few persons were seen
strolling through the Agora; once a family — father, mother, and two or three children — came
up to the prison, looked in, said a few words,
and passed on; two crows flew cawing across the
Acropolis, over the prison, throwing their shadows on the ground; and, finally, three armed
men passed between the prison and the Pnyx,
and were lost to sight behind the Acropolis.

To my mind, the ancient scene was more a reality than the modern ; to me, as to Phædon, "it was the most delightful thing to call up the memory of Socrates," and to repeople these deserted dungeons with the forms of those who shared in the conversations of the two closing days.

Plato was not there. It is incidentally mentioned by one of the speakers that he was ill ; but he worthily gathered up the great thoughts then uttered, and has handed them down to us. He tells us that Socrates discoursed of the future life which was so soon to open before him. "I, O Simmias and Cebes, were I not convinced that I shall go into the presence of the wise and good gods, and of departed men better than those on earth, should do wrong not to be reluctant to die ; but now, rest assured, I hope to join the company of good men, though of this I would not be over confident. I am confident, however, as confident as I can be of anything, that I shall depart to excellent masters, the gods; and I am strong in the hope that, after death, it will be much better with the good than the wicked." With such views he argues that it will be becoming in him not to escape from the prison, and evade the sentence which a court of law has pronounced against him, but to submit himself with cheerful resignation, and with no touch of resentment, to the voice of his country and the will of the gods. "It is our duty," says he, "not to return an injury, nor to do evil to any man, however much we may have been wronged. *This, indeed, is, and will be, the opinion of but few.*" What an anticipation of the teachings of Christ is here!

Then, once more, in the Phædon, which embodies the conversations of the last day of his life, how nobly does he combat the scepticism of some of his friends, who feared that at death the soul would flit away, pass into nothingness, vanish like smoke on a breath of air, or dissolve like harmony, when the instrument which makes it is broken! His teaching is not direct, and authoritative, like that of the Apostle on the Areopagus, but drawn out with the keenest subtlety of argument, and expanded with a variety of illustrations in which the logical intellects of the Greeks — and of Socrates more than all — delighted to indulge.

As I read these arguments on the spot where they were delivered, I seemed to hear the earnest voices of this little company issuing from the inner dungeon. I seemed to witness their assent to the master's conclusions, and the half-stifled expressions of their agony at the thought of so soon losing such a guide and such a friend. To me, as to them, the argument was prolonged, and the shades of approaching evening stretched over towards the Acropolis. The sun was still on the western hills, when Socrates said, " Therefore, that man may be of good cheer concerning his own soul, who, in his life, abandoning sensual gratifications and earthly vanities as foreign to his being, has cultivated the love of knowledge, and adorned his soul with the befitting ornaments of virtue, righteousness, courage, liberty, and truth, and so awaits his departure to another world, when the appointed time may call him. You, my friends, each in his own time, will go thither hereafter, but me Destiny is already calling, as a tragedian would say, and the moment has arrived when I must turn to the bath; for I think it better to bathe before drinking the hemlock than to trouble the women to wash a corpse."

He retires to an inner apartment where he remains a long time, while his friends converse together on what they have heard, and on the greatness of the calamity which is to make them orphans for the rest of their lives. He returns, composed for death; the fatal drug is mixed by the executioner, and is drunk off with a serene smile by the illustrious prisoner, although Criton reminds him that the sun is still upon the mountains and has not yet gone down. He continues to walk about as long as strength remains; then lies down, covers himself; moves once more; the attendant uncovers his face, — his eyes glaze, — Criton closes his mouth and eyes. "Such was the death of our friend, — a man, as we should say, the best, the wisest, and the most just, in that time, of all with whom we were acquainted."

When, towards sunset, I walked away from that consecrated prison, the scenes and conversations so vividly represented by Plato seemed to have just taken place; and as I looked up to the Areopagus, on which the sun was still shining, I seemed to hear the voice of Paul, enforcing and perfecting by Divine authority the doctrines as to duty and immortality toward which Socrates had felt his way by the guidance of reason alone. The sunlight on the Areopagus compared with the shades of Socrates's prison, seemed a type of revelation contrasted even with the best and clearest deductions of the unassisted human mind.

It was singular to pass from the impressive solitude of this part of the city of Athens, walking by the ruins of the Odeion and the Theatre, and noticing over the eastern end of the Acropolis the upper line of the clouds that rested on Parnes, as Aristophanes represents them in his play; and to meet, on the broad platform of the Temple of Olympian Jupiter, the population of Athens, in their gay Sunday dresses, amusing themselves like children, running, jumping, pitching quoits, and laughing at a little donkey overloaded with a dozen boys and girls stuck into panniers on his sides. No contrast could be more startling; the solemn spirit of antiquity which reigns undisturbed at the western end of the Acropolis, and the frivolity, levity, vanity, and idleness which strike one just under the eastern extremity.

I continued my walk, pondering these things. Approaching the King's palace, I overtook Mr.

Hill, and joined him in a stroll through the royal gardens, which contain the only trees in or near Athens. They were vocal with the evening song of birds, and reminded me of the description of the groves at Colonus, in the first chorus of the Œdipus Coloneus of Sophocles. A part of the foundations of the Lyceum of Aristotle is enclosed in the royal grounds, and within a few years a long and curious mosaic floor — I think it must have been the floor of a walk where the philosopher meditated his lectures, — has been discovered. It is now enclosed, covered by an arbor, and used in summer as a dining-room for the royal family.

While we were in the garden the sun went down, and in his departing light stood against the golden sky the columns of Olympian Jupiter, the Arch of Adrian, the Acropolis with the Parthenon and the Erectheium, while in the distance gleamed the waters of the Phaleric Bay, — a picture I never grow wearied with contemplating.

Hurrying to my hotel, I took a hasty dinner, and at six o'clock heard a sermon in Greek, on the Missionary Enterprise, by Rev. Mr. Arnold, a Baptist clergyman stationed here. At eight o'clock I attended another religious service at the house of Mr. King, — the sermon by Rev. Mr. Lowndes from Malta, in English, — and finally reached my home for the night at ten o'clock.

XXVI.

ATHENS, November 7, 1853.

EARLY this morning I went to the church of St. Demetrius, to hear a celebrated Greek preacher, Metrophánes. It is a great fête day, — *eorté*, — as they call it in Greek, and the whole population of Athens put on their best clothes in honor of so distinguished a saint. I was at the church-door at eight o'clock, and had some difficulty in getting in, till a Greek friend who was with me whispered that I was an *Americanós*, when the crowd not only gave way, but some of them led me to a kind of stall near the pulpit, usually occupied by some ecclesiastical dignitary. The chants were performing, but I cannot say that I was much edified or delighted by the style of the singing. If S—— is correct in supposing that the Greek Church has preserved, in part, the ancient Dorian and Æolian moods, why, then I must think the Dorian and Æolian moods were not much better than that bit of Pindaric music which you once performed, but refused to repeat. After an hour and a half of this infliction on my delicate musical sensibilities, varied by swinging censers and perfuming the church (which needed it), and sprinkling perfumed water over the heads of the people, — (I had about half a pint dashed into my face over my spectacles, which I was obliged to take off and wipe,) — a strange-looking chap, with long hair hanging over his shoulders, and a grotesque, many-colored dress, mounted the pulpit, and began to chant alone. At first I thought it was the sermon, and I recalled various statements about the ancient fashion of pitching a tone at the commencement of an oration. But I soon discovered that he was not the preacher.

The preacher is one of the four authorized to preach in Athens; for the Greek Church very prudently permits only a small portion of its clergy to perform this function, thereby — an arrangement worth thinking of elsewhere — saving the heavens from a great deal of unnecessary vexation.

His Sanctity, Mr. Metrophánes, is a good-looking man, with a fine voice and an earnest, eloquent style. His sermon was excellent and practical, naturally arising out of the occasion, and treating of the proper use to be made of festivals. " You must not pass the day in drinking, in gluttony, in wantonness ; you must make it the occasion for kindness and charity, for mutual love, and the practice of all the virtues." Just at this moment a crowd of Athenian women just over my head, in a little gallery, began to chatter so loud, that for some minutes I could not hear a word. His Sanctity turned in the direction of the noise, stopped a moment, and then said to some lay functionary of the church, " Tell those women to hold their tongues, or I will come down." This, of course, put an end to the disturbance, and the sermon went on to the conclusion.

Returning to a late breakfast, and with an appetite sharpened by so early a morning service, I came near violating the prohibition as to gluttony; as it was, I believe I eat a whole Attic partridge.

As I was sitting in my room afterwards, I had a great surprise. You must know that, when I arrived in Athens, I took a guide, and told him to show me the way to Mr. Notara, the banker's, to whose care I had requested R—— S—— to forward my letters. No letters were there. Twice since have I called,—no letters there ; and I began to think the powers that be must have found something treasonable, and so detained them. There was no help but a patient waiting for the next Austrian steamer. A knock at my door. " Come in." An elderly gentleman appears, with a package in his hand. I recognize R—— S——'s writing, and the address to Mr. Notara. Elderly gentleman informs me in bad French that he has had the letter for ten days, but not knowing where I was to be found, until he accidentally heard from Dr. King to-day, had of course kept it. " Are you Mr. Notara ? " said I. " Oui, Monsieur." I was utterly perplexed. I had seen Mr. Notara three or four times, and had struck up something like an intimacy with him ; and here was another gentleman claiming to be Mr. Notara, and handing me the long-looked-for letters from home. The mystery was cleared up by a little explanation. My guide had carried me to the wrong banker, either by a blunder, or because he thought one banker as good as another, and I took it for granted all along that the obliging friend whose acquaintance I had made was Mr. Notara.

November 8. — I had written so far, when Mr. Hill called to ride with me as far as Daphne, a village on the way to Eleusis. It was a singularly beautiful afternoon. We rode from the city out to the olive-groves which occupy the plain covering the spot where Plato's Academy once stood. The trees have suffered some injury ; but they still form the most prominent feature of this part of Attica, and, being so constantly referred to by the ancient writers, are objects of interest in the landscape beyond any other trees that could be placed there. We had the Acropolis and the Temple of Theseus on our left, with a distant view of the sea, and on our right the Academy, and Colonus, the birthplace of Sophocles and the scene of one of his noblest tragedies. This height is now surmounted by a monument to K. O. Müller, who died from a sun-stroke received while imprudently exposing himself at Delphi. This gives an additional interest, in the eyes of the classical scholar, to a spot already famous.

The picture around us, as we galloped across the plain, was not only lovely in the extreme, but crowded with historical associations, from the mythical times down to the present moment. Mount Ægaleos, where Xerxes sat to watch the battle of Salamis, the strait itself, and the island, in one direction, Phyle and Mount Parnes in the other, all lovely under the brilliant light of an autumnal sun; seemed to bring history and poetry visibly before us. The road wound along the eastern end of Ægaleos, into a hilly and most picturesque region, and in about an hour we reached Daphne. Here the view that suddenly opened combined every element of picturesque and associated interest. The hills on the right were clothed with the delicate purple veil, so often seen in this country; on the left, the descending sun threw Ægaleos into deep shade; through the vista opened before us, between the hills, lay, calm and soft, the inner bay of Eleusis and the end of the island, and beyond rose the mountains of Megara robed in deep, rich purple. I could have looked on this picture of natural beauty for hours. Evening was approaching, and orange, purple, and golden lines shot across the western sky, and bent over a scene of varied loveliness unsurpassed by anything the imagination can conceive.

We turned our horses' heads towards Athens. In a short time we came in sight of the Attic plain, with the dark-green line of olive-plantations, the

Acropolis painting its columns upon the sky, and the west pouring its liquid gold, until the entire plain and the air itself seemed filled with its splendor. The colors of sunset, shifting with every passing moment, faded away, and the crescent moon, with her attendant stars, came out into this soft Attic heaven, tipping the mountain summits and the ancient temples with her silver light. Beyond the city Mount Hymettus rose, colored as I had never seen it or any other mountain before. A delicate veil of blue had been carefully thrown over it, not concealing its form in the least, but softening its rugged features, as if the mountain itself were preparing for the repose of night, from the excitements of the day.

Under this light, with the summer-like air breathing around us, we galloped across the Attic plain, through the olive-groves, into the busy streets of Athens, — and so with dinner and the evening's study ended the day.

Thursday, November 10. — I believe I have not yet given you an account of my manner of life here among the Athenians. Well, there are only two good streets in Athens: one is Hermes Street, where the King lives, and the other is the street of Æolus, where I live. I have taken a room in the Hotel d'Angleterre, which looks first upon an enclosed garden where the birds sing every morning; then towards the left on Lycabettus, a mountain that overhangs the city; and, finally, on nearly the whole range of Hymettus, where the bees make their honey, as in the time of Plato. I see the sun rise over Hymettus every morning, and at evening he casts his last beams directly on the garden beneath me. My room is quiet, but not far from the hotel is a soldiers' barrack, and I have almost every day the benefit of a lesson in Greek, by listening to the words of command, in the drill. A young Greek teacher, who speaks French very imperfectly, and no other language at all except Greek, comes to me at seven o'clock in the morning, and spends about an hour and a half. At nine I go to the University, and hear a lecture on ancient Greece by Professor Asopios, — an old and very learned gentleman, whose language is not only elegant, but lively and eloquent. He speaks too rapidly for me to follow him, but I understand a considerable part of what he says, and daily understand more. Then I generally study three or four hours, reading and writing the best modern Greek I can. I have attended only one debate in the legislature, but the new session is to be opened to-morrow, and I shall try to be present, and to attend often afterwards.

The hardest exercise I have had in Greek was to make out a list of clothes for the washerwoman. The ancients had no shirts to their backs, but the moderns have, and they have made a very good word for the thing; but what an under-waistcoat should be called went beyond me. However, I constructed an excellent classical term (*hypochiton*). When the waiter came in, I gave him the bundle and the list. My *hypochiton* was heathen Greek to him ; he could not make it out in the least. I showed him the article, and he exclaimed, "O! O! fanella, fanella!" So it is, that we go to remote and learned sources for what lies very near at hand.

A few days ago, I had occasion to go to a tailor's. My wardrobe, like the Acropolis, has suffered some dilapidations by the wear and tear of time, and needed, like the temples, a little restoration. My frock-coat was out at the elbows, and my pantaloons were a little ragged about the feet, and a trifle threadbare at the knees. I addressed the tailor in Attic and Xenophontic Greek on the subject of *periskelides*, and the necessity of mending them. He understood me readily, being a *raptes* (tailor) of education ; but when he took the garment in hand, he told me he would send back "*to pantalon*" the next day.

There is an Irishwoman in the city, married to a Greek. Her boy goes to school, but she complains that he begins to use language she cannot understand. Her own dialect is an Hibernian Greek. The common word for water is *meron ;* the classical word *hydor ;* and when the boy comes home thirsty he calls for *hydor*, — to her great amazement.

A few such instances occur, but, in general, nothing has surprised me more than the excellence of the language and the purity with which it is spoken, not only in the pulpit and the professor's chair, but in society. My ear is not yet sufficiently accustomed to the rapidity of conversation, but it is becoming so.

The watchmen in the. streets use very good Greek. Coming home the other evening, about eleven o'clock, I was saluted by the usual question, " *Tis ei?* " — " Who art thou ? " — the very question, by the way, that Anacreon puts to the dove. The answer to be given is " *Kalós*," which in ancient Greek generally means *a handsome fellow*. Well, I gave the answer, but, immediately remembering my French portrait, I rejoiced that the night covered up the monstrous lie I had to tell. This tenderness of conscience lasted, however, but a short time, and now, when the *skopos*, or watchman, asks me who I am, I tell him, without the slightest hesitation, that I am a *kalós*, though the falsehood grows greater every day. He believes me, and I pass on.

My letters have procured me a very agreeable reception. Some of the best among the Greeks — professors, officials, and members of the legislature — have been very attentive and kind. I have the free use of the University library, which is really a very good one, and Mr. Pittakys, the conservator of antiquities, has given me free admission to the Acropolis for a year.

The Americans stationed here are all hospitality. At the house of Mr. Hill I am always sure to find an agreeable society of Americans and Greeks, or travellers that come this way; and Mr. Wyse, the English Minister, for my acquaintance with whom I am indebted to Mr. W——, has given me a general invitation to take tea at his house, and use his library as much as I please. I find him not only a man of solid learning, but of rare accomplishments, and of very remarkable conversational powers. Mr. Finlay (whose works, you know, I have found useful) has given me a very handsome dinner, and paid me every other attention that could be useful or agreeable.

Last evening I took tea at the palace, with Dr. Roeser, the King's physician, — an old university friend of Agassiz, whom he knew at Munich, and who was delighted to hear about him. It has been proposed to me to be presented, especially on account of a great ball soon to be given by the court; but as this will involve a new pair of gloves, and perhaps a cravat, I hesitate. To-day the Doctor took me over the palace, which is really very handsome, but just like all the other European palaces, and quite too large for so small a country.

Yesterday I walked out to the Academy and Colonus. At the latter spot I read the Œdipus Coloneus of Sophocles entirely through. Certainly this is the most exquisite of his pieces. I

wish you would read the translation (Dale's),
and imagine how it would strike you, if read on
the top of white Colonus, with the whole city of
Athens in view, and the site of the temple of the
Furies, where Œdipus mysteriously died, opening
a dark chasm into which he may readily be imagined to have vanished from mortal sight.

The bright Attic sun, the olive-groves still covering the Academy, the birds singing (though not
the nightingale, so beautifully described in the
splendid choral ode), the Acropolis, the Theban
road still passing by the foot of the hill, revive the
scenes of Sophocles, though the groves of Colonus,
and the Temples of Neptune and Prometheus,
have disappeared. There is but one tree on the
hill; but the soil is filled with bits of marble,—
the crumbling fragments of former splendor.

I have been many times to the Acropolis, and I
believe there is not a street of modern Athens
which I have not more than once traversed. I find
my way better here than in Boston. As to the
principal remains of the ancient city, I needed no
guide on the first day of my arrival. There is at
present no sojourner in the city with whom I can
hope to make arrangements for travelling in the
Peloponnesus.

I continue to find myself very well placed in
Athens, and hope to derive great benefit in my
future studies from this visit. I have now been
here between two and three weeks. As yet I am

the only American traveller in the city, and I do not believe there will be many, if any, here this winter; but I have already formed a very agreeable circle of acquaintance, Greek, English, and American.

Mr. Marsh has left in Athens, among the best people, a profound impression of his ability, learning, firmness, and good sense. I am glad to know this, because I heard in Germany stories tending to a different view.

I do not find that there is any evidence of Mr. King's having violated the constitution by open attempts at proselyting, or by any outrages upon the religious feelings of the Greeks; and some of the evidence given against him on his trial was notoriously forged by a rascal named Simonides, who was detected afterwards in an attempt to pass off a quantity of his own manuscripts for ancient documents, found at Mount Athos. Such a villain was allowed to testify.

I am fully convinced, from all that I have seen and heard here, that the prosecution was one of the most frivolous and perfidious attempts ever made to put down a man, who, though personally offensive by his well-known opinions, was wholly innocent, in a legal and moral point of view; and that the accounts transmitted to Mr. Skhinas, at Munich, were colored and exaggerated by Greek mendacity, as notorious now as it was in the days of the Romans. I have carefully examined the constitution, in reference to the charges against Mr. King, and I have come to the same conclusion with Mr. Marsh. But I believe it to have been an affair of the priesthood, not of the government.

The politics of Greece are in the queerest state in the world. The elections have recently taken place in Athens. I attended the hustings, and was greatly amused by the process. A vote-distributor, taking me for an Athenian, gave me the government ticket, which I put into my pocket. The most curious thing is, that, before a single deputy has been returned from the provinces, the new session is opened.

I attended the ceremony. It consisted of a religious service, chanted, the administering of the oath, the declaration that the session was opened, and a few cries of " Live the King."

There were two or three members of the lower house, and about as many senators, present. The service, amusingly enough, happened to contain a passage signifying, " Fear ye not, O Greeks, because ye are *few*." There was a great parade of the military, and strains of martial music gave notice of the successive steps in the grand performance.

I asked a gentleman how the chamber, not yet elected, and therefore not existing, could be opened. He said that the constitution required it on that particular day, but that the elections had been retarded by the length of the previous session. " Yes," I said, " it is constitutional, but impossible." He admitted the practical contradiction ; but this is just the way the government tampers with the constitution, and turns it into a farce. There is great discontent, and you hear in private society the plainest language. An outbreak here would not in the least surprise me, at any moment. Should it happen, the Bavarians would get marching orders at once. These things one cannot help observing. I have not gone out of my way to hear them, my objects here being wholly literary ; but I cannot shut my ears.

Since my last letter I have ascended Mount Pentelicus, — the highest mountain in Attica. You may easily imagine the magnificence of the view, when I tell you that on the west we saw the whole Attic plain, with the city, and, beyond, not only the sea, with Salamis and Ægina, but the shores and mountains of Peloponnesus ; on the north, Mounts Ægaleos and Parnes ; on the east, the whole plain of Marathon, and the bay, strait, and opposite highlands of Euboea ; on the south, the great plain called Mesogæa, with the Lameian hills in the distance ; Hymettus on the southwest ; and on the southeast, Sunium, the blue Mediterranean shore ; so that we had, in one magnificent panorama, the whole of Attica, and its surrounding seas and islands, with distant and beautiful views of the neighboring provinces.

Pentelicus is renowned the world over for its exquisite marble. The old quarries, from which so many temples and statues sprang to life, still show the traces of the ancient workmen. A curious cavern leads into the centre of the mountain, its roof of marble hanging in all directions with stalactites. Its mouth is large, high, and spacious, but as it descends, it narrows until one is obliged to crawl, holding a lighted candle, to see where he is going. It ends in deep water, from which, doubtless, the ancient laborers in the quarries drank.

We galloped back to Athens about three o'clock. I am becoming, of necessity, a centaur. The horses here are so accustomed to climbing, that, when they reach a level spot, away they dash, on a gallop, rather alarming to an elderly gentleman, who has been out of practice for twenty years. However, I illustrate the growth of the ancient myth about the Centaur Chiron. You would be astonished, I dare say, to see me tearing over the soil of Attica, and raising a greater dust than I shall ever raise in America. The only mode of travelling, except on two or three short roads out of Athens, is on horseback; and to-morrow I start for a ten days' journey, to visit Thebes, Eleusis, Argos, Mycenæ, &c., &c. I shall write you on the journey, but whether it will be possible to post my letters before I return, I do not know. I have much to tell you; but it is long after midnight, and we start early to-morrow.

XXVII.

YOUR geography may not be quite sufficient to tell you exactly where I am at the present moment of writing. If so, I will endeavor to help you out of the difficulty. I posted a letter for you, scribbled in the haste of preparation for a journey, at Athens. The day was interesting there on account of a great public ceremony, at the funeral of a brother of Marco Botzaris, a distinguished man, and a senator of Greece.

Dr. Roeser told me, a few days ago, that there was to be a splendid funeral ceremony in a few days. I inquired who was dead. " No one," he replied, " but Senator Botzaris is going to die tomorrow." I was struck by the professional coolness of his statement, but soon forgot it in other things that occupied my mind. Yesterday I accidentally heard of the ceremony, and, walking down the street of Æolos, overtook the procession just as it was entering the church of St. Eirène. The great officers of state, the leading ecclesiastics, with the Bishop of Athens, the officers of the army, and a large body of soldiers, accompanied the body.

A long funeral service was chanted. Then a discourse was delivered by Mr. Argyropoulos, an eminent Athenian scholar, and last year President of the University. The body lay uncovered, surrounded with military insignia, a plumed cap placed on the breast. After the eulogy was over, the procession formed again, and we followed the old hero out of Athens, over the Ilissus, leaving the Temple of Jupiter on the left and the Acropolis on the right.

The heavens were overcast, and seemed to sympathize with the melancholy pageant; and as we passed the ruins of the Temple of Jupiter, and I looked at the few standing columns, and one recently prostrated by a violent tempest, — all weather-stained and shattered, — I thought they were typical of the few surviving heroes of the revolution, and of the one just fallen. He was borne by men who relieved one another, — his strongly marked face looking up to the overcast sky, his moustache and hair grizzled with age, and his features emaciated by long sickness. The burying-ground lies at a considerable distance from the city. At the tomb another service was chanted, and then, when the mortal remains of the last of the brothers of Botzaris were deposited in their resting-place, three volleys were fired by the soldiery, and the crowd dispersed.

We returned by the Ilissus and the Callirrhoe; and as I looked up to the stained and hoary col-

umns of the Acropolis, the gray rocks on which
they stand, and the clouds shrouding the light of
Attica, I thought the funeral pomp of old Time
and coeval Nature vastly more impressive than
any ceremonies of man.

This morning, the hills of Attica were still
clothed in heavy mist, and my companion — a
young Englishman who resembles S—— C——
so much, that I took to him immediately — and
I hesitated about setting out. But after eating a
hearty breakfast, we bade defiance to the clouds,
mounted our Thessalian steeds, and, like the gallant
knights in Spenser, " pricked across the plain."

Our guide is Strattis, the most experienced of
his tribe in Athens. Our troupe consists of Strattis as commander-in-chief, Mr. C—— and myself,
and three mules carrying luggage, cooking apparatus, chairs, table, beds, and provisions. The condition of Greece is still such that this is the only
possible mode of travelling ; the most you can de-
pend on getting is a room, with a fireplace and
bare walls.

The air was soft, though moist, and the mist and
clouds on the marble hills rolled about like tossing
waves of the sea. We took the road to Parnes,
the wildest and most picturesque of the passes between Attica and Bœotia. We rode between
Colonus and the olive-groves of the Academy, on
the one hand, and the Queen's summer-house on
the other. As we moved slowly along, we were

saluted by a chorus of birds, — among them *a single nightingale*, — which quite reminded me of Aristophanes. On one of the distant slopes was feeding an immense flock of sheep, tended by a shepherd, who charmed his weary hours exactly like the shepherds of Theocritus, by playing rustic airs upon his reedy pipe.

The next sight we encountered was less agreeable, though perhaps more romantic, — four *klephts*, or robbers, led, bound, by a strong detachment of troops, who had just taken them in the mountains we were on the point of traversing. We congratulated ourselves that the arrest was made this morning rather than to-morrow, though it would have helped the interest of the journey to meet the ferocious-looking fellow who appeared to be the leader of the band, face to face, on the rocky heights of Parnes.

The Pass of Phyle reminds me of the Alps, so wild, so massive, and so rugged are the piles of rock that rise on either side. They are not so high nor so precipitous as the Alps, and the immense quantity of marble mixed with other rocks takes from them the sombre solemnity of the Swiss mountains. The path is very winding, and runs along the sloping side; but there are no mountain streams, at this season, to blend with the wind and fill the ear with their united voices.

Gradually we rose towards the summit of the pass, stopping to eat bread and honey at an ancient monastery, where there is a monk a hundred years old. The honey was excellent, resembling that of Hymettus. The old gentlemen were very curious to hear the news from the world below, and when we told them of our having seen the klephts, they said it was only yesterday that the same gang had been at the monastery, and demanded bread and wine.

We went through several beautiful forests of pine, and the winds murmuring through the branches sounded like the roaring of the Hellespont along the shores of Troy. The scene from the summits of the mountains was superb; the clouds were sweeping over them, and rolling and surging like the ocean in a storm; while here and there a break let in the sunlight on some distant peak, or on the rugged side of a mountain. For a few moments we had a view of the plain of Athens, from the ancient fortress that still surmounts "the brow of Phyle," where Thrasybulus and his companions in exile assembled previously to their attack upon the Thirty Tyrants.

From this grand old work of Grecian skill we continued our journey, at first mostly descending, then crossing an extensive plain which must have been the bed of a lake, and at its northern extremity ascending a slope, on which the celebrated town or hamlet of Sielisi is built. In fact, we are just on the confines of Attica and Bœotia. We are at a khan, or rather a private house used as a khan, and were so fortunate as to arrive just before the Bishop of Thebes and his retinue went away. His Sanctity — a venerable and kind-hearted man — is on a tour through his diocese to comfort the poor people, who are frightened out of their wits by the earthquakes that have recently made such ravages in Greece. Thebes has been laid in ruins ; houses in Athens have been damaged, and the house in which we are now quartered for the night has been terribly shaken, as its cracked walls testify. It was curious to see the assembly of men, women, and children waiting to kneel before the Bishop and receive his blessing; and his leave-taking was really very touching. He met us courteously, told us of the misfortunes of Thebes, and expressed his regret that he could not stay longer with us.

Well, here we are, in a house without a single pane of glass ; the upper story, of two rooms, occupied by us and the family, and the rooms below by the animals, or, as a Yankee would call them, the *critters*. Nevertheless, our guide, aided by the cook, has given us a dinner of three courses, — excellent *pillau*, cutlets, fried potatoes, roast chicken, pudding, figs, dates, almonds, and *café noir*, as good as you can get at the best restaurant in Paris. I think we shall rough it pretty well. Good night.

11*

XXVIII.

LEUCTRA, November 16.

I BADE you good night at a little hamlet on the confines of Attica and Bœotia. After a sound night's sleep, in our homely quarters, at the house of an Albanian peasant (whose two little daughters I made happy by giving each a copper coin worth two cents), we mounted our Thessalian chargers, and, followed by our quiet little dog Walnut, entered the territory of Bœotia. The descent was rocky and rugged, and the riding hard; but by and by we reached the Bœotian plains, so much more fruitful than those of Attica. We soon came in full sight of Helicon, with a dim outline of Parnassus in the distance, and Cithæron just on our left. And so over hill and valley we went, sometimes walking and sometimes galloping like the wind.

At length, about noon, as we were passing between two hills, suddenly the Acropolis of Thebes came in sight, in the centre of an extensive plain, with a circle of beautiful hills encompassing it. I was surprised by the beauty of the situation, which has had no justice done to it by travellers. To me it was deeply interesting, not only as the birthplace

of Pindar, but as one of the centres of poetical tradition, around which so many tragic stories turn.
On yonder hill stood the Sphinx, and gave the
fatal riddle which cost so many their lives.

Thebes has been an unfortunate city, even from
the mythical time of Œdipus. Philip took it; Al-
exander destroyed it; and now, this last summer,
a terrible earthquake has almost prostrated it.

We entered near the river Ismenus, and, stopping to look at the springs that feed it, we saw
the Theban nymphs washing clothes. They were
standing knee-deep in the water, in a costume of
the most classical brevity and simplicity. My
horse had a fancy to walk into the stream. I did
not object to it; but when he got in, he liked it so
well, that he lay down and rolled, with me on his
back. I sprang off as quickly as I could, but not
quickly enough to escape a handsome ducking. I
had, however, the consolation of reflecting that it
was in the Ismenian fountain, — one of the most
classical waters in Greece; and, all dripping, I
pulled the horse out and remounted. We drove
directly up to the Acropolis, and, stopping at the
principal *hotel*, left our horses and walked round
to see this once famous town. The ruins caused
by the earthquake have been partially repaired,
but many of the houses are in a shattered and un-
inhabitable condition. The houseless inhabitants
have either fled to Athens, or taken up their abode
in tents outside of the city.

The gallop over the plain of Thebes to Platæa, with Cithæron just before us, was one of the most inspiring we have yet had. We arrived in an hour and a half at the remains of the ancient walls, rode entirely round them, and recalled the great defeat of the Persians on the plain, and the memorable siege sustained by the city against the Spartans, and so powerfully described by Thucydides.

Thence we rode to Leuctra, having Cithæron behind us and Helicon directly in front. The day. has been a somewhat wild one, with sunshine part of the time, and shifting masses of clouds careering over the hills, — beautiful, solemn, and melancholy, — solitudes where once peopled cities flourished; flocks of sheep picking the scanty grass between the piles of stone out of which ancient walls and towers were made. In some places we galloped over the sites of great towns, where the plough is now drawn.

Just before leaving Athens I had attended the funeral of Botzaris. On entering Thebes I stopped at the ruined church of St. Luke to see an ancient sarcophagus. There was a fresh grave open, with the coffin already there. When we reached the Acropolis, the first sound we heard was the funeral chant, and the first sight that met our eyes was the procession with the corpse, winding down to the church. · These melancholy pomps, and the wildly drifting clouds on the mountains, brought up, with extraordinary impressiveness, the Klephtic lines :

" Why are the mountains shadowed o'er ?   Why stand they dark
        ened grimly ?
  Is it a tempest warring there, or rain-storm beating on them ?
  It is no tempest warring there, no rain-storm beating on them,
  But Charon sweeping over them, and with him the departed."

Riding over the mountains, the only way of travelling here, one not only understands the conversion of Charon the boatman into Charon the horseman, but cannot help feeling the extraordinary solemnity of the scenery, which so naturally suggested the associated conceptions. It is curious how the studies of one's lifetime take form and substance as he travels over the consecrated ground of history and poetry. My wanderings in Europe have been constantly haunted by the great figures my mind has grown acquainted with in literature. Like the shadowy hosts in Napoleon's midnight review, they come, and from nearly as many and as distant burying-places in the memory. It is now after nine o'clock, and so good night.

XXIX.

I INTENDED to write every evening, through my present journey. My date last evening would have been Lebadeia. But the best intentions are often frustrated by inexorable Destiny, as you will learn.

Yesterday morning we left Leuctra, with the clouds hanging over Helicon, and showery Jove threatening to interfere with human projects. However, the view was superb, and after a rough and stony ride up hill and down, we came upon a lovely plain, covered with flocks and herds. Then, winding up the myrtle-covered sides of Helicon to the fountain of Aganippe, near which, in an old church, is an inscription on an ancient column, showing that here the Muses once used to come, and in a basin below bathe their celestial bodies, we drank of the fountain and rode away.

As we crossed a lower point of Helicon, and came in full sight of Parnassus, the travelling grew rougher and rougher. Gray says:

> " From Helicon's harmonious springs
> A thousand rills their mazy progress take."

One of these streams had taken its mazy course directly across our path; had worn a channel, and then run off and left it dry. It was necessary to cross it. Our horses are generally sure-footed, but no sureness of foot is proof against slippery mud; and so down went my gallant Thessalian, pitching me head foremost over to the opposite bank. My hat, already the victim of circumstances, was damaged; my knee was considerably bruised; my side was pommelled, and, what was more irreparable, my old frock-coat — the faithful companion of so many journeys — was not only covered with mud, but rent at the left elbow. Think of my condition, — on the slope of Helicon, in sight of Parnassus, and *out at the elbows.*

On we journeyed, through gorges of magnificent beauty, where murmuring streams answered the oak and the whispering plane-tree, and Nymphs and Dryads have scarcely ceased their sports.

The trees had put on their autumnal colors, as varied and brilliant as those of an American forest; while the marble summits, rising on either side above the zone of cedars that encircles their waist with a belt of green, closed in the picture with a sculptured frame, contrasting with the many-tinted picture within.

At length we descended the last slope, on the northeast, towards the Copaic plain, — one of the most remarkable in Bœotia. Looking back on Helicon, and off to the left on the scarcely visible

Parnassus, we saw the clouds thickening, and showery Jove more ominous and threatening. Thunders began to roll, and lightning to play about the distant summits. We hastened to a village called Cotumala, and stopped at the principal house it contained, thinking we would lunch there, and wait until the coming shower had passed.

In we went, and in a few minutes our lunch, consisting of a cold boiled egg and a bit of bread, was laid on a circular table six inches high, with coarse rugs and cushions round it. We lay down — *lay to*, I might literally say — and ate ; and while we ate, the thunder and lightning raged with fearful violence, and the showers came down like another Deucalion's deluge, which, you know, happened just about in these parts. In a few moments the mountain torrents began to rush down with a roar and a fury quite inconceivable in our country. It was plain we could get no farther.

Let me tell you what sort of a house it was. Remember, it was quite superior to the average of houses throughout Greece. The walls were of baked clay, and over these was laid the wooden roof, running up to a ridge-pole. There was one story only, and only one apartment. In the middle was a depression in the floor ; the floor being made of earth mixed with straw. This lower portion of the room was occupied by the animals, — horses, cows, &c. Towards the end of the upper portion was raised a circle, on which a fire was made, and the food was cooked. The smoke found its way up to the roof, and meandered in graceful curls among the timbers, some of it escaping, in the course of time, through the cracks, which served the double purpose of letting out the smoke and letting in the rain. Glass windows were not. Openings in the wall, closed by wooden panels when necessary, were the primitive communications with the light of heaven.

The family consisted of father, mother, aunt, and four children ; the youngest a baby, rocking in a cradle or trough. The mother, like Nausicaa in the Odyssey, had gone to the fountain to wash the clothes of the week ; the father was about his farm ; the aunt was keeping the children quiet, and spinning, — not with a wheel, but with merely a spindle, whirling it on the ground, in Homeric fashion, with her hand.

After luncheon, I lay down at full length, with my feet towards the fire, and, being a good deal exhausted with my Heliconian tumble, fell fast asleep. When I awoke, the mother had returned, completely drenched, and was changing her dress.

Well, here we were to stay for the night. It was an embarrassing circumstance that our luggage — bag, baggage, and provisions, beds, chairs, and table — had all gone forward to Lebadeia. As the people had no beds, there were no bed-rooms ; as they sat on the ground, there were no chairs ;

as they ate with their fingers, there were no knives and forks. Never mind. "Justice," says Æschylus, "often flies from gilded splendors, and takes up her abode in smoky houses"; and we were exactly in the condition of Justice, with some wonder, to be sure, at her ladyship's taste.

Besides the family, here were Strattis (our guide, a Lesbian, and therefore the countryman of Sappho), Walnut the dog, Mr. C—— and myself, and three horses, all to sleep in the same room, — all to be fed. Strattis reconnoitred the village, and returned with a chicken. The good mother tipped the baby out of the trough, and poured some Indian meal in, which she kneaded into a mighty loaf, and then, burying it in the embers, baked it well. The chicken was put into a kettle, and that was set on a tripod, (just as Homer describes,) and boiled; and " when they had cooked the food, and skilfully prepared the feast," the table was spread, and " we stretched forth our hands to the things that were lying before us."

Do you think the bread was not good ? Prejudiced mortal, I never ate better. But when the sacred rage of hunger was appeased, we bethought ourselves of sleep. C—— the Englishman, F—— the American, Strattis the Lesbian, and Walnut the dog, lay on a carpet, on the ground, on one side of the fire ; the family on the other ; the horses stood below, and the god descended to close our eyes in soft slumbers.

We started early this morning, and without breakfast; rode three hours to Lebadeia; bathed, breakfasted, and visited the cave of Trophonius; galloped on to Chæroneia, where Philip destroyed the forces of Thebes and Athens; rode over the field; saw the colossal lion, once on the mound of the Thebans, now lying, weather-beaten, with his noble face turned to heaven, as I saw the dead Botzaris the other day; rode up to the ancient theatre in the hillside, and the church where they preserve Plutarch's marble chair; and then, skirting the eastern side of Parnassus, which rose clear and lofty over us all the way, reached this spot at nightfall. As it is growing late, and there is prospect of better sleep to-night than the last, I will say good night.

XXX.

THERMOPYLÆ, November 19, 1853.

WELL, here we are on the ground sacred to 'Leonidas and the three hundred Spartans; within ten feet of the hot springs from which this famous pass takes its name.

We left the village of Drachmano this morning, with heavy clouds threatening to accompany us on our way. Showery Jupiter sat enthroned on Parnassus, and, as we ascended the opposite range of mountains, he hit my nose with a single drop, perhaps expecting that, like the Greeks of old, we should postpone our journey to avert the omen. But we kept on and up in spite of all his warnings and threats. We had a gloriously dark and frowning view of Parnassus, as we left it, and showery Jupiter was as good as his word; for when we had got fairly entangled in the mazes of the Œtian range, down came a shower, the like of which we seldom see in our unpoetical latitudes. But the scenery all around us — the bare and desolate peaks, the wild ravines, the foaming streams that started like racers on their course, the many-tinted oak and plane-tree, the evergreens on the mountain-side, and the fiercely careering clouds, so unlike our dreams of the classic beauty of Greece — was splendid.

On we went, regardless of the rain, — all except Walnut the dog, who seemed greatly chagrined. Walnut is a dog of taste; has made the tour several times; takes a special pleasure in showing off his country to foreign travellers, and, when he found we were going, insisted upon going with us. He is a very quiet dog, almost never barks, and has taken a special friendship for me. He sleeps under my bed when I have one, and when I have not, sleeps as near me as he can get. He has kept by my side all day long, and, as we rode through the magnificent scenery under the heavy rain, hung his tail between his legs in the most desponding manner, evidently feeling a heavy responsibility for the present state of affairs, and concerned for the character of the Grecian climate.

Suddenly the rain ceased ; the sun, the Grecian sun, came out ; the hilltops, trees, and silver raindrops were lighted in a moment; the region round about broke into a blaze, and thousands of birds added the full chorus of their song. Ah! then you should have seen Walnut the dog, — how he capered about ; how he ran up the hill and down the hill; how he jumped on me, and even barked, in the gladness of his heart ; how he snatched up a stick, and shook it till it broke in pieces. The dog had never done anything of the kind before ;

he is a sober, affectionate dog, with a temperate enjoyment of the world, and a friendly eye for every wayfarer. I could not help sympathizing in his joy, and my own pleasure in the sudden outbreak of beauty was really heightened by the sight of Walnut's ecstasies.

It soon began to rain again, and so continued, until the sea broke upon us, between the mountains, with Eubœa before us and Thermopylæ on our left.

We stopped to rest at Bodenitra, and ascended its Acropolis, which has the remains of an ancient structure, and a castle of the Middle Ages. Here is one of the most splendid prospects in the world. The weather again cleared off, and we began our descent from the last ranges of Œta to the seashore. It was steep and rugged, reminding me of the Alps. We reached the pass, galloped along the ground of the immortal battle, visited the mounds supposed to cover the bodies of the three hundred Spartans, and then reached the narrowest point, where the battle must have commenced.

What sound strikes my ear? What sight meets my eye? The noise of a mill! The hot springs, celebrated in all ages, are now made to do the work of ancient slaves, and *grind*. I was shocked; my newly acquired character of poet rose in arms at such a desecration. Bathed in Ismenus, rolled on Helicon, refreshed by draughts from Aganippe, my coat out at the elbows before the Parnassian heights, — I could not now but feel every sentiment of my poetical nature outraged by the sight of a mill carried by the hot springs of Thermopylæ !

But — but — we were to stop at the mill for the night, or travel an hour to a desolate khan, — and we stopped, mounting by a crazy staircase to the single room. There was a bright wood-fire on a raised circle. There was a colossal loaf of wheaten bread, just ready to be put under the embers. The miller, a stately-looking man in fustian, took down his single chair, and with a bow offered it to " His Nobleness," — meaning *myself*.

Poetry began to ooze out of the hole at the elbow, and a mill at Thermopylæ was not so bad a thing after all ; and when he told me that thirty villages depended on his mill for grinding their corn and wheat, I came to the 'conclusion that Thermopylæ was never put to half so good a use before.

Just as I write these words, he gives us an invitation to pass to-morrow with him, and join in a Klephtic festival, which he will celebrate in our honor. We consent, and he sends at once to order a kid, and to arrange the Klephtic songs for so grand an occasion. I could not help quoting the words of an ancient fragment :

> " Grind, miller, grind ;
> For e'en Pittacus grinds,
> Of great Mytilene the king."

Clatter, clatter goes the mill below ; but it does not disturb the sleep of Leonidas and his Three Hundred, who lie beneath yonder tumulus. We have reached the northern limit of our journey, and our next move will be southward.

XXXI.

THERMOPYLÆ, November 20.

I MENTIONED yesterday the tempting invitation of our host at the mill. Well, the sun rose bright and cloudless, and our first movement was to the hot bath. It is the most delicious thing in the world. The water comes steaming from the foot of the mountain, nearly as hot as the body can bear, clear as crystal, and softening to the skin, like the fountain of youth. If these springs were in some easily accessible spot, they would be the most frequented watering-place in the world.

Our bath was followed by a breakfast, such as would have " created a soul beneath the ribs " of Leonidas himself. One item was a colossal loaf, smoking hot from the coals, which, with honey of Hymettus that we had brought from Athens, had an admirable relish.

Then we took a long stroll, and examined all the remains of ancient fortifications, and walls as old as Herodotus, besides ascending some of the overhanging mountains, to get a distant view of these glorious scenes.

Towards evening, the preparations were made

12

for our Homeric repast. The kid had been killed the night before ; a huge wood-fire was lighted in one wing of the mill, and the kid was spitted on a long pole, with sausages made of his own insides twisted around the body. Two men turned the spit, one at each end of the pole. The table was laid, and a man brought a huge armful of freshly gathered myrtle-branches, and placed them on the table. Meantime the *splanchna* (entrails), as Homer calls them, were brought, and we each ate about three inches. It was excellent. An hour after, the kid was brought, piping hot, on the spit, " skilfully divided " by the cook, and laid on the myrtle-branches ; and the head was cleft, and also set on the table. All things being prepared, we laid our hands — not knives and forks — on the meat that was placed before us. I never ate better in my life. The kids, fed on the mountains, have an excellent relish, and, cooked in the manner I have described, the flesh loses nothing of its natural flavor. With a sprinkling of Homer's "divine salt," one desires nothing better. Our host sat with us, and supplied, from a wooden vessel, copious draughts of Grecian wine — to those who liked it ; — for my part, I detest it and prefer water.

After the feast was over, came (in Homeric fashion again) the singing of Hellenic songs. Four or five wild-looking fellows, sitting on a carpet, chanted some dozen poems, on various subjects, — war-songs, lamentations for the dead, love-songs, — and among the rest, *Olympos and Kissabos*, which you remember. Perhaps you recollect that one of the interlocutors in that curious piece is the head of a slaughtered warrior, who boasts that he has been *twelve years* a robber on Mount Olympus. It was a piquant circumstance in the entertainment of this evening, that the corypheus, or leading singer, has been for *eleven years* a *Klepht*, or robber, in precisely the same place ; and I thought he sang that piece with a quite peculiar zest, and a knowing twinkle of the eye, — as much as to say, " Though I tend the mill now, I have not always done so."

I am not sure that you would have liked the music altogether ; your taste has been too much perverted by the Italian opera. But one who, like me, has been nurtured on Pindaric strains, finds in these songs, and the peculiar music in which they are chanted, something exceedingly interesting.

The name of my Olympian Klepht is Basilios Christopoulon, — or Basilios, the son of Christopoulos. The singing closed our Hellenic supper, the wild-looking chorus disappeared like the chorus in a tragedy of Æschylus, and all of our company, except myself, betook themselves to chibouks, and paid their devotions to cloud-compelling Jove. So, good night again.

XXXII.

THERMOPYLÆ, November 21.

STILL near Leonidas. This morning, when daylight dawned, Strattis the Lesbian came in and informed us that it was raining. We got up, and, looking forth, saw that a heavy storm had set in, and it was quite out of the question to set out. We made up our minds to submit to what was inevitable, with as good a grace as possible.

Thermopylæ is an interesting spot, but not exactly the place to choose for a long storm. Its range of amusements is rather limited. The vicinity cannot be seen to advantage under a heavy rain. Leonidas and the Three Hundred are well enough for a day of sunshine. The mountains are splendid, if you can get a sight of them. The mill keeps up its clatter, indifferent to the weather; but when one has heard it for four and twenty hours, it is no longer exciting.

I brought books with me, but we have only one window, though there are many holes in the roof; and one or another is constantly at that window to watch the weather, so that the room is mostly darkened, and literature is, therefore, of little avail. We discussed England and America; we talked Greek politics with Strattis and our host; we read a few sentences now and then, and sometimes ventured a few feet outside the door, or stood observing for the hundredth time the working of the millstones. A change took place towards noon; instead of a heavy rain, a deluge came down, and still comes down.

As our host, the miller, gave us a Klephtic dinner yesterday, we determined to give him a European dinner to-day. We invited him in due form, and then told Yanni Bulgari, the cook, to do his best, as we were going to have a dinner-party. Luckily, I bought a partridge a couple of days ago, and we had a fat chicken, and plenty of rice. We had also a bottle of rum and a bottle of brandy. The cook did his duty nobly. We had three courses, fruit, nuts, and tea — but no cream. We drank the health of the King and Queen of Greece, the Queen of England, and the President of the United States. In short, the dinner went off with the greatest eclat. Strattis, the miller, and C—— are at this moment smoking their pipes, — the former two sitting on the floor, and the Englishman on a chair. The wood-fire is also smoking.

It is now half past eight o'clock, and the rain is falling in such torrents that we suppose the heavens must be exhausted by the morning. The mill is shut up for the night. I forgot to tell you that there are port-holes which command the approaches in all directions; and guns and pistols ready for use at a moment's warning. The mountains are near, the robbers *might* descend, and it is well to be prepared for any event.

XXXIII.

THIS morning was again stormy. We stayed at Thermopylæ the whole forenoon, doing little else than taking turns to look out of the only window in the mill to see what the weather was. It rained, — rained, — rained. I read part of a play of Sophocles, — the Trachiniæ, — the scene of which is laid in this neighborhood; Mr. C——— read Thackeray, — both of us lying on the floor.

At length, about one o'clock, we determined to make a start for Bodenitra. We had intended to take a different route, for Delphi; but the weather looked so bad that we thought it better to be getting into the road to Athens. From this place we can either go across the mountains to Delphi, or return to Lebadeia, Thebes, &c., as we think it best. We rode along the pass, and took the bridle-road up the side of the mountain. The rains of two days had formed several beautiful mountain torrents, where none were to be seen when we rode by before, and we enjoyed the sight of them greatly.

But we soon found, that, however picturesque they were in the landscape, they made our passage unexpectedly difficult. We forded three rapid streams, with some trouble, and just before we reached the height on which the Acropolis of Bodenitra stands among the clouds, we came upon a fourth, which roared and foamed from the mountain in a dark ravine that was perfectly dry three days ago. After searching some time, we found a place over which our guide thought we could safely pass, and in he͏͏ dashed. But the water was too deep and strong; his horse lost his footing, and fell plunging and floating among the rocks.

Strattis, the Lesbian, is a very stout man; he floundered for some time, and at last succeeded in getting to the opposite shore, and dragging his horse out by the bridle. Man and horse certainly ran a narrow chance of being drowned, the depth and force of the current were so great. Of course C—— and I made no attempt to cross; and there we stood, in a heavy rain, like a couple of disconsolate ghosts on the shores of the Styx, with no Charon to ferry us over.

Fortunately a peasant, in his " shaggy capote," came along, and for two drachmas showed us a place about a quarter of a mile higher up the mountain, where we crossed with a slight additional wetting.

We pushed on to Bodenitra with all speed,— which at best was small, as the road went up a steep mountain all the way,— and, hurrying to the house of the *Papas*, a village priest, soon had a huge fire, by which we threw ourselves down on rugs, and enjoyed the comparative comfort. This house is in some respects better than the other Greek houses I have seen. There is an opening so arranged that not more than three quarters of the smoke comes out into the room.

We found our luggage had not got wet at all, and a change of clothes set everything right. This looks a little like an adventure, and came very near *being* one.

I wish you could see the interior of this house, so that you might form some idea how a Greek papas, or clergyman, with his family, lives, and compare it with the condition of the minister of a New England village. I should despair of succeeding in depicting it adequately to you; and perhaps you would hardly believe the details I should have to enumerate. But I must say good night.

XXXIV.

ANOTHER day of dismal rain. Our New England climate has been abused. Only let Northern Greece take it into its head to give you a specimen of its powers in the disagreeable way, and my word for it, New England must give in "dead beat." We got up this morning, and as we looked out of the papas's house, a darker, drearier, rainier, colder day one could not wish, and need not hope to see. But we were not to be frightened. We armed ourselves with a comfortable breakfast, mounted our Thessalian steeds, and, following Strattis the Lesbian, set off to cross the mountains into the valley of Elateia. It rained first, then it drizzled, and then came a fog, thick, piercing, heavy, and so dark that we could not see twenty rods. The earth was slippery, and the stones were more slippery. But still we went on.

I can hardly imagine a more ludicrous satire on travelling for pleasure than a picture of our drooping company would have been. Strattis the Lesbian, — covered with a shaggy capote, — dripping; C—— in a mackintosh, — silent, — dripping; F—— in a thick great coat, india-rubbers, umbrella, — silent, — dripping; Yanni Bulgari on the top of the kitchen furniture, which was on the back of a mule, — silent, — dripping; Parnagiotes, leading the other mules, with a boy to help him keep silence and drip. The only sign of animation was given by the mule that carried the provisions, making a vicious attempt to kick whenever man or horse came near him, and lifting his heels about a quarter of an inch from the ground. We did see some shining oak-leaves mysteriously gleaming through the fog, and we met, on the mountains, two or three muleteers, looking like ancient satyrs.

The mountains were not endless; Œta was finally crossed, and we descended into the plain of Elateia, with a more temperate atmosphere, but more copious rains.

Our arrival caused as great consternation among the turkeys as Philip's did among the Athenians. Two fell victims. We stopped at the khan where I am writing at the present moment. The rain pours down as if it were just beginning, and we are told that the river which we crossed easily the other day has risen so high that the postman yesterday could not get over it, on his way to Athens. If it continues so, we shall be detained in this enlivening place — the raining heavens and showery Jove alone can tell how long. Delphi must be absolutely given up for the present.

I am sorry to lose time here by such weather ; but every inconvenience has its counterbalancing good. I should not else have seen so much of the interior life of the Greeks. Imagine the worst you can of discomfort, — the utter absence of every- thing we hold needful, not merely to the luxury, but to the decency of life, — and the picture in your mind will be one of regal magnificence com- pared with the condition of a common Greek peas- ant, — even of a common Greek clergyman. The highest dignitaries of the Church live in a style that a coachman would despise among us. A room is swept about once in three months. Out of Athens there is hardly a glass window in all Greece, — possibly one or two may be found in Patras. While I write these words, a great splash of water falls on my portfolio. We have just had our beds placed in the middle of the room, before the fire, to get as much out of the way of the rain as possible. You understand, from these few traits, how necessary it is for travellers to take with them *everything*. Once in a while a turkey, or chicken, or quarter of lamb may be bought, and if you happen in at baking-time, you may get a loaf of unleavened bread. The miller at Ther- mopylæ is a most rare exception. The fire is going out, and I must go to bed ; so good night.

XXXV.

MOUNT PARNASSUS, November 24.

WHEN we got up this morning at Elateia, and found that it had been raining heavily all night, I did not think I should write to you this evening from a high place on the mountain of the Muses.

Last evening, though near Parnassus, we could not see his majestic form, for the mist and clouds; this morning, his summits were covered with snow, which had fallen during the night, and the sight was magnificent.

We could not set out early on account of the swollen streams, which made the plain of Elateia impassable. The rain had, however, ceased, and some signs of fair weather greeted us. We waited until noon, and then sallied forth, — Walnut, the Lesbian Strattis, C—— and myself, Yanni Bulgari the cook, the master of the asses — the three donkeys — and his servant, — all expecting that we might be obliged to return.

At Elateia we became acquainted with two brothers of our host at the mill of Thermopylæ, — two very handsome, genteel, and civil pallecars, who were very attentive to us. We invited one of them, whom we happened to meet first, to dine with us. He accepted, but afterwards excused himself, as he had letters to write to send off the next morning. To-day he came to see us, with his youngest brother, Constantine Demakedes. A more gallant-looking fellow, with his Klephtic leggings, his white fustanelli, embroidered jacket, and goat's-hair capote over the whole, you would not often see.

We stayed until about twelve o'clock, and then set out in the order I have just mentioned.

The manner in which these torrents are suddenly swollen by the rains, and suddenly subside when the rains are over, is a striking illustration of Homer's description of the conflict of Achilles with the Simois and Scamander. We found the plain traversed by them; but since morning they had so diminished in volume, that there was no danger in fording them. The first we crossed my horse took a fancy to bathe in, as he had at the fountain of Ismenus in Thebes; and down he went, giving me an involuntary plunge. Luckily I was well protected. I approve of the animal's taste for cold baths; our notions agree on this subject, but his time does not coincide with mine, which makes it inconvenient. I dragged him out, and gave him a few blows with a shepherd's crook presented to me by our host at Thermopylæ, to signify my disapprobation of his proceedings; then remounted, and trotted on.

The sun began to show his face, and to shine on the snowy summits of Parnassus. This led us to resume our original plan of going to Delphi, instead of returning directly to Athens. We crossed the plain, passing the Phocian Cephissus, over a high arched bridge of stone, then took the road to the right, between Helicon and Parnassus, to Daulis. As we entered the mountains by this pass, the scenery soon became magnificent; the glittering sides of the limestone and marble cliffs contrasting with the zones of green oak below and dark cedars above.

Daulis stands in a secluded nook, most picturesquely placed, with gardens of pomegranates, and, on an eminence above the town, a large, circular, stone-paved threshing-floor, while on a projecting spur of Parnassus stand the foundations of the ancient Acropolis. The road began to climb up the slope of Parnassus; and by and by, after passing a singular chasm between Parnassus, which is limestone, and the opposite mountain, which is red slate to the very summit, we reached the famous spot where three ways meet,— the scene of the murder of Laius by his son Œdipus.

It is a wonderful spot, so strongly marked that there cannot be the slightest doubt of its identity. The road from Daulis here meets the road from Delphi, at the triangular little valley where the road from Thebes also comes in. Laius was journeying from Thebes; Œdipus had just gone from

Corinth to the Delphian oracle, and, frightened by the awful responses he had received, fled by the road towards Thebes, and, meeting his father here, got into an angry parley, and slew him with all his train. Then pursuing his way to Thebes, he solves the riddle of the Sphinx, is made King, and marries the widowed Queen.

As I came to this place, from which so much of the tragic poetry of Greece radiates as from a centre, it seemed to me one of the most splendidly fearful spots I ever visited ; and as I cast my eyes up to the jagged summits of the surrounding mountains, the rude rocks took mysterious forms, and some of them, shaping themselves into a line of sphinxes, looked down with grim silence, as if they had been struck dumb by the dreadful tragedy enacted before them, and had stood there in stony and speechless horror ever since. I half hoped they would break the silence of so many centuries, and tell us something of what they had witnessed, as we passed. But no; they looked down, dumb as before, — stony as when Œdipus lifted his unconscious but parricidal hand, and did the deed that should ring through all succeeding ages.

Just beyond this tragic spot, on the very road by which Œdipus came from Delphi, we have stopped, at a solitary khan, to pass the night. The stars have come out clear and cold ; and we look down from our airy elevation into the mysteriously winding defile, and see by the light of the stars those stony, silent sphinxes, on the brow of the opposite mountain, peering into the " triple way" of destiny. I have read the portions of the Œdipus Tyrannus which refer to these fatal stones since we reached the khan, by the light of brands of fir, with a shuddering sense of its vast poetical power. Pray read it, and try to conjure up in imagination the realities I have witnessed this day. I do not wonder at the lofty estimation in which Sophocles was held by his countrymen. It is now ten o'clock; so good night.

XXXVI.

Delphi, November 25.

WE saw the sun rise bright over the hills that shut in the Triodos, — the Three Ways, — while Parnassus was covered with a heavy fog. The sun looked like a globe of fire. We made ready to start for Delphi ; breakfasted, mounted our Thessalian chargers, and pursued our way higher and higher up the side of Parnassus, until we got into so dense a cloud that we could not see fifty feet before us. Once in a while the fog swept away, and opened the most magnificent glimpses, down into the deep ravines, over the opposite mountains, and off into the Peloponnesus, beyond the Gulf of Corinth. In the valleys were the finest olive-groves we have anywhere seen ; on the slopes, firs, oaks, and cedars.

In two hours we reached Arachova, — a town perched on the crags among the clouds. The weather cleared up just as we climbed into the town, and showed the vineyards and cultivated fields far down in the valley, and on the lower sides of the mountains.

An hour more brought us in sight of Delphi, — once the richest oracular site in the world ; a city of temples, statues, hippodromes, theatres, votive offerings of the costliest works of art, gold and silver, precious stones, from far and near, from Greek and barbarian; city of song and dance, and Pythian games, and solemn deputations from Athens, from Corinth, from every other renowned city upon the earth.

In the southern and western slope of Parnassus is a natural theatre, rising from the valley of the Pleistus, — green with olive-trees, terrace on terrace, to the very summit. As you come in from Daulis you turn to the right, and ascend to the angle of this natural theatre. Here is a deep chasm, cutting the rock into two crests, that rise sheer and high above Delphi. From this flows the Castalian spring, and here the Pythian prophetess breathed in her inspiration.

There are traces of the oracle here, — the hewn face of the rock, niches, caverns, partly cut and partly natural. I drank of the fountain, and found its waters sweet. These terraces were once covered with the most magnificent temples, — above them all, the hippodrome or stadium, on the very brow of the mountain. The natural form remains; the terraces, with huge masses of masonry here and there, exist still. Two or three wretched monasteries; as many churches, like hovels; a narrow, muddy street or two; rows of tile-roofed, dirty huts; bits of hewn marble built into rude walls; fragments of exquisite sculpture, turned topsy-turvy and stuck into enclosures; foundation-stones, covered with inscriptions still legible, and telling the splendid story of other times, — these are the Delphi of to-day, — a glorious position, fit for the dwelling-place of gods, — a prospect that Apollo might gaze upon forever with delight.

We arrived here at one o'clock, and spent the whole afternoon in walking up and down the ancient site ; examining every fragment we could find, every foundation-stone, every inscription. Here poor Otfried Müller lost his life by a sun-stroke, in his ardor for investigation. This gave, to my mind, a deeper tragic interest to the spot.

But to stand here and think that in Homer's time the Temple of Delphi was reverenced beyond the limits of the Grecian name ; to recall its increasing splendors for a thousand years, and the immense influence it exercised through the whole period of ancient history ; and to look at it now, and see, as we saw to-day, half a dozen barefooted Delphian maids washing clothes in the basin supplied by the Castalian spring, in the midst of the annihilation of so much splendor, — we can hardly call it ruin, — is a solemn spectacle of the vanity and perishableness of all human grandeur.

Just over the edge of the mountain is the place where the Amphictyonic assemblies met, but not a trace remains. I could infer the spot only from a passage in Æschines. Not a word is said about it in any of the guide-books. But he pictures the scene so vividly in his oration against Demosthenes, that I could not mistake it by many rods. There extends the Crissæan plain, to which he pointed when he addressed the Amphictyons, and all the features of the landscape are as they met his eye. It is a curious passage; and as I looked down over the region, I could fancy I heard the indignant tones of the orator, as he called the attention of the Amphictyons to the outrages committed by the Locrians of Amphissa on a spot consecrated forever to Apollo.

We stop for the night at a private house, scarcely better furnished than the huts we have slept in before. A family of a mother and three daughters, a son-in-law, and a young man who is to marry one of the remaining girls, occupies the house; one room is given up to us.

The whole family came in to see the strangers. The father, we are told, has recently died, so that the marriage is put off for a year. They stand round the room, gazing. Statho, the future bride, is a dark-eyed, comely damsel, looking, in her Parnassian costume, like a bas-relief on the Parthenon, — so statuesque is she in her attitude and the flow of her drapery. She has a brother, — an inquisitive, large-brained chap of ten years. He asks me more questions than I can answer; peeps into my books; shows me his school-books; and reads me a passage from his geography.

XXXVII.

On Board the St. Nicholas,
Gulf of Corinth, November 26.

OUR adventures are almost as various as those of Ulysses. We passed last night at Delphi, under the shadow of "the prophetic rock," as Sophocles calls it. The morning was bright and pleasant. Breakfasting early, and mounting our Thessalians, we commenced our descent from the lofty Parnassian heights. On our way, we passed many tombs excavated in the rock, themselves in ruins, — Death himself besieged and conquered in his last strongholds by old Time, mightier than he. Hewn rocks and smoothed hillsides showed where magnificent works had once stood; and crumbly stones under our feet testified to their long decay.

In two hours we reached the town of Chrisso, — the ancient Crissa, and, riding through it, galloped into the famous Crissæan plain, once consecrated to Apollo, and trodden by multitudes thronging from every part of the world to worship at the shrine, consult the oracle, or share in the splendid spectacle of the Pythian games. It is a charming, fertile region, now partly filled with very beautiful plantations of olives. The mountains of Doris, on our right, were covered with immense quantities of snow, almost within reach, while we were riding in summer heat. The change from the stormy weather we had experienced since our arrival at Thermopylæ was most welcome, and we congratulated ourselves that we had seen Delphi, after all.

The view of Parnassus from the plain was grand, but its summit was still enveloped in clouds, that rolled and swept in billows in that upper sea. Two hours more brought us down to the Crissæan Bay, and there we took a large ferry-boat over to Galaxidi, whence we expected to cross to the Peloponnesus. Our horses were sent round by land to the same place. The change from horse-back to the boat was pleasant enough; and we lay down to enjoy it at our ease, my friend C—— smoking his chibouk. The motion of the boat almost put me asleep, as I lay, gazing up to heaven and round on the magnificent scenery that borders the Gulf of Corinth, — the citadel of Corinth rising like a mighty pyramid on the edge of the horizon. I made our Greek rowers sing some Klephtic songs, — the second time we have been treated with this primitive poetry.

Two hours of pleasant rowing brought us to Galaxidi. It is the Greek carnival to-day; and the landing-place was crowded by an idle population, who swarmed around us, and stared as if they had never seen a stranger before. All the coffee-houses — dirty as they could be — were filled with people, playing cards, and doing honor to their *apokreas*, or farewell to flesh. We stepped in to get a cup of coffee; and instantly the windows were filled with peering faces.

We had to engage a craft of some kind to take us over the Gulf to the coast of Peloponnesus. It is like the making of a treaty between two mighty powers. Our Lesbian finds the captain of a two-masted vessel, with lateen sails, and brings him to the coffee-house. The preliminary step is to order coffee for the captain. This being gravely disposed of, the real subject is formally opened. The captain informs us that his vessel is a beautiful one; the cabin is large and commodious; his crew excellent.

"Very well: now, Captain, how much do you ask to take us over, — man and beast, — to the land of Pelops?"

"O, only a reasonable sum. There are six men, three horses, three asses, and a dog; — six drachmas a head, not counting the dog."

Captain counts us all alike, — man, horse, and ass, — a dollar a head. We protest that we will do no such thing; the price is monstrous; and we will rather wait till Monday, and take the Austrian steamer back to Athens.

Proposition No. 2. Seventy drachmas for the whole company. We offer forty. He proposes sixty-five.

We offer forty-five.   He consents to come down to sixty, though it is ruinously low.   We say we will pay fifty, though it will nearly bankrupt us.

At this point the negotiation flags, both parties affecting great indifference, and looking loftily around upon the assembled town, who were listening with irrepressible interest to the dialogue.

At length I renew the conference.   "*Pentekonta pente*, — fifty-five, — and not a *lepton* more."

"Done," says the Captain, in excellent Greek, and instantly sends for his boat, to take us off and see the craft, which is lying in another harbor. We row round the point, reach the vessel, — the St. Nicholas ; climb up her side, and look round for the cabin.   It hardly answers the Captain's description ; but Parnassus is in sight, and poetry transforms the realities of things into imaginary shapes.   The cabin is a box, at the stern of the vessel, down into which you jump.   Sitting on a low stool and bending a little, your head only touches the top.   On each side is a place for a mattress ; in the centre, a space three feet square, in which two persons can sit, if they arrange their legs judiciously.

In some mysterious part of the hold Yanni Bulgar, the cook, has established his kitchen. Panagiotes, the packer, Yanni Bulgar, the master of the asses, and his boy, have scattered promiscuously, I don't know exactly where.   Early to-morrow morning the horses and asses are to be swung on board ; and then, as soon as the wind is favorable, off we spring for the land of Pelops.

I compare myself, at this present moment, to nothing else than a pirate or corsair, in gold spectacles ; and if you hear of cities taken and countries ravaged by audacious buccaneers, you may make up your mind that C—— and I are the heroes of the tale.

A serious disaster has been discovered since we came on board. Yanni Bulgar, the cook, has left a turkey, a leg of pork, and the spit at Delphi. Apollo and the Muses were so captivated by our pork-steak breakfast, that they absorbed his senses in oblivion, and are at this moment revelling in a supper such as they have not had since the days of Jupiter. Good night.

XXXVIII.

SYKIA (FIG-TOWN), November 27.

ABOUT three o'clock this morning, while I was uneasily sleeping in a wooden box, our piratical craft got under way. In an hour more, it took our horses and donkeys on board, swinging up the ship's side in the most amusing manner. Horses snorted and donkeys kicked, but on board they went, and sails were hoisted, and slowly we moved out of the harbor of Galaxidi.

There was scarcely a breath stirring ; the sails flapped lazily against the masts, and the felucca crept slowly out into the Gulf of Corinth. The glorious sun rose, and lighted a superb panorama, — the deep blue waters of the Gulf, the dazzling, snow-capped summits of Parnassus, the majestic piles of Helicon, Cithæron, and Geranion, and on the other side the blue ranges of Achaia. The eye commanded nearly the whole length of the Corinthian Gulf, and its mountain barriers.

When we had left the shore, the breeze freshened, and on we sped over the dancing waves. We sailed the whole forenoon, enjoying one of the finest views in the world ; but about twelve o'clock the wind suddenly fell, and instead of reaching

Corinth to-night, whither our captain was to take us, we were likely to beat about the Gulf, either with no wind, or a wind dead against us. We, therefore, decided to land at once on the Peloponnesian shore, and travel as fast as we could by horse. So we — horses, donkeys, men — left our ship at Zakoulitico, and rode to this place, which is in the demos or district of ancient Sicyon.

It was a most delightful ride, along the shore of the Gulf, with such famous mountains far and near, and such a wonderful play of light and shade.

Sykia is grandly placed. Behind it rise terraces on terraces, on which the currant is cultivated; below is a beautiful curve of the beach ; beyond, the Gulf, Helicon, Cithæron, and Geranion. It is a town of some consequence, *and has several houses with glass windows.* Indeed, I begin to think what I said a while ago about the absence of glass windows in Greece a hasty generalization, — true of Northern Greece, but not true of the Morea. We are in a house with glass windows, — four, and only three have broken panes, — a degree of luxury quite extraordinary.

We look out upon the lovely waters of the Gulf. We have walked over the winding beach for a mile, and picked up its polished marble pebbles. We have three chairs; books are lying on a table at the side of the room ; to finish the catalogue of comforts, there is a fireplace with a chimney ; and there is room to walk and dress. This morning, on board the St. Nicholas, we washed, one at a time, while the other lay in bed, — the washer standing in the cabin, and the wash-bowl on deck. To-morrow morning we shall bathe in the open sea. We mean to make a long day of it ; so good night.

XXXIX.

CLEONÆ, November 28.

WE were up at daylight this morning, and were prepared for the sun, when he rose, gorgeously attended by flaming clouds, over the Isthmus of Corinth and the mighty Acropolis. Heavy masses of threatening clouds overhung the heavens, and soon extinguished the splendors of the sunrise. By the time our. cavalcade was ready to start, the rain began to fall ; but we had seen too much of this to be frightened. We rode along the shore several miles, and then turned off to visit the ancient city of Sicyon, which stands on high table-land several miles from the coast. The foundations of the ancient buildings cover an immense surface, and there is a theatre, the contour of which and some of the seats, with two entrances, are still quite complete. The spectators here had a magnificent panorama before them, — the Gulf, the Acropolis, the Isthmus of Corinth, and the beautiful mountains on the other side. Scattered all around are weather-stained blocks of hewn stone, pieces of columns and friezes, and other melancholy indications of ancient greatness.

We came down by a very steep descent, and

galloped over the meadows of Corinth, — once the most luxurious city, now the muddiest village, under the sun ; in the midst of which rise seven Doric columns, lonely, solemn, darkened with age, twenty-five centuries old, — and nothing near them to explain them or to keep them company in the filthy and dreary present surrounding them. I have never looked on any memorial of past and vanished splendor that so moved me as this, — the strange contrast of these majestic pillars with the littleness of everything else, except nature, in the panorama. We walked round them, then through the town to the ruins of an amphitheatre, and, returning, mounted our horses to ascend the citadel.

This was a much higher ascent than I had counted upon. The path winds round the mountain, for it is a mountain of vast size, and about three quarters of the way up we leave our horses, and perform the rest of the route on foot. The enormous circuit of the now almost deserted fortress astonishes me. It is large enough for a city, and the passages are as numerous and as winding as the streets of Boston. It was an hour's hard work to reach the summit. The clouds prevented one's enjoying the whole extent of the prospect ; yet we saw the Isthmus, the greater part of the Gulf of Corinth on one side, with the mountains on its margin ; on the other side, the Saronic Gulf, Ægina, Salamis, Attica with its mountains, with just a glimpse of Athens; and, opposite, a great part of the Peloponnesus. The ancients have not in the least exaggerated the commanding position of this wonderful Acropolis, and yet I prefer that of Athens, with its thousand associations of the greatest achievements in letters and art.

We descended from this astonishing spectacle, and struck off, late in the afternoon, for Cleonæ, by a nearer road, if road that can be called which road is none. As long as the light lasted we did well enough, though we were often obliged to dismount and lead our horses, — the rains having performed the quite unnecessary exploit of making the bridle-path worse than it naturally was. But when the darkness came on, it became a serious matter. We found ourselves between two ranges of mountains, and even our experienced guide, Strattis the Lesbian, lost his way. There were ditches and streams that intersected the valley in various directions, and thick bushes that perplexed our steps and confounded our horses.

We stopped and shouted, that being the only thing we could think of; and I recommend it to you when you are caught in a similar scrape. In good time a voice answered from the mountain; a light next appeared, and finally the person of a peasant-boy bearing it. He conducted us safely to a hamlet on the edge of the plain, and thence we hired one of the villagers to accompany us with a lantern as far as Cleonæ, whither we had sent forward our luggage, — neither C—— nor myself desiring a second edition of the Heliconian night.

The road was excessively bad, the night excessively dark, and the rain very heavy; but we reached Cleonæ in time, wet, wearied, and cold, glad of the shelter of a hut where we pass the night; glad of the warmth of a fire, which fills the room with smoke, and particularly glad of a hot dinner, after eleven hours of hard walking and riding.

Corinth, you remember, is the place where Œdipus was brought up, at the court of old King Polybus; — so that we have now finished the circle of that awful tragedy; beginning with his death at the Temple of the Furies, in Athens, — then exploring Thebes, where he lived as king, and where the thread of his destiny was unwound, — passing a night on the spot where he slew his father, another night at the oracle which sent him, in flight, upon the very road where he should commit the crime, and finally visiting Corinth, to which he was brought by the shepherd, who found him bound by the ankles on Mount Cithæron.

To-morrow we come within the tragic circle of another line, — the Atreidæ. We shall visit the scene of the Agamemnon, and of so many other direful tales. But it is getting late, and I must say good night.

XL.

EPIDAURUS, December 1.

WE left Cleonæ on Tuesday, the day cloudy and the weather uncertain. We directed the master of the asses to go first to Mycenæ, and thence to Argos, to await our arrival, we purposing to pass by Nemea. We crossed the hills near Cleonæ, and soon came upon the cavern where the Nemean Lion used to dwell, and where Hercules tracked him to his den. An hour or two more brought us in sight of the valley where the Nemean games were celebrated, and of the three moss-grown columns, still standing, in the midst of a huge pile of the ruins of the Temple of Nemean Jupiter. The circle of hills which shuts in the valley is singularly picturesque. In the side of one of them stood the theatre, of which traces yet remain, commanding an admirable view of the whole region.

We stopped for some time at the temple to examine these interesting ruins. To the imagination it was an affecting contrast, — these prostrate walls and columns, with only three left standing, so old, so weather-beaten, in the midst of utter solitude, on a spot once peopled by festive throngs, resounding with song and dance, the tramp of long processions, and the hymns of worshippers. At Corinth, the columns of the old temple stand in the midst of dirty hovels; here the majesty of nature encompasses these fallen memorials of the past.

We remounted our horses, and took the path into the mountains. A few hours more gave us a glimpse of the sea, and of the rich vale of " hollow Argos," — the gigantic walls of Mycenæ, gray with age before Homer was born, and scarcely moved from their solid basis now, occupying a high summit just at the entrance of the valley, and commanding a view of the kingdom of Agamemnon.

We rode up to the " Gate of Lions," — of which you have seen many prints, — and, dismounting here, walked round the walls, and entered the citadel. Here again were silence and solitude, peopled only by the shadowy forms of dusky antiquity. Yonder is the tomb of Clytemnestra; in the slope of that hill is the huge dome-shaped subterranean chamber, called the treasury of Agamemnon; here are the foundations of ancient palaces and castles, as solid almost as the rocks themselves on which they were built. Here Agamemnon lived, and reigned, and was slain. Here and at Argos, which lies in sight, those bloody scenes of the Æschylean drama were enacted, — the Thyestian banquet, — the murder of Agamemnon, — the return of Orestes, — the slaying of his guilty mother, — the ghost, — the Furies, — the flight.

I read a part of the Agamemnon here, — then we galloped over the plain to Argos, which lies much nearer the sea, on the plain, and just beneath the citadel.

Mycenæ was the Homeric fortress; Argos, the later centre of wealth and power. At Mycenæ there is nothing but antiquity; Argos is a large modern village, with no trace of antiquity except the stone seats of the theatre in the slope of the citadel.

We rode through the village, attended by a ragged troop of Argive boys, to see the theatre. This is the only place where we have had any impudence from boys. The young rascals followed us, clamoring for *baksheesh*, — a word they have retained from Turkish times. We refused, and they pursued us with insults, until we reached a police station.

The sun came out once or twice as we were crossing the plain of Argos, illuminating the rare beauty of valley and mountain range; but in general the overclouded heavens lent only a gray light, which, however, harmonized well with the immeasurable age of the ruins. We determined to continue our journey to Tiryns, and to stop for the night in the neighboring town of Nauplia. Towards evening we reached the gray old walls of Tiryns, — an ancient fortress before the war of

Troy. It resembles Mycenæ, but the walls are even more massive and complete. We walked round these, too, and entering the still remaining gate, in the posts of which are the holes in which the hinges turned, ascended to the citadel. Evening came on while we stood on these sad old walls, and we and they seemed to re-enter the dim and shadowy past from which they had emerged. Descending, we mounted, and another hour brought us to the shore and the fortified town of Nauplia.

There we found a hotel, and took lodgings for the night. Our luggage, through some misunderstanding of the master of the asses, did not come; and as my writing-materials were with the luggage, I could not follow my usual custom of scribbling a few words before going to bed.

Yesterday, the luggage again not appearing, Strattis the Lesbian despatched a horseman to Argos, directing the master of the asses to proceed at once to Epidaurus. As all our provisions were with the asses, Strattis bought half a lamb at Nauplia, and, tying it in his pocket-handkerchief, fastened it behind his saddle, across the back of the horse. A basket of fish and some oranges were swung at the saddle-bow; and, everything being arranged in this *nice* and comfortable manner, we started for Epidaurus.

The road — a mere bridle-path — soon ascended the mountains, and continued through a beautiful and picturesque region, the hillsides covered with the myrtle, arbutus, and other evergreens, and many of the rocky summits crowned with the ruins of ancient castles.

Five hours of hard riding brought us to the valley of Hieron, the ancient seat of a temple of Æsculapius, — one of the most renowned of all antiquity. The ground is covered with the foundations of many temples, masses of hewn stone, parts of columns, and fragments of an aqueduct; and up the side of a lofty eminence reach the seats of one of the most gigantic theatres in Greece, built by one of the most famous of the architects. Almost all the seats still remain; but trees and bushes have grown up between them, starting some from their places, and overshadowing others; and instead of the choruses and tragedies which once resounded here, a solitary bird — true and unchanging poet of nature — sat in the branches and sang. We climbed the seats to the top, and stood long, contemplating from that commanding height the half-buried ruins that lay below, and the lovely mountains that threw their encircling arms around.

In the valley still bubbles up from the earth the fountain of Hygeia, once the object of religious homage, and still sending out streams of the sweetest water in the world. We went down and drank, and gave our horses to drink also. Then we took the road through the mountains again, and winding through a most romantic pass of sev-

eral miles, wild as any place in Switzerland, and
varied with every charm of rude nature, we at
length came in sight of Epidaurus, and the sea,
studded with islands.

Here we stopped for the night; and as our luggage had not yet arrived, Strattis set about preparing for us a dinner from that lamb behind
the saddle and the fishes at the saddle-bow. He
boiled the fishes, and roasted the·lamb. I dare
say you would have hesitated about eating either.
You would have made a great mistake then: *both*
— especially the lamb — were excellent.

As our luggage did not come, we had to get
along as well as we could. Luckily we lodge at
a house occupied by a new-married pair of the
better sort. For a wonder they have mattresses,
coverlets, and even sheets. Spreading these on
the floor, we sleep much more comfortably than
we did in the Heliconian hut. This morning we
find a heavy rain that makes it impossible to quit
our quarters; and it looks as if it had set in for a
long storm, so that, again, it is quite uncertain when
we get back to Athens. The mountains are del-
uged, and the sea beats wildly against the shore
just under our window. We set out for a journey
of ten days; we have already been seventeen days
from Athens, and, like the returning heroes of the
Trojan war, are still arrested by winds and waves,
with no Calypso's Isle, no Alcinoüs's gardens,
to cheer our homesick souls. We look out upon

the roaring deep, like Ulysses, desirous " to behold
the smoke rising from our dear native land."

Evening. — We have passed the first of December here, in one of the most tremendous storms I
ever witnessed, — rain in a deluge, with thunder
and lightning all day. We have not been able to
leave the house, and, though the water came in at
many points, we were thankful to have reached
such comfortable shelter.

To add to our embarrassment, we find that two
of our horses have fallen sick, and may not be able
to carry us farther. In that case we shall have to
procure a couple of Epidaurian mules for the rest
of our journey. Disastrous downfall of human
pride, — to leave Athens on chargers from Thes-
saly, prancing proudly over the plain ; to return
on a pair of shabby donkeys from Epidaurus, just
tall enough to keep one's feet from dragging on
the ground ! My Munich hat, too, I left at Nauplia, having bought a cloth cap ; and it was high
time. The hat had gone through the battle of
Marathon, — had weathered the siege of Platæa, —
survived the fight of Leuctra, — stood the three
days of Thermopylæ, — witnessed the tragic scenes
of Thebes, Corinth, Delphi, Mycenæ, and Argos,
— and, after these various experiences, was really
the worst-looking hat I ever owned or saw. That
is saying a good deal. Respect for the feelings of
Mr. C——, and the possibility of getting a cap at

Nauplia, — for the first time since we left Athens, — led me to sacrifice an old friend that had borne the brunt of so many fields.

During this expedition I have read Sophocles, Æschylus, Strabo, and Pausanias, and have settled in my own mind the disputed question between Mycenæ and Argos, as the scene of the Agamemnon. In the arrangement of the signal-fires, the last before striking on the roof of the Atreidæ is placed on the Arachnæan mountain, " a height neighboring the city." Now Pausanias says the Arachnæan mountain was over Lerna ; and Lerna we visited yesterday, and the mountain that overhangs the town is not in sight of Mycenæ at all, but in full sight of Argos. A signal-fire lighted on its summit would be seen instantly at Argos, and not at all at Mycenæ. If this is not conclusive as to the poet's conception of the scene, I do not know what can be. Other arguments convinced me before, as they had convinced Otfried Müller and many others. I am not sorry to have a deliberately formed opinion confirmed by the unquestionable arguments of the natural scenery, which must be supposed to have been in the poet's mind when he wrote.

A day of so few incidents — nothing but rain, thunder, and lightning — gives but little to write about ; so good night.

December 2, Evening. — We are still in this place,

sacred to Æsculapius. The bad weather and sick horses make it impossible to depart. Last night it not only rained, but blew violently. This morning we found that a house had been blown down, and a mill swept away with all its contents, and carried out to sea. A stream, swollen into a violent torrent, has broken down fences, torn up trees by the roots, and ravaged the country, in a manner unknown " to the oldest inhabitant." The sea was angrily chafing the shores, and had dashed a boat moored near our lodgings to pieces. Clouds were hurrying over the mountains, as if to attend a stormy meeting on the summit of Parnassus. We had nothing to do but submit.

Towards noon the weather looked a little better. We mounted our donkeys, to visit some pieces of sculpture about a mile from the village, and to examine the foundations of the ancient city of Epidaurus. We sat on pack-saddles, and guided the animals by ropes ; but they were obstinate, and kept their own pace.

We found blocks of hewn stone ; lines of ancient wall ; fragments of statues, especially one mutilated but beautiful figure, without a head, draped and lying on a couch, — some patient, who had resorted hither for health. It was lying alone, on the ground, a singular and touching figure, so long preserved after the original had mingled with the dust. The walls of the city are all overgrown with trees and bushes ; the ever-renewing life of nature triumphing over the works of man. We looked at all these things with great interest. A heavy rain overtook us before we regained our quarters, and put an end to a half-formed project of starting off on our donkeys. So here we are for another night. We mean to get off to-morrow, if possible; but as the peasants here say, " As God wills." It is extraordinary how much bad weather we have had on this journey. The people tell us they never knew such a succession of stormy days. In other countries the weather makes but little difference in the facility of travelling; but here a few days of rain render the bridle-paths dangerous, and send the torrents roaring and foaming down from the mountains to the plain, exactly as Homer describes them, — " tearing up fields, breaking down fences, and destroying the works of man." This forenoon a boat put in here in distress. The crew came near perishing in the Saronic Gulf. We still hope to reach Athens next Monday, though that is doubtful.

XLI.

SOPHIKO, December 3.

AFTER about fifteen days of rain, this morning, for a wonder, it — rained again, harder
than ever. But, as the horses were pronounced
convalescent, we made up our minds to set out,
and see what would turn up. Epidaurus was a
great place in ancient times ; but at present, when
you have seen the statue of the sick man, its resources are nearly exhausted. Two days in such
a place is enough to gratify the most exorbitant
curiosity.

Last evening, as there was no fireplace in our
room, we took a fancy to go into the family room
adjoining, and have a bit of a chat with our enter-
tainers. C—— filled his pipe, and I put on my
capote, and together we proceeded to make a soci-
able call. I told you that a young couple, married
only twenty-five days, occupied the house. We
found the mother-in-law sitting by the fire. We
sitting down, — (we carried our own chairs, that
being the fashion in the polished circles of Epidaurus,) — the old lady gave us a history of her
life, — how she married a husband, who built the
house and died in seven years, — how she took

another husband, who died in nine months, — how she had a thousand olive-trees, and was left alone with an only daughter, — how she took the son of a *pappas* (priest) to help her, — how he fell in love with her daughter, and the daughter with him, — how she gave him her daughter and half the property, meaning to give him the whole if he behaved well, and so on. While this story was telling by the light of a wood-fire and the smoke of C——'s pipe, happening to look round, I noticed that the young couple had gone to bed in one corner of the room, and Strattis told us that the mother-in-law slept in the same bed. All this was queer, but according to Grecian customs ; and it will serve to give you a notion of the simplicity of life in this classic land.

It costs this family to live a thousand drachmas a year, about $166 ; and they are decidedly the first family in Epidaurus. They keep a shop, and sell *rakhi*, — a kind of rum, — and a few onions, in virtue of which they constitute the Epidaurian aristocracy.

As we journeyed on, we saw, everywhere, the ravages of the storm, and the sudden overflow of the mountain torrents ; but we got along without much difficulty, by the aid of a local guide. Our road turned into the mountains, and in a few hours brought us to a large monastery, inhabited by about twenty monks. Being thoroughly wet, we stopped here to dry ourselves, and to rest our horses. The good fathers were very obliging, gave us a good fire, and plenty of bread, honey, and wine. On this journey I have taken nothing but hot tea and coffee, except for the first day or two, when I was told to use a little brandy. But I soon found that hot tea, without milk, was the best possible safeguard against exposures, and exposures are inevitable on such a journey. We dried ourselves pretty thoroughly, and took a fresh start. The monastery is in a valley among the mountains. It was almost inundated. Yesterday, on the other side of the mountain, a man and a woman were drowned. To-day, we crossed the spot ; the stream had subsided, and we had no difficulty.

Sophiko is one of the villages Dr. Howe fed with provisions from America during the Greek Revolution. I wish you would tell him that, though they remember his services to them, they are the greatest rascals we have met in Greece.

As we entered the town, our guide called on the Demarchos, or chief magistrate, to find a room. He was a *fustinellied* fellow, with a villanous hang-dog look, and tried to make us pay for the worst room we have yet been in more than three times as much as we have paid for the best. When Strattis told him that the gentlemen would not pay so much, the rascal said, " Leave the gentlemen to me, and they will pay it." He mistook his men all round, and this precious Demarchos slunk away like a whipped dog. Other Sophikians were nearly as bad. They tried to over-charge the straw for the horses, and every other thing we wanted to get. But luckily our bar-gain was with Strattis at so much a day; and he is Greek, and knows perfectly well how to meet Greek, in the tug of war.

There is a great noise in the town. The elec-tions which have been going on for about a month are finished to-day. Guns are firing, men are shouting, and half the citizens seem to be tipsy. They drink a great deal of very bad wine here in Greece. Soldiers are everywhere too, — a bad element, when out of proportion to the peaceful classes. Three or four citizens of Sophiko are looking over my shoulder as I write.

XLII.

I DARE say you are tired of this long rain. I am, at all events, and this morning all the discomforts and petty villanies of Sophiko were amply made up by the appearance of the long-lost sun. The rogues in Dr. Howe's town made us pay even for the water we used. One would think that, after fifteen days of rain, *that*, at least, might have been had gratuitously. Not so thought the philosophical Sophikians.

Our road wound up a high mountain, whence we had the Saronic Gulf, Ægina, Attica, before us ; and in the north the heights of Parnassus came once more in sight, loaded with snow which has been falling there during this long storm. We had the loveliest view of the Isthmus of Corinth, above which rises the majestic Acropolis. Our road lay through groves of pine, which extend almost down to the beach. A soft wind blew, and the pines murmured over our heads, while the sea resounded at our feet. On the distant mountains lay masses of silvery cloud, the remnants of the storm ; and Greece, the greater part of which we saw from the mountain overhanging the Saronic

Gulf, looked thoroughly drenched; but she came out from the drenching with a smile upon her sweet face. The sky seemed bluer, and the light softer, and the hills of a more delicate purple than ever. Ægina lay in the distance, as if reposing, while just before us extended the famous Salamis, with its deep blue strait, which drowned the Persian hosts.

We passed Kechriæs, the ancient harbor of Corinth; passed the ruined house on the Isthmus, built by Dr. Howe, as a magazine of American charities during the war, — a monument quite as interesting to me as any that antiquity has left; passed the ruined piles of the ancient wall which ran across the Isthmus; passed the spot where the Isthmian Games were celebrated; rested an hour at Kalamaki, the port of the Isthmus, where the steamers stop; and all this afternoon have ridden along the sea-shore, with the most exquisite panorama of mountain, sea, and plain around us that imagination can conceive.

As the sun went down behind the hills of Morea, which we had crossed this morning, the play of colors over the water, the islands, the hills of Megara and Attica, the transparent blue, the deepening purple, the gold that edged the clouds, presented a spectacle of extraordinary splendor, and we forgot the many drenchings of showery Jove, as we looked with admiration upon it.

As night fell we reached this place, — a ruined

14

village with not a single house, — only a few bare rooms, with walls of mud, temporarily occupied by a few laborers from Megara. We have taken possession of one, which has a sort of fireplace, but no window, where we pass the night. Yanni Bulgar has cooked our last turkey, — an excellent one it was ; we had our last cup of tea ; C—— smoked his last tobacco, and to-morrow we hope to reach Athens in time for dinner.

XLIII.

YESTERDAY morning we were up betimes, breakfasted by candle-light, finishing our eggs, our honey, our coffee, and our last cold turkey (except a drumstick or two reserved for luncheon), and mounted our Thessalian grays at daybreak. Our road lay for a time along the shore; then climbed the sides of the precipitous mountains which overhang the blue waters. In places, the ancient road, cut in the solid rock, or supported on the precipices by equally solid masonry, still exists, with the deep traces worn by chariot-wheels; but generally it is broken down, and the horse picks his way slowly among the ruins that encumber the path.

For a considerable distance pine-trees were growing down to the water's edge; and the morning breeze sang among their green branches to the answering sea that swept murmuring up to their feet. The distant waters, the islands that stud the gulf, the shores of the Morea, lay still and dim, but beautiful, in the gray twilight. We passed under the red cliffs, known as the Scironian Rocks, whence Sciron, the ancient robber, kicked his victims into the sea, — a level distance of not more than twenty rods, — a mere trifle for such a formidable fellow. Theseus, you remember, interfered with this amusement, and treated Sciron in the same way. The spot is a remarkable one, the cliffs hanging overhead and frowning upon the passer-by. As we journeyed on, over this most picturesque of roads, at this quiet hour, gradually the blue hills of Attica were illuminated by the rosy fingers of Aurora; the morning mists sparkled with the ruddy glow; the clouds put on their gold and purple fringes, and the new-born day, shooting his beams across the Saronic Gulf, hung his diamonds on the curling waves, and striking the distant mountains of the Peloponnesus with his fiery arrows, kindled their snowy summits into a blaze. Upon my word, " I am afeard," as old Weller says, " this is werging on the poetical." All I can say is, that a horseback ride at sunrise along the Saronic Gulf is not an every-day occurrence, and I can neither write nor speak of it as if it were..

At length we turned to the left, crossing the mountain of Kerata, and came in sight of the lovely plain of Megara, and the graceful sweep of the harbor of Nisæa. A gallop of half an hour brought us to the modern town. A few hewn stones are all that remain of its former magnificence. From here to Athens there is a good carriage-road. We rested a short time; then galloped over the plain, through olive-groves; then along the picturesque shore of the Bay of Eleusis;

then, crossing a promontory, came in sight of the
ruins which cover the ground and the hillside of
the ancient town.

We stopped at Eleusis to examine the splendid,
but prostrate ruins of the great Temple of Ceres,
built of the purest Pentelic marble. From the
Acropolis that crowned the ancient city the view
takes in the island of Salamis, and the pass where
the great sea-fight took place; the Karian and
Thrianian plains, so famous in Grecian history,
and the passes of Cithæron and Daphne. Having
examined every trace of antiquity, and repeopled
the hill and plain with imaginary processions, like
those which anciently crowded the Sacred Way
from Athens hither when the great Eleusinian
mysteries were celebrated, we entered into a treaty
with the owner of a pair of horses and a rickety
carriage, to take us to Athens, — desirous of arriving before evening.

The treaty was at length concluded; and, amidst
a crowd of dirty Eleusinian men, women, and children, we left the city of the " Two Goddesses,"
driven by a dirty Eleusinian Jehu, and drawn by
a mismatched pair of Eleusinian steeds, about as
large as wharf-rats. We rattled over the Sacred
Way; — one of the rats lost his shoe; we continued to rattle; — one of the traces broke; still we
rattled; — the lash flew off the handle; still we
rattled on. Arriving at the pass of Daphne, we
took a farewell look at the fine scenery connected

with so many interesting associations, through which we had passed.

We rattled on to the ruined convent of Daphne, where we stopped to see the old Byzantine pictures in the church; the dusty stone coffins of two Middle-Age Dukes of Athens who were buried here; and two or three dustier and stonier and more than middle-aged nuns, who are buried here also, though still pretending to be alive. They seemed to me contemporaries of the Dukes, — only Death, observing the crumbling walls, and falling roofs, and fading pictures, forgot the breathing remnants of mortality that haunted, ghostlike, the ancient chambers, and, sweeping by in pursuit of other game, left them to creep down from century to century, and finally to dry up and float away on the evening breeze. I am sure they will come to that at last.

Again we rattled on. Hymettus, clothed in blue, came in sight; Parnes lifted his front, darkened with clouds; the sunny plain of Athens smiled a welcome; the harbor of Peiræus lay glistening and calm, as in a summer day; the Acropolis — the columns of the Parthenon more august and solemn in their eternal beauty than they ever seemed before — rose against the sky; the olive-groves of Plato lay just below us, and Pentelicus showed his marble splendors, that reflected the westering sun.

We rattled on, the dirty Eleusinian vociferat-

ing to his rats, and the carriage threatening to
tumble in pieces at every pebble. We rattled
through the olive-grove; we rattled past the majestic Temple of Theseus; we rattled into the
street of Æolus, under the shadow of the Acropolis; we rattled through the crowds that filled
that fashionable promenade, and, rattling up to the
door of the hotel, were joyfully received by our
friends, and gladly reached our old quarters. But
how that dirty Eleusinian driver, with his rickety
carriage and discordant rats, managed to get us
from Eleusis to Athens is an Eleusinian mystery
which I am totally incompetent to fathom.

Here I am, however. I have tried to give you
a faithful account of a journey, to me of unusual interest, but of more than common hardship
and exposure. Its *ups* and *downs*, especially the
latter, its haps and mishaps, its many enjoy-
ments, its frequent drenchings, have been jotted
down from day to day.

Last evening I went over to Mr. Wyse's, and
finding there Lord John Hay (the commander of
a ship of war, whom I had met at Constantinople)
and the Earl of Carlisle, who has been a couple
of weeks in Athens, I had a delightful evening.
Nothing could exceed the cordiality of their
greetings. Pray tell Mr. Winthrop how much I
am Mr. Wyse's debtor for every kindness a stranger can possibly receive, and for the richest intellectual entertainment one man can give another.

XLIV.

ATHENS, December 15.

SINCE my last letter but little has happened in Athens. I believe I have told you that I am established, during my stay here, at the hotel. It is impossible to get private lodgings, and the only way of living with tolerable comfort is to take lodgings in the hotel. We have for permanent boarders at the *table-d'hôte* one of the Secretaries of the British Embassy, Mr. and Mrs. W——, Russians, also connected with diplomacy, and the Secretary of the Russian Legation. There are some families living in the house, but they take their meals in their own drawing-rooms. Besides these, the travellers who pass through Athens, on their way to the East, generally stop here ; so that we have a pretty good variety of company, some of it very amusing.

About a month ago, a short, fat, brisk, rosy-faced, bald-headed, rather elderly man made his appearance at table, on his way to the Holy Land. He began at once to talk about a mishap he had met with at the Isthmus of Corinth. He had landed from the steamer, and, though he had not been on horseback for twenty years, he immediately galloped up the Acrocorinthos, but, "*figu-rez-vous, Madame*," addressing himself to Madame W——, "I tore a large rent in my only panta-loons; I could find nothing to eat, and only very bad wine to drink."

We laughed at his misfortunes. He went on to say, that he had studied five years to prepare himself for this tour, that he was a lover of the fine arts, and that wherever he went he made it a point to order the wine of the country; — he wanted something *characteristic.* He then called for a bottle of Greek wine, at which, being about half turpentine, he made the most ludicrous grimaces. A young Englishman, named Robertson, was here for a few days. Our round little friend was de-lighted, firmly believing he had the honor of con-versing with the celebrated historian of that name, whose works he had read with so much satisfac-tion. Almost every place in the topography of Athens and Attica he got wrong, — visiting one, and thinking all the time it was another. One day we were speaking of the extent of the king-dom of Greece. He was astonished to hear that some of its provinces lay north of the Gulf of Cor-inth. We were very curious to know who this busy, brisk little blunderhead could be. Madame W—— thought he must be some *Abbé;* others thought him a wine-merchant; but I was quite puzzled, for it seemed to me that either of these would have known something about Greece after studying five years. It turned out that he was an *employé* in the military prison of Belgium. After he had left us, the question arose, what could have brought such an odd specimen of humanity to Athens. A French gentleman suggested that " perhaps he was sent by the Belgian government to visit officially the prison of Socrates." We are all expecting a rich treat from the publication of his book.

I have dined once, since my return, at Mr. Hill's, and attended a small party — the best of the English and of the Greek society in Athens — at Mr. Wyse's. For the first time since I left the cabin of the good ship Daniel Webster, I saw a game of whist. I had a long and to me very instructive conversation with General Sir Richard Church, — an Englishman who was the commander-in-chief of the Greek armies in the war of independence, and is now naturalized in Greece, — himself a living monument of history. Several ladies played the piano,' and Mrs. ——— sang.

Last evening, for the first time in Athens, I went to the opera. The theatre is not like the old Dionysiac theatre, at the Acropolis; nor is King Otho, who was present, much like Pericles. The music was poor ; but the *prima donna* sang and dressed and looked well. The scenery was good. The Queen listened attentively, but the King went asleep, except while he was staring at the *prima donna* through his opera-glass. The opera, I should have mentioned, was the Marino Faliero of Donizetti.

As I came away, at eleven o'clock, the old Acropolis, looking solemnly dòwn upon the city, with the columns of the Parthenon and the Erechtheium, under the moonlight and the mysterious troop of flitting clouds that partially obscured the picture, silently contrasted the greatness of the past with the insignificance of the present, I shall not go to the Athenian opera again. I prefer the Acropolis, the Theseium, the columns of the Olympian Jupiter, Hymettus, Pentelicus, Parnes, the Prison of Socrates, the Bema, the Mars Hill of St. Paul, the tragedies, histories, and great creations, which acquire so much additional interest by reading them on the spot. Good night.

December 18. — Since I began this letter, but little has happened out of the ordinary course of things. I am hard at work, reading and studying Greek, and examining repeatedly the antiquities of Athens, especially on the Acropolis.

More than two thirds of my time is now gone; I shall remain for the present quietly in Athens; and towards the end of my stay here, if I can make a convenient arrangement, I shall make an excursion to Chalcis, another to Sunium, and end with a tour round the Peloponnesus, visiting Argos again, then Mantineia, Sparta, Elis, &c., taking the steamer for Italy at Patras, and joining

G—— and the rest of the party at Rome, or perhaps at Naples. I suppose we shall pass at least a month in Rome, and then go to Florence by way of Perugia.

I have enjoyed my visit to Greece in the highest possible degree. On the whole, the people please me, though they have not recovered from the effects of their long slavery to the Turks. I mentioned,. in a letter written on our journey, that I had noticed only a few attempts to cheat ; I must mention one here. Two or three days ago I dropped into a barber's shop to have my hair cut. Of course he knew at once that I was a stranger ; and when I asked what was to pay, the rogue answered " two drachmas " (about two shillings). I assured him that he was mistaken ; that I knew the price in Athens, and most certainly would not pay him what he asked. I gave him one drachma, which was twice the customary charge. He looked foolish and ashamed at being caught in such a petty dishonesty, and pocketed the money in silence, and I walked away. I was reminded of the amusing description, in one of the letters of Alciphron, of a barber's shop in Athens, and the rogueries practised there.

Since our return from our journey, the weather has been very various. Yesterday it was clear, exquisitely beautiful, and of a summer heat. I walked through the Agora, over the Pnyx, and along the western side of the Museum hill, to examine the numerous steps, paths, and squares cut in the living rock. One is surprised to find so numerous vestiges of this kind, all over Athens. They indicate the sites of temples, shrines, votive pillars, tablets, &c., with which these rocky eminences were once covered. But the objects themselves have completely disappeared. I had Pausanias with me, and spent several hours in attempting to identify the positions of the buildings which he describes as existing in this part of the city.

As to the Pnyx, or place of assembly for the Demos, there can be no doubt. I sat on the Bema where Demosthenes delivered his great orations, and endeavored to call back the scene, as he describes it in the Oration on the Crown. As I descended, I picked up a bit of marble, — the fragment of a tablet, or statue, or seat, formerly existing there, — perhaps seen by Demosthenes himself, as it was within a few feet of where he stood. I shall have it cut and polished, with the word *Pnyx* carved on it, as a memorial of this most interesting spot. I spent several hours in this survey, and am similarly employed almost every day.

The antiquities of Athens are very numerous, though not occupying a very large surface. The Acropolis alone contains enough to occupy one many months. The fragments of statues, friezes, pediments, vases, and the immense blocks of the walls and pillars of the Parthenon, scattered around it, or lying prostrate on its marble floor, excite an unceasing astonishment. The tablets containing inscriptions are numberless; they employ Mr. Pittakys nearly all the time. He copies and publishes them in a journal he edits here. The collections he has already made are of great historical importance, and his labors deserve more encouragement than they have yet received from European scholars.

The literary activity here is immense. It has quite outrun the progress of the Greeks in material prosperity. The university numbers, in all its departments, six hundred students; and among the professors, many of whom I already know, are several very distinguished scholars. There are nearly thirty journals published, some of which are ably conducted and admirably written. The books for the schools, gymnasia, and university already fill an extensive catalogue. We found them in the most miserable cottages. The school system is excellently organized, and the people universally are quite aware of the importance of education.

I cannot say much for the government, judging by what I have seen and heard. The King, educated at the court of Bavaria, has apparently no idea of the duties of a constitutional monarch; while the Queen — the stronger of the two — hates the constitution. It is constantly violated in the most flagrant manner. The government, at every popular election, prepares a list of candidates, and through its agents, by corruption, intimidation, and sometimes by throwing out the ballots of persons independent enough to vote in opposition, generally procures the return of its own men. The best people refuse to attend the elections, in such a state of things. I had abundant opportunity to notice this, as the elections were going on during my journey. Yet, curiously enough, the right of free speech is not tampered with directly; and there are not only private citizens, but journalists and politicians, who do not hesitate to speak openly. A Senator told me, the other night, that an attempt would be made to pronounce the elections just completed unconstitutional. He did not expect much from the motion; but at all events it would show that there were still independent spirits in the Senate.

The English are out of favor. The Queen never invites the ladies of Mr. W——'s family to the state balls, — a mean and pitiful revenge for fancied political hostility to the now prevailing maxims of the Greek government. I could tell the Queen something that would startle her, about the popular feeling through the country. I think that the mania for despotism which possesses the government at the present moment is preparing a crisis which may overturn the throne.

Foreign papers — as I saw in Galignani the

other day — speak of the tranquillity of the late elections, and the readiness of the people to support the government candidates. The author of the article in Galignani is a letter-writer here in Athens. He is either profoundly ignorant or wilfully mendacious. Perhaps the country people spoke more freely to me than they would have spoken to a European, knowing me to be an American and a republican ; but I do not doubt that the government is reposing on a volcano, and that an eruption will soon take place, unless the administration is greatly changed.

But enough of politics for the present. I shall write to L—— by the next steamer. Love to her and A——.

XLV.

ATHENS, December 25, 1853.

THIS is Christmas day with you, and with the Franks here in Athens. The Greek Church has never received the Gregorian Calendar, and the Greek Christmas comes, therefore, twelve days later than that of Western Europe and America. It is the courteous usage, however, for the Greeks to share in the festivities of the European foreigners, paying visits, and receiving them in turn when the Greek Christmas arrives. Both parties to this pleasant arrangement have a double share of the good things this time-hallowed festival brings with it. I have just returned from the morning service in Dr. Hill's church. He gave us an excellent sermon.

Last evening, Dr. Hill invited me to a little party at his house, given for the children and young ladies in his school, or rather the school under his care. There was a table covered with presents for the young people, which, however, they were not allowed to see till the moment for their distribution arrived. The ceremonies commenced by the recitation of pieces appropriate to the occasion by three or four of the younger scholars; then several pieces were sung by the young ladies, accompanied by the piano; and finally Mrs. Hill distributed the gifts, with appropriate remarks in Greek to each of the recipients. This afforded a good deal of amusement, and the young people were all highly delighted. You will be convinced that I am not so old as some malicious persons and records make me out, when I tell you that among the other young people I too received a prize as one who had made commendable progress. On opening the parcel, I found it contained a beautifully polished square piece of marble from the Parthenon, to one surface of which was attached an embroidered cloth, with the figure of Minerva's owl beautifully wrought by the hand of an Athenian damsel, — thus combining a memorial of the past with the living present, — the goddess of Wisdom, with her consecrated bird, who still haunts the Acropolis, and makes his nest among the crumbling architraves of the Parthenon. I felt not a little proud of this trophy, and shall preserve it with especial care.

Since I wrote you last my occupations have been the same as before. I have attended the lectures at the University, with no other interruption than the saints' days. It is a great misfortune to the Greeks, and to the Athenians in particular, that they have so many saints in their calendar, and so many festivals in their honor, to interrupt the

usual business of life.   They lose about a quarter
or a third of the time in putting on their best
clothes, gadding about the streets, gossiping in
the coffee-houses, getting tipsy on execrable wine,
and singing noisy songs in the streets, in honor of
the blessed saints and martyrs who swarm in their
ecclesiastical history. ' The sensible men here are
gradually diminishing the number of their idle
days, and the sober part of the tradesmen and men
of business find their advantage in attending to
their affairs, while the rest are dissipating time and
drachmas, to the impoverishment of their purses
and the damage of their health, in the bacchanalian
orgies of orthodoxy, — orthodoxy here denoting the
Greek Church, the Oriental Orthodox Church, —
the national Church of Greece, of the Greeks
in Turkey, and of the Holy Russian Empire.   In
the short time that I have been in Athens I have
found the University closed three or four times,
and, on inquiring the cause, have been told it was
the feast of St. Demetrius, St. Spiridion, or some
other apocryphal vagabond who had the luck to
get his name inserted in the calendar.   I suppose
our students would like it, if I could introduce
some of these orthodox observances at Cambridge
on my return.

To speak seriously, I cannot share in the re-
grets of those persons who lament the absence of
festivals and amusements in our country.   What
I have seen of their effects in Europe — East and

West — has given me a strong distaste for them, and the worst possible opinion of their influence upon the moral, mental, and physical well-being of the people. In the first place, the loss of so much time to productive industry, in the midst of poverty, is a serious consideration against them. In the next place, the waste of money, in small sums to be sure, but swelling in the aggregate to immense amounts, helps to keep the people poor and to make them poorer. And, finally, the frivolity, dissipation, and low habits everywhere encouraged by these festivals, crown the climax of grave objections to their observance, which I think must strike every reflecting person who travels with his eyes open through these countries. You will never again hear me lamenting the want of amusements in America, or finding fault with the serious countenances of our American people. The weekly rest of Sunday, Christmas, Thanksgiving, the anniversary of our Independence, and one or two other holidays for the interchange of friendly salutations and the re-union of scattered families, are infinitely better than all the festivals in the calendars of the Catholic and Oriental Churches.

On Tuesday evening I attended at Mr. A——d's small party, mostly consisting of European residents in Athens. You must know that all foreigners here, however much they may differ on the Oriental question, or in articles of religious faith, unite in a common love of tea. No one gives expensive suppers, but everywhere you are entertained with an excellent cup of tea, and some sort of cake. I do not think I ever drank so much tea in so short a time in all my life, and certainly I have nowhere drunk better tea. The Greeks, with few exceptions, are but little addicted to this form of social intercourse. The women of the present generation are not generally well educated. They like to dress up on saints' days, and make or receive calls; they like balls once in a while; but for the daily and informal social intercourse which is the charm of cultivated life in Western Europe and America, they show but little taste.

There are exceptions. There are Greek families that add to the semi-Oriental culture which is native here the amenities of European refinement, — the ladies speaking the modern Greek with elegance, and reading the ancient poets with facility, at the same time reading and speaking French, German, and even English. There are some good houses, furnished in the European style, among the best of which are those occupied by the American and English families. But by far the greater part of the houses in Athens are like those in the country, — dirty, damp, destitute of the simplest conveniences, with a crowded population of men, women, and children. They have not learned to sleep on beds, to sit in chairs at table, to wash their faces in the morning, or to take off their clothes at night. When it rains, their floors become mud-puddles, and when the rain is over, they go out and sit down by the side of the street in the sunshine until their floors are dried. They live on coarse bread, cheese of sheep's milk, a little fruit when they can get it, and now and then a pitcher of turpentine and wine. Once in a while they eat meat, generally lamb or mutton. But when they walk through the streets, they strut as if they were lords of the creation. If you come too near them, you incur the most imminent risk of getting an immigration of vermin, who are always eager to strike up a sudden friendship with strangers, but whose name it is improper to mention to ears polite. I therefore am wont to give these strutting *Pallecars* a pretty wide berth, and to look upon them with the most distant respect.

December 30. — Yesterday was one of the most delicious days I ever passed. The air was of the most transparent clearness ; the temperature soft and warm ; the sky of the serenest blue. Wherever a branch or a green leaf offered a foothold, birds were singing as if the winter were gone and the spring had taken its place. I was in the open air through the greater part of the day.

At noon, Dr. Roeser, the King's physician, called to accompany me to the Minister of Foreign Affairs. From his office we drove to the palace to pay our respects to the *Megálé Kyria* or *Grande Maitresse.* I had not before performed this ceremony, and was a little curious to get this peep into the royal household.

The Grande Maitresse is the widow of some very illustrious German, of blessed memory, whose name, however, I have entirely forgotten. She is the confidante and bosom friend of the Queen, and, as such, the object of homage to the fashionable world of Athens.

The next move I have to make is to be presented to their Majesties. I had not intended to take this step; but Dr. Roeser mentioned to the Queen that I was in Athens, that I was a friend of Mrs. P——'s, &c., and had come to Greece as a scholar, for the purpose of studying the people and language; and her Majesty was pleased to convey, through Dr. Roeser, an intimation — I use the Doctor's own words — that she would be gratified to make my acquaintance. I told the Doctor I should feel myself highly honored by a presentation to their Majesties, but being a simple traveller, with no claim whatever to ask it, I had forborne to speak or even think about it. However, I should be highly flattered, &c., &c., &c. We have no diplomatic representative here, except the Vice-Consul, Dr. King; and, by the etiquette of the court, an official of that grade cannot *present,* — he can only accompany the visitor to the palace, and consign him to the hands of the Grand

Chamberlain. Dr. Roeser has requested Mr. Paicos, the Minister of Foreign Affairs, to present me; and I suppose that will be the course.

January 8. — Since I began this letter, I have been more closely than ever occupied with my studies. But before I enter into any particulars I must tell you of my *presentation.* This morning I attended church; after church, took a long walk, and, as the weather was superb, lingered longer than usual from spot to spot, tracing the vestiges of the ancient wall of Athens, so that I did not reach my room until five o'clock. Arriving there, I found a notice on my table that their Majesties would receive me at seven o'clock this evening. So I had to examine my wardrobe, brush my coat, fit my gloves, make sure of my white cravat, — the same I bought for the Gran Scala at Milan, — get a hurried dinner, order a carriage, and dress. You would have laughed, I think, at the sight.

Well, I accomplished these multifarious duties in a very short time. I do not think you would have known my coat, hardly me, so spruced up were both of us. Dr. King went with me to the palace, to present me to the Grand Chamberlain, — a son of old General Colletti, one of the heroes of the revolution.

We went up the grand staircase, into the ante-chamber, and in a moment the Chamberlain appeared to conduct me into the royal presence. The hall of reception — the throne room — is as handsome as any I saw in Western Europe. There was no other person to be presented, and I confess that my experience with our republican court at Washington was not a very useful guide in circumstances so novel. The door opened, and in I must go. The Grand Chamberlain stopped at the door; the Grande Maitresse was visible in the distance, near the other end of the hall. As soon as I was inside the door I bowed — I had been told a little what to do — to their Majesties, who stood about a third the length of the room from the door, and, advancing to the presence, bowed two or three times more before I got within hailing distance.   .

My reception by both King and Queen was most gracious, and the conversation went on as smoothly as possible. After some words of salutation, (you know the person presented — like a ghost — never speaks until he is spoken to,) the Queen asked, "Have you been long in Greece?"

"About three months, your Majesty."

King. "You are occupied with the study of the Greek language?"

"Yes, your Majesty."

"With the modern as well as the ancient?"

"Yes, your Majesty, that is the principal object of my travels in Greece."

"The pronunciation of the Greek is very differ-

ent in America and England from the pronunciation here."

" Yes, your Majesty, so different that the Greek
seems like two languages."

Queen. " How many students have you in the
University of Cambridge ? "

" Exactly the same number, your Majesty, as
are now in the University of Athens."

Queen. " The same number ? But you have
many universities in America."

" Yes, we have many."

King. " What are the principal subjects or
branches studied in the American universities ? "

" The general studies, your Majesty, are the
Classics, the Mathematics, Physics, Philosophy."

King. " Which of the professions attracts most
of the young men ? "

" The law, I think, since that is the profession
which opens a political career."

King. "In Greece the study of Medicine and
Theology are favorite studies."

" Yes, — the Greek physicians have always
been very distinguished."

" In what departments do your writers excel ? "

" Your Majesty, we have many writers in various departments. We have poets," (I thought of
asking, if he had ever heard of Longfellow,) " we
have historians, &c."

" Are the sciences much cultivated ? "

" They are, — especially the natural sciences.

Since Professor Agassiz has resided in the United States, he has given an extraordinary impulse to the department, and excited an ardent scientific spirit."

Some things more were said; his Majesty bowed, saying, " I am delighted to know you "; I bowed my thanks, and, backing carefully towards the door, bowed every two or three steps; their Majesties receded bowing; then I, peeping over my shoulder and seeing that I was near the door, bowed very low, and vanished from the presence. It is not so difficult to get into the royal presence; but to get out again is a matter of no small delicacy. However, I got out without any catastrophe, and, to tell the truth, a good deal pleased with the amiable manners of their Hellenic Majesties. The Queen is a little past her beautiful prime, being now about thirty-six years old; but she is a very fine woman, and in her port and attitude every inch a queen.

I mentioned, in one of my letters, the difficulties existing between the ladies of Mr. W——'s family and the Queen. These have all been adjusted. The Emperor of France instructed his minister here to interpose, and put an end to this state of things; and his intervention was so successful that the Queen sent for the ladies, received them in the most cordial manner, and made, not only Mrs. W——, who was a little lame from an injury, sit down, but her daughter also, — quite an extraordinary thing in a court. So far as I can understand the matter, they were not in the least to blame, and the course of the Queen is a silent admission of the fact. The W——s have the good taste to show no sense of triumph, though it is in reality a triumph of downright English honesty over a Russian intrigue, the object of which was to force Mr. W—— to ask a recall.

I fancy the Russian influence here is on the decline ; and though Mr. W—— is a man who will engage in no contest of intrigues, I should not wonder if his open and honorable character drove the lying diplomates from the field. I have rarely met a man whom I liked so much, and in whom I saw so much to admire.

After my grand reception, I took tea at Dr. King's, and about nine o'clock walked home. The evening was glorious, the air was mild as summer, and the moon filled the tranquil heavens with light. Over the darkness of the Acropolis hung the loveliest star in the sky, and the solemn temples lay silent and mournful, as if dreaming of the past, under the azure canopy of the night.

XLVI.

THE present season in Athens is one of idleness, gayety, and festivity. The holidays in the University have caused me the loss of lectures for about a fortnight, and now my time has nearly expired. One week more will probably wind up my residence in Greece.

Last Wednesday I attended a great public funeral. General Hadgi Chrettos, one of the most distinguished officers of the Greek Revolution, suddenly died the day before. Here, it is the invariable custom to bury the dead the day after death. The church of St. Eirène was crowded with officers and people of every class, and, besides the usual services, a discourse was delivered by the Archbishop of Patras, and an immense procession followed the old warrior to the grave. On the same day I took two young Englishmen over the city, and afterwards dined with Dr. King in company with a few other friends. There was a rumor circulated through the city that the Archbishop of Athens had suddenly died, and was to be buried on Thursday. The ceremonies on such an occasion are very peculiar, and we all resolved we would attend. I mentioned it to some English travellers who had just arrived, and we went early in the morning to the church of St. Eirène. But no preparations seemed to have been made; the doorkeeper said that no orders had been given; and, finally, Mr. A——, who had also come to the church to ascertain the hour of the burial for some friends from the Peiræus, inquiring of a priest, learned that, so far from intending to be buried that day, the Archbishop was in uncommonly good health.

In the afternoon I went to make a little visit which I had long contemplated, at the house of Rev. Mr. B——, at the Peiræus. It was a pleasant afternoon. We took a boat, and went out to the extremity of the harbor to see the tomb of Themistocles, — a place excavated just in the edge of the rock, looking over the strait of Salamis to the island, and precisely in the range of the spot where the battle was fought. We had a beautiful sail over these classical waters, and then, walking along the shore, examined the foundations of the ancient walls, which are so remarkable in this quarter.

We got back to Mr. B——'s house to a late dinner, and in the evening Mr. and Mrs. Black and their handsome daughter came in to tea. Mrs. Black, you know, is Byron's maid of Athens. At tea I had the felicity of sitting between the old maid of Athens and the young maid of Athens.

Mrs. Black will not speak a word of English; but she is a sprightly woman yet, and must have been very *piquante* and handsome when Byron was here. The daughter speaks English a little, but prefers to speak in Greek.

We had an amusing time. I repeated to Mrs. Black some sentences in Greek, pronounced in the English and American style, and the shouts of laughter which the ladies raised would have edified an Oxford Professor. There is nothing more comical than the figure an English scholar cuts when he first comes to Athens. He may have taken the first honors of his University, and written prize odes without number; yet he cannot utter a sentence that any mortal in Athens will understand, nor can he understand a single word he hears in the streets or in society. The Professors laugh at him; the women laugh at him; the boys in the street laugh at him. He can buy a cravat only by drawing his hand round his neck, as if he were preparing for the halter. If he wants something to eat, he must open his mouth and point down his throat. If he wants a hat, he must lay his hand on his head and say, " Eh ! " For a pair of stockings, he must pull off his shoes, and, holding his foot up to the shopkeeper, show the holes in the old ones ; — and so on. The Oxford and Cambridge prize man is the most helpless creature under the sun, when some strange fortune lands him on the shores of Greece, unless he picks up a servant who can speak some Western language with which he happens to be acquainted. All this, because the Greek is taught wholly as a dead language, apart from its living representative, and with an absurd and arbitrary pronunciation, to which we cling as if its rules were the Ten Commandments. The spoken language of Athens appears to me very pure and elegant, and I am quite convinced that it would be a great advantage to adopt at once the pronunciation established here.

On my return I found a note from the palace, requesting, in the name of the King, my presence at the ball. At a quarter past eight o'clock I went up to the palace, and found my way to Dr. Roeser's room. The Doctor was just putting on his coat,—a splendid uniform, decorated with half a score of orders,—a cocked hat, and a sword. I could not help laughing at his fierce military look. We entered the ball-room together, and it is as splendid an apartment as can be found in Europe,—brilliantly lighted up with hundreds of wax-candles, in five enormous chandeliers, showing off the tasteful decorations of the rooms—which are painted in the Munich style—to the best advantage.

The company was assembling. The masters of ceremonies, with their richly embroidered Greek costumes, shining with silk and gold; the Greek ladies, with their splendid head-dresses; the for-

eign ministers, with their diplomatic costumes;
here and there an old Turk,—nearly all with
swords by their sides,—made up a brilliant, semi-
Oriental picture, not to be seen at any other court
in Europe.

At nine o'clock the King and Queen entered,—
he in the uniform of the Greek cavalry, and she
in the handsomest and most beautifully fitted dress
that I ever saw. O for the pen of some inspired
milliner to do justice to this exalted theme! The
company opened to the right and left, and their
Majesties passed down the rooms, graciously bowing a smiling welcome to their guests, and we
bowed a respectful response. They walked about,
conversing with the company; after some time
the English minister and the Queen, the King
with the wife of one of the other foreign ministers,
and other great lords and ladies, commenced a
stately promenade round the room, to the sound
of music, changing partners each time they passed
round; and then the dancing commenced.

The Queen danced better than any lady of the
court, taking part in every dance but one,—
waltzes, quadrilles, and Heaven knows what besides. The King was conscientious in performing
this part of his duty, but seemed a little tired.
The Queen looked fresher and fresher with every
dance, and when they withdrew at half past three
o'clock, you would have supposed she was just
dressed for her first ball, so blooming, bright, and

animated did she appear. The company divided, right and left, and they retired, bowing and smiling, and bowed at and smiled upon, as when they entered. It was a beautiful and brilliant scene.

There was no great supper, as with us at balls. Refreshments were served at intervals, — lemonade, orgeat, punch, tea, coffee, and cake; but nothing to excess, and of course none of that crushing round a table which we have constantly at great balls at home.

On Saturday evening I was at Dr. Hill's, and while we were chatting on this and that, the Archbishop of Patras,•the Protosakellos, the Bishop of Hydra, and Mr. Metrophanes, the eloquent public preacher of Athens, were announced. The Greek priests always appear in the ecclesiastical costume, and their entrance into Dr. Hill's drawing-room was a somewhat imposing spectacle. These gentlemen entered into conversation in the most agreeable manner. I had a very interesting conversation with the Archbishop about Greek pronunciation in Greece and in the West of Europe. He maintains — and I agree with him entirely — that the present pronunciation, though not in all respects the same as that of the educated classes in ancient times, yet makes a much nearer approach to it than the European; that it came down from the earliest organization of the Church; "and," said he, "as the child at the mother's breast learns his pronunciation from her lips, so the Greek people received the traditional pronunciation with the word of God from the lips of the Church," — at once a good illustration and an argument.

The discussion tasked my Greek to the utmost; but I was glad to find that, though I had none of the Archbishop's fluency, I could understand him perfectly, and had words enough at my command to keep up the conversation.

I think I shall leave here early next week, but shall write you at least once more from the city of Athens. Give my love to each and all, and tell everybody everything I should like to say, but have not time, because the post closes soon.

XLVII.

Off the Coast of Attica,
a little north of Sunium, January 19, 1854.

YOU will be surprised at the date of this letter; and perhaps you will be more surprised by my explanation of it. Well, you must know that, after the grand ball at the palace, the King very graciously placed at my disposal, through Dr. Roeser, the royal cutter, " The Lion," for an excursion to Sunium, Ægina, Trœzen, and generally round the Attic seas.

I asked permission to take with me two young Englishmen, who had recently arrived in Greece, — one a graduate of Oxford, and the other of the London University; and the permission was instantly granted. The incident has caused no little commotion in Athens, and my friends here are not a little pleased. General Church laughs, and says the republican has turned royalist; the Russians are at their wits' end, and I have no doubt the small diplomates will put the thing down to some tremendous intrigue between America and England. The next steamers will carry despatches to Russia, Austria, France, and perhaps to Turkey, with the profoundest speculations on the consequences to be drawn from this portentous combination. Seriously, it is a most courteous thing on the part of King Otho, and I thought the offer ought not to be declined.

It is the only opportunity I should have had to see Ægina, and its famous temple of the Panhellenian Jupiter; and I could otherwise have seen the temple of Minerva at Sunium only by a two or three days' journey on horseback, with the chance of getting thoroughly ducked. The Lion is an English-built yacht, very safe and comfortable. I took Strattis the Lesbian, and Yanni Bulgar the cook; bought a supply of provisions for three days, and off we sailed this afternoon at half past two o'clock.

We came down to the Peiræus this morning, and I had the pleasure of showing my young English friends the tomb of Themistocles, and other interesting antiquities of the place. We came on board, bag and baggage, and amidst the curious and inquisitive looks of the nautical multitude on shore, and of the sailors on board the numerous ships in the harbor, out we dashed under a spanking breeze from the north, — Boreas, as they still call it here, — with our sails all set, and the Ægean waves roaring and foaming about the prow.

I have told you before, I was born to be an admiral, not a professor; and I have serious thoughts of running away with this craft, and making for the Black Sea, to help the distracted nations settle the Oriental question.

It was beautiful, sailing out of the ancient harbor, whence so many fleets of classic renown have swept into the Ægean. It was most exciting to dash past the strait and island of Salamis, where the great defeat fell on Xerxes and the Persian array, and where the tomb of Themistocles still looks over the sparkling waters. On all sides we beheld the memorials of Athenian greatness, — the huge masses of ancient walls and towers which lined and guarded the coast of the three harbors of Peiræus, Munychia, and Phalerum, in which the ancient navies rode secure. In front of us lay Ægina, with the Peloponnesian mountains in the background, the clouds resting on their summits. As we turned southward, the city of Athens and the long range of Hymettus bounded the picture, gradually fading from sight as the shades of evening came down on sea and land ; and now it is a dark and wild scene, for the moon does not rise until ten o'clock. We hope to get a moonlight view of the Sunium Temple.

Our armament consists of no cannon, a captain, and four men. If pirates should attack us, we have pen-knives and steel-pens. Yanni Bulgar has spits and teapots, and we should make a desperate fight.

Yesterday, I attended a curious ceremony of the Greek Church at the Peiræus, — the celebration

of St. John the Baptist, a very ancient observance. I rode down from Athens at seven o'clock.
The morning was fresh and beautiful, like the
first of October with us. At half past eight we
went to the church, where a long service was performed, and a little cross, apparently of gold, set
with precious stones, was baptized by the Archbishop of Achaia, dressed in his gorgeous pontifi-
cal robes, and a mitre blazing with jewelry and
miniatures of the saints. The water was in a vessel about as large as a barrel, and stood within an
enclosure in the centre of the church, guarded by
soldiers. After the baptism was over, there was
a great scramble of the multitude to fill their cups
with this blessed water, which they keep for the
most sacred occasions. From the church a procession was formed and marched with banners
flying through the town, stopping at the fountains
to bless them, and then coming down to the wharf
of the Peiraic harbor. We took a boat and joined
the fleet of boats, anxiously waiting for the arrival
of the procession. The ships in the harbor were
gayly decorated with flying streamers of many
colors, and the people everywhere had dressed
themselves out in holiday attire. At length the
Bishop's mitre was seen, like Minerva's helmet,
shining from afar. As he approached the sea,
divers, one after another, jumped or plunged in.
After a few moments, the Bishop threw the cross
into the water, and such a splashing and plunging

as there was to find it! The successful diver has the right to carry it round the town, and ask for money. Sometimes he gets from fifty to a hundred drachmas from the liberality of the pious zealots for Oriental orthodoxy. The effect of throwing the cross into the water is to sanctify the sea, and make it safe for navigators.

XLVIII.

Sunium, January 20.

WE reached this famous promontory of Athens about ten o'clock last evening, but thought it best to postpone our visit to the temple until to-day, as the moon did not rise until very late.   We were up long before sunrise, found the morning bright and clear, and, putting ashore in the cutter's boat, first paid our respects to Neptune by plunging into the sea.   The moon was still shining in the west over-the surface of the water, and pouring her pale light on the columns of Minerva.   Refreshed by our bath, — think of a sea-bath before sunrise on the 20th of January ! — we ascended the lofty promontory on which the temple stands.

Just as we approached the summit, up came the glorious sun from the midst of the Cyclades, and, flashing over the Mediterranean, struck the shining columns which sparkled with joy at his coming.

The columns are perfectly white, — scarcely a weather-stain is noticeable ; but their surfaces are much crumbled, and the marble seems to be scaling off.   On this high point, looking southward to

W

the middle of the Mediterranean, and east and west to the seas that encircle Attica, the winds are constantly blowing; and this may perhaps explain the wearing away of the surface, and the consequent unchanging whiteness of the marble.

The foundation of the temple and twelve columns remain, — nine on the southern side, with the architrave, and three in other parts, with the square column in which one of the walls of the temple terminates.

There are numerous other foundations of walls and buildings, covering the entire surface of this extremity of Attica; and looking northward, to the interior, the eye ranges over the ancient mines whence the silver of the Athenian currency was drawn. The mines were exhausted even in the Roman times; but extensive traces of the excavations are seen all over the southern part of the promontory. We had not time for any special examination; that I reserved until A—— and I can visit the spot together. Here, as elsewhere, I was obliged to make a rigid selection of objects to visit; and it was more to my purpose to spend the little time I had among the beautiful ruins of the temple.

We are now just hoisting sail, under a strong wind and a bright sun, for Ægina and the Temple of Panhellenian Jupiter; thence we hope to reach Poros to-night; and to-morrow to re-enter the Peiræus. The Lion is pitching and rolling among the waves that come sweeping in from the Mediterranean ; and so, for fear of growing illegible, I stop, and go on deck for a last look at the Temple of Sunian Minerva.

Evening. — I rushed on deck just in time to get a last glimpse of " Colonna's columns " shining in the morning sun. The Lion was roaring through the sea, and tossing the foam from his mane. The wind was strong and fresh, and the waves were running high. About two o'clock, after a splendid sail, we cast anchor in a little solitary harbor, just under the hill on which stands the grand old ruin of the Temple of Panhellenian Jupiter. We went ashore at once, and ascended the mountain. A walk of half an hour up the steep slope, among pine-trees and over terraces walled up with masonry, brought us under the shadow of the venerable columns, many of which, though worn away by the weather, still stand. The foundation is loaded with immense masses of stone from the architraves, roof, and columns that have fallen in. Between the crevices a thick growth of bushes has sprung up, encircling and overshadowing the old gray rocks with their green arms.

The view is most magnificent. We look over the Saronic Gulf, and see the whole extent of the plain of Athens, and its shining wall of mountains. The Acropolis rises in its centre like a great altar, and its temples are just visible as tracery against the eastern sky. Salamis is in sight, and beyond rise the mountains Cithæron and Helicon; we have a glimpse of Megaris, and the high lands about Corinth just mark the horizon. Southward we see the coast of Peleponnesus, and the broad expanse of the Mediterranean.

On this glorious height, commanding this panorama, and looking directly over the lovely and fertile valley which lies nestled in the interior of Ægina, and furnishes all its agricultural wealth, stood the great temple in honor of Jupiter, the god of the whole Grecian race, the Panhellenian ruler of all who spoke the Grecian tongue. As I walked among its columns and over its ruins, looking abroad over the grandeur of the spectacle, and listening to the melancholy voices of the wind among the neighboring pines and the wasting columns, I could not resist the sadness of the lonely and melancholy spirit that seems to haunt this strangely interesting spot.

We remained there a long time, and as the shadows began to fall from the western heights down into the lovely valley, we descended to the sea-shore and regained our ship. Here we remain until midnight, when, if the wind changes a few points, we hoist our sails for Salamis. The vessel sways lazily over the waves that roll in from the Saronic Gulf. Our captain and the sailors are taking their rest; my companions are dozing, and Strattis the Lesbian is arranging the beds.

I am never weary of listening to the water plashing against the sides of the yacht, and the distant tumult of the waves chafing along the steep and rocky solitude of the shore, while the solemn spirit of the past broods darkly over the crumbling temple, and breathes in the sighing pine-forests beneath it.

XLIX.

SALAMIS, January 21.

WE held a council of war yesterday afternoon to decide whether we would go to Poros, Trœzen, and Calaureia. All these places we have seen in the distance; and the last in particular I was desirous of visiting, because here Demosthenes died. But the north-wind was blowing, and there seemed no prospect of a change; we might be detained a week, or even longer; and I am now anxious to be on my way to Italy. So I decided to make for Salamis, as we could easily reach that island from Ægina; and from Salamis over to the Peiræus is only five or six miles. The captain hoisted sail about nine o'clock in the evening, and stood out into the middle of the Gulf between Peloponnesus and Attica; and, though the wind blew very strong and the sea ran high, in the course of the night we reached the little harbor of Salamis.

This morning we saw the sun rise over distant Athens, and, going ashore, we walked round the point to the narrowest part of the strait, where the Greek and Persian fleets met, and there, plunging into the sea, had a delicious bath.

The appearance of the island is desolate enough; and one cannot but wonder how the Athenians found shelter for their wives and children here, during the Persian invasion of Attica. It is very interesting to remember that Æschylus fought in the battle, that Sophocles took part in the chorus which celebrated the victory, and that Euripides was born here on the same day, — a wonderful crown of poetical associations for this solitary rock. We swam out, at a point about half-way between the bay of Eleusis and the harbor of Peiræus, so that we had the entire scene of the battle just around us. The water was cool, but delicious; and we could not help recalling the involuntary bath which so many Persians took in exactly the same spot. On our left lay the Greek fleet, and on our right the Persian. Had they been present at the moment, *our* bath would have been seriously interrupted.

This island, you remember, was the birthplace of Telamonian Ajax, and as we walked on the higher parts of the island, and noticed the foundations of ancient walls and towers, we pleased ourselves with the fancy that here was the palace of ancient Telamon, and that from the harbor where the yacht was anchored sailed the Salaminian fleet to the war of Troy. There are two small villages on opposite sides of the island, and a few fields planted with olives. It seems that during a part of the time the Greeks in the war with the

Turks took refuge here, just as in the Persian invasion; similar circumstances leading to similar results. On inquiring how they sheltered themselves, I was told they had small huts all over the slopes of the hills, and many lived in caverns. We are now just getting under way for Athens; so I must go on deck to look at these historical scenes again.

L.

ATHENS, January 21.

THE sail from Salamis over to the Peiræus was indescribably charming. I had never before had exactly that point of view of the various objects of interest, — the scenes of the great naval battle, with the plain and city of Athens in front. The wind was fresh, and the waves sparkled under the Attic sun. The mouth of the Peiraic harbor is so narrow that it is sometimes extremely difficult for a sailing-vessel to enter. Our gallant yacht was obliged to tack fourteen times. We reached the anchorage about one o'clock, and, taking a carriage, drove back to Athens, — ever-welcome Athens, — past the remains of the long walls, — past the olive-groves, — past the hill of the Nymphs, — past the Temple of Theseus, — up into the street of Hermes, — then to the street of Æolus, and to the Hôtel d'Angleterre.

My friends in Athens were not a little surprised to see me. They were confident I should be detained at Sunium by the wind, which was strong from the north. But I told them I had long ago written to you that I had mistaken my vocation, that I was intended by nature for an admiral, and

16

that my return was to be attributed wholly to that distinguished seamanship which had led to my appointment in the Greek navy.

I found, as I expected, that this little expedition has been a good deal discussed by the quidnuncs in Athens. That the royal cutter should have been placed at the disposal of a private traveller, and that traveller an American, is something quite unintelligible. A Russian diplomate and his wife, who live at this hotel, questioned me very closely; and when I told them the simple truth, they could scarcely believe it, — indeed, they did not believe it. It is very plain they think something is on foot, — a mystery that they cannot fathom; and I really believe they are of opinion that it is another proof of the purpose of America to intermeddle in European politics. The simple explanation is, that I was presented to the King, who already knew from Dr. Roeser the purpose of my visit; that, after the presentation and the ball, the offer of the cutter was made to me through Dr. Roeser, to promote and facilitate that purpose; and that I accepted it very frankly, asking at the same time permission to take two friends with me, which permission was most readily granted.

I have been highly delighted with the voyage. It has given me the opportunity of seeing places that I should not otherwise have seen, and of witnessing a specimen of pure Greek navigation, under very agreeable circumstances. I am glad to have seen some of the most interesting parts of the Greek waters in a *sailing* vessel. I had seen them sufficiently in a steamer, and shall for five or six days more be tossing about in the same way again.

My friends here approve entirely of my scheme of returning here with Agassiz in two or three years. Agassiz will find, in the birds, fishes, fossils, and mountains of Greece, quite enough to occupy him for a year; it will take me a year to complete my study of the spoken language, and to make various collections I have in mind of the popular poetry among the mountains; and we will publish our researches in a joint work on Greece, — physical, picturesque, and poetical. My three months' visit is only a preparation for a visit. The fair image of Greece, to be sure, is stamped on my mind too deeply ever to be effaced; but there is not an inch of its hallowed ground which does not deserve a careful study.

The future of Greece is a problem nearly as interesting as her past has been illustrious and unfortunate. Events now beginning to cast their portentous shadows on the Eastern world are agitating the best minds here. The war, though not openly declared, is considered as having actually begun. Several battles have been fought, blood has been profusely shed, the fleets of France and England have entered the Black Sea, and powerful armies are concentrating at neighboring points, to be ready when the struggle actually commences. What will be the result of this threatening state of things on the condition of Europe, God only knows; but the Greeks confidently anticipate the liberation of their countrymen in the Turkish provinces from the Ottoman dominion. There is an intense excitement throughout the nation, and visions of an empire with Constantinople for its capital float before the imaginations of old and young. I shall not be on the spot to witness the development of the drama, but I shall watch it with great interest from a distance.

LI.

YESTERDAY I made a most delightful excursion in company with the Rev. Mr. A—— and my two young English friends. We took horses in the morning, and, passing out of the city by the Arch of Hadrian and the Temple of Olympian Jupiter, took the road along the sea to the southern point of Mount Hymettus, where it comes down to the shore. It was a fine, fresh morning, and the breezes of Attica, the sparkling waters of the sea, the sight of Ægina, where we had so lately been, lying off in the distance, with the hazy mountains of the Peloponnesus in the background, and the beautifully moulded slopes of Hymettus on our left, made us feel that we were indeed treading enchanted ground.

At short intervals we rode over the foundations, — crumbling masses of hewn stone, — all that remains of the towns with which this part of ancient Attica was once studded. After a ride of about ten miles, we struck into the wild gorges of the mountains, and, taking one of the roughest bridle-paths I have anywhere travelled over, commenced our ascent.

We hired a shepherd to conduct us to the cavern; and it was well that we did, for on the way thither he showed us another cavern, not mentioned in any of the books, but very extraordinary in its form and character. The mouth is an almost circular opening at the southern end of the mountain, about twenty or thirty feet in diameter. It descends perpendicularly to a great depth, but there is no way of entering it. There is water, apparently running under the mountain, at one side; but the greater part of the bottom is covered with a growth of trees, on the tops of which we look down. I think it possible that this cavern may be a shaft of one of the silver-mines that were worked by the Athenians in this part of Attica; only it is farther north than any mentioned in the ancient authors. I made no attempt to go down; but threw stones in, and from the sound it appeared to me that the depth was very great.

We kept on our rough and stony way until we reached the grotto we were in search of. It is most picturesquely placed, commanding a view of the whole district of Sunium, and, off in the distance, of the Mediterranean. We entered the cave by a wide flight of steps, and found two subterranean chambers, hung and curtained with stalactites. On one of the walls a tablet is smoothed, and an inscription cut in very ancient letters, that Archedemos, the *Nympholept*, i. e. possessed or *crazed* by the nymphs, had wrought this cavern.

Other inscriptions repeat the name several times, and still others show that tablets and offerings were placed here in honor of Pan, Apollo, and the Nymphs. There is an entire figure in relief, sculptured on one of the walls, representing the workman with his hammer and chisel. He was not, at the best, a beauty, and I could not much wonder that he was "crazed by *hopeless* love." There is also the lower part of a sitting figure; but as little more than the legs remain, it is not very easy to form a complete idea of the gentleman's *personnel*. I fancy it is the same Archedemos.

A pleasant circumstance connected with this grotto is the probability that Plato was brought hither in his childhood by his parents, who desired to offer sacrifices to Pan, Apollo, and the Nymphs; so that I have now seen all the known localities connected with his name and biography. I have been three times to the Academy where he taught; have visited every point of the Ilissus to which he alludes; have breakfasted at his farm near Cephissia; and have now spent an agreeable hour in the grotto, where his youthful mind was impressed by the religion of the place, and whence his poetical eye must have gazed with admiration upon the wonderful and varied beauty of surrounding nature. I think I understand Plato all the better for these opportunities of studying the originals from which he drew his pictures of Attic scenery.

Not to do injustice to the outer man, we decided to lunch here; and Strattis, having produced his stores of rolls, cold tongue, chicken, English ale, and oranges, we discussed them with an appetite not diminished by our Platonic reminiscences. We returned to Athens by another route, through the Mesogæa, an inland valley of Attica, which I had often looked down upon from the surrounding heights, but had never crossed. It is a most interesting part of Attica, extending from the southern mountains, between Hymettus and the hilly eastern shore, and Pentelicus, and joining the plain of Athens near the Lycabettus.

On our ride we passed over many ruins of ancient towns, and the sites of others of which not a vestige remains. Here were the birthplaces of Socrates and Demosthenes, but not a stone to mark the spot of either. In the midst of solitude, near the site of an ancient temple, now occupied by a deserted church, with Byzantine pictures, a marble lion, belonging to the best ages of Athenian sculpture, lifts his head, and looks, with an expression of almost human sorrow, around upon the ruins of the ancient walls. We stopped long to examine this interesting monument. The head and body of the lion are entire; the forelegs are gone; but he is propped up by a pile of stone, so as to be in the posture evidently intended by the artist. As I shall never have an opportunity of riding a living lion, I took the occasion of jumping on the back

of the marble one. Bacchus and other mytho-
logical personages were fond of riding and driving
tigers and lions ; and if they found their backs as
comfortable a seat as I did the Mesogæan lion's, I
approve their choice. I should like to have ridden him into Athens ; but there he remained
fast rooted in the earth, like the first lion of creation, as described in the Paradise Lost.

On we galloped with Hymettus west of us, his
head covered with a frowning mass of clouds. We
had already been attacked, near the grotto, by short
but sharp showers of hail, and now the rain was
approaching. So we galloped still harder, —
leaving the Mesogæan lion again to his solitary
contemplations among the mouldering walls. Just
as we rounded the northern end of Hymettus, the
Attic plain, the Acropolis, with the Parthenon
drawn against the western sky, and the declining
sun, beyond the line of clouds, pouring his light
between the columns, and blending with the soft
but sombre hues that antiquity has thrown around
them, burst upon us. The cloud over our heads
let fall an almost summer shower ; and behind us,
the Mesogæa was spanned by the unbroken arch
of the rainbow, that seemed to follow us, as if Iris
herself had just descended from Olympus with a
message from Jupiter to his favorite daughter
Athene, the protecting goddess of the city. It
was a scene lovely past my feeble powers of description ; but alas for my Athenian hat ! — that

"brilliant affair" I had so recently bought in the street of Æolus, — the hat I held in my hand in the presence of royalty, and afterwards at the ball, — the hat with which I fondly hoped to dazzle you all on my return. Alas! its lustre is dimmed; it looks as sad as the Mesogæan lion; the storms of centuries seem to have spent their fury upon it; it is fast reaching the last stage of a hat's decline, when the inevitable phrase of "shocking bad" dooms it to the head of some ragged beggar or houseless vagabond whose home is the gutter.

We entered the city just as the sun was going down. The shower had already passed, and the glorious sunset of Athens lighted up the Acropolis, the sea beyond, and the hills around.

In the evening I went to the palace to take tea with Dr. Roeser. He asked me a thousand questions about America, Agassiz, &c., &c.; told me how Agassiz looked when a student under Döllinger at Munich; and listened with the greatest interest when I related his brilliant success in scientific discovery, and described his unbounded popularity in America as a lecturer. Nothing astonishes Europeans so much as the large audiences drawn together in our country by scientific lectures. When I tell them that Agassiz has lectured night after night to two thousand people, it sounds fabulous to them; and I am sometimes tempted to cut the number down a couple of hundred, as the Irishman wrote to his friends that he had meat twice a week, instead of three times a day, for fear they would not believe him. The Natural History Society of Athens has made him an honorary member; and (I suppose, on the strength of my relationship with him) it has conferred the same honor upon me. The diplomas, duly signed and sealed, have been sent to my room to-day.

LII.

ATHENS, January 27.

YESTERDAY I made another excursion, and probably my last in Greece — for the present. I awoke at half past five, and, looking out of my window, saw the slender arch of the waning moon hanging over the dark ridge of Hymettus. In a few moments the whole east was flushed with a glorious rose-color, which almost quenched the pale moon; then the rose changed into gold, which for nearly half an hour transfigured the mountain heights; and finally up came the sun, and filled the earth and hills and valleys with his presence. The rosy fingers of Aurora and the golden dawn had fled; the silver moon had vanished, and the unclouded splendor of an Attic day spread over the green fields and the sparkling sea, awakening the busy present and illuminating the mouldering memorials of the mighty past.

We set out to go to Decaleia, but, an accident happening to one of our horses, we were obliged to return. Then we took a carriage and drove down to Peiræus. From the beach of Peiræus we walked along the strait, up to the narrowest part and nearly to the Bay of Eleusis, so that we saw from the land side all the points in the scene of the great battle, and read on the spot the account of Herodotus, and the poetical description in Æschylus, who fought here. It is impossible to form a precise and positive idea of the arrangement of the forces, because a variety of combinations was possible, and the chances of battle would have changed any order previously agreed upon. But in these repeated visits to different points of the scene, I have been enabled to stamp on my memory a most distinct picture of the whole, and to clear up, to my own mind at least, several topographical particulars before obscure. We selected a beautiful spot on the shore, where the water had polished the marble and limestone cliffs, and hewn out gracefully curving recesses, and the floor of the sea was laid with a natural mosaic of rounded and many-colored pebbles, and the waves rolled over it, with a gentle sweep and swell, and plashed and tinkled under the resounding caverns. Here we plunged into the crystal water, through whose transparent depths the marble pebbles shone, and the sea-plants on the edge of the shores undulated with the undulating waters. We swam out into the strait and took a water view of the battle, as we had a few days before on the Salaminian side. It was the most delicious bath I ever took. We thought of the Persians, and how little they liked the bath they were compelled to take. The vivid lines of Æschylus brought the scene almost up from the deep, and placed the fleets before our very eyes. After all this exercise by land and sea we were well prepared for a lunch. The cold tongue and fowl, the French bread and London ale, had full and speedy justice done them on the very spot where we thought Xerxes must have sat to overlook the fight. Having finished our survey and our lunch with equal satisfaction, we returned to our carriage, and drove to Peiræus.

Hearing that the garden of Mr. Contostavlos contained some antiquities, not long since discovered, we stopped there, and found some very interesting objects. This garden seems to occupy the site of the ancient burying-place of Peiræus; he told me he had found about two hundred sarcophagi.

LIII.

ATHENS, January 29.

TWO days ago, I took a long walk round the city. I went by the Temple of Theseus, the Areopagus, the Agora, up the Acropolis, and spent about an hour in and around the Parthenon. The sky was somewhat overcast, and the distant islands and mountains, and the Saronic Gulf, were partially shrouded, and presented a wild, though beautiful appearance. A raven, perching on one corner of the western pediment, added to the sombre impression of the scene by his croaking. It was one of my last visits, if not the last; and I walked slowly away. I returned by the Dionysiac Theatre and the Temple of Olympian Jupiter, and reached my room as it began to darken. There, to my surprise, I found your letter lying on my table. I had not expected to receive another here, because I wrote some time ago to England to have my letters forwarded to Rome; but I suppose there was some delay, and by that happy accident your letter was sent as usual to Athens. There was but a moment to glance over it, as it was time to dress for dinner at Dr. Hill's, where I was engaged, and for a party at Mr. Finlay's.

We had a nice quiet little dinner; soup, fish, &c., and, among other things, mince-pie and squash-pie. I never thought to look upon mince and squash pies with a sentimental feeling; but since I have been in Athens, they have passed through a sort of transfiguration to my mind's eye.

After dinner we went to the party. It was larger than is usual in Athens, the guests being English, Americans, and Greeks. We had Italian music from Mrs. F—— and Miss L——, and Greek songs from Miss S——, a young and very pretty Greek lady, who is engaged to be married to a young man in England, a countryman of her own, whom she has never seen. This is in accordance with the custom of the Greeks. Marriages are arranged by the families; and as Greek families are established in distant cities, and in all the countries of Europe, it often happens that the persons most interested never see each other until they meet to be married. Some years ago, in their enthusiasm for progress and emancipation, they tried the experiment of letting young people decide for themselves; but the result was so unfortunate that they went back to the old system, and now nobody dreams of anything different. These facts go to confirm Judge F——'s theory. The party was a very agreeable one, as parties generally are here, and we stayed rather late.

Yesterday we had some thought of making an expedition; but the sky was threatening in the morning, and we did not think it safe. Before noon, the rain began to pour, and in the afternoon, when I went to hear Professor Kontogoni lecture on the Old Testament, a regular Old Testament deluge came down, and torrents flowed through all the streets.

LIV.

ATHENS, January 30.

THIS is my last day in Greece. I have taken my ticket for Molfetta, and shall pass several days among the islands of the Ionian Republic. Yesterday I dined at Mr. W——'s for the last time,—the company, General Sir Richard Church, my two young English friends, Mr. L——, Secretary of Legation, and myself. It was a delightful dinner in every respect,—saddened, to me, only by the thought that I should so soon take leave, for a long time, perhaps forever, of friends who have become so dear to me. Mr. W—— is certainly one of the ablest and most accomplished gentlemen I have met in Europe. I am indebted to him and to his family for kindnesses and hospitalities I can never repay. This morning I have been taking leave of many friends: I do it with real sorrow. But I have established relations with Athens, which I shall not allow to die out; and the communications are so frequent and regular now, that an acquaintance may be easily continued. Mr. Black (the husband of the maid of Athens) has just called. I tell him his wife is well known in America, and he must carry her thither. Everything promises well for my voyage.

LV.

PATRAS, February 1, 1854.

I AM at the present moment sitting on the deck of the steamer Oriente. The mountains around Patras, and on the opposite shore of the Gulf, are covered with snow; the sides that slope down to the city are green with wheat and grass. An old castle, strongly and picturesquely placed, lies just under the Snowy Bodia, commanding the town and the Gulf. Westward rises the rocky Cephalonia, crowned by the heights of Blackmountain, now capped with snow. A little to the north of it, low on the horizon, we see rocky Ithaca, the kingdom of Ulysses, and a little to the south, the island of Zante, the ancient Zacynthus, which furnished a part of the fleet of Ulysses for the Trojan war. We arrived here early this morning, having left Athens yesterday. Monday, in Athens, was one of the most exquisite days I have seen in Greece, saddened, to me, by the necessity of saying farewell to so many friends, who received and have treated me more like one of themselves than a stranger. Madame de Staël truly described travelling as *un triste plaisir;* — the haunting thoughts of home, and the constant separations .

from those who have honored us with their regard, in the new places we have visited, mingle· many a drop of bitterness in the sweet cup of increasing knowledge which we drink as we travel from place to place.   Athens will always be a delicious memory to me, — so " hospitable in her sweet recess," — so full of glorious vestiges of her most illustrious past.

When we drove through the city yesterday morning it was still dark, — only the light of the stars twinkled and quivered in the silent sky. The Temple of Theseus slept, a formless mass ; the Acropolis rose solid and black ; the Erechtheium and the Parthenon stood shadowy and ghostlike, and seeming to touch the sky.   We passed out upon the Peiraic road.   I tried to catch a glimpse of the olive groves of Plato ; but their dark foliage seemed only a sombre covering for the slumbering earth.   The prison of Socrates was blotted out by the kindly touch of night ; and the Bema of Demosthenes peered dimly through the darkness, that was like the darkness of ages.   We went down the road once traversed by armies and triumphal processions ; we reached the massive foundations of the long walls ; we reached the harbor, and by the light of lamps were rowed out to the Austrian steamer, which was startling the silence of night and antiquity by its hissing.

At six we started.   I watched, from the deck, the lines of the Attic coast.   We passed outside of Salamis, and the light broke splendidly over its historic rock, and then illuminated the distant mountains of Peloponnesus. Day advances, and we sweep along the Bay of Salamis, and the sacred shore of Eleusis. Next, Megara, with its background of mountains, salutes the sight. Soon, peering above them all, the white summit of Helicon is lifted to the sky. We come in sight of the Isthmus of Corinth, and I watch with interest the opposite shores, whose picturesque beauties had filled me with admiration, in my journey of November and December. We arrived at the Isthmus at half past ten. Here we took carriages, and drove across to the other side. The mountainous Acropolis — so splendidly commanding two seas — towered on our left, and the ranges of Helicon and Cithæron far off on the right.

At Loutraki another steamer from Trieste had arrived, and was waiting for us. Here there was a magnificent view of the Corinthian Gulf, and its variegated shores. Here again I recognized the features of glorious Greece which I had seen before. I was glad to see them from another point of view, which invested them with new beauty.

The clouds were sweeping wildly over the face, of heaven, and the sea roared and chafed against the shore. It was not easy to get on board ; but at length the feat was accomplished, and at eight o'clock in the evening the steamer moved from Loutraki. The wind went down in the night, and we had a tranquil and rapid passage the whole length of the Corinthian Gulf. When I awoke this morning we were just coming to anchor in the harbor of Patras. I went on shore to deliver a letter and a parcel with which I had been intrusted by Dr. Hill. Having attended to this, I climbed to the castle, and enjoyed the magnificent beauty of the panorama, under the light of a most beautiful day. I rambled over the city ; entered a church ; dropped a letter for you — my last from Athens — in the post-office ; returned to the steamer, and here I am, on the 1st of February, writing on deck, while you, in your Northern climate, are shivering over a register, and suffocating with the gases of coal. I look up into the blue sky, and a few silvery clouds hang over the mountains, or paint the face of the sea with green and purple. The waters are laving with their summer-sounding plash the sides of the ship as she lies quietly at anchor. Miss M—— is making a sketch of the scene, which I am trying to sketch with pen and ink for you at home. We start in an hour or two for Zante and the other islands that border the western shore of Greece.

LVI.

CORFU (the ancient Corcyra), February 2, 1854.

THE weather has continued as beautiful as
heart could desire. We left Patras about
three o'clock, and steered for Missolónghi, so
famous for the exploits of Marco Botzaris and the
death of Byron. We had on board a Greek general and his suite, together with several civilians,
bound for that place. The steamer was not long
in reaching the entrance of the Gulf of Patras.
She stopped five or six miles from the town of
Missolonghi, on account of the shallow water, and
boats with lateen sails came off to take the passengers. You cannot imagine anything more splendid
than the panorama in the centre of which we
paused for half an hour. The sun was just going
down, and all the west was flushed with gold,
orange, rose, and purple. The mountains on the
northern side of the Gulf were clothed in the
deep blue I have so often admired on the slope
of Hymettus at sunset. The summits above Patras, covered with snow, were glowing with rosy
light like that of Chamouni. Zante, Cephalonia,
Ithaca, lay to the west under the sunset. The ship
rolled indolently on the gently throbbing water,

like the deep, but tranquil beating of a heart in
the calm sleep of innocence ; and the broad-winged
boats, gliding towards the classic shores of Missolonghi, gave animation to the still beauty of the
picture.

We moved on again.   In the course of the
night the boat touched at Zante ; but I had gone
to bed, and so lost the view.   In the morning we
cast anchor in the harbor of Argostoli, the principal town of Cephalonia.   Here Miss M—— met
her brother, and her voyage terminated.   Taking
leave of her seemed like severing the last link of
the chain that bound me to Athens.   In two hours
we were again under way.   The weather continued fine.   We swept out of the Gulf of Argostoli, and along the western coast of Cephalonia,
high, precipitous, and plunging steep into the sea.

Soon we reached the northern extremity, and
saw Ithaca on our right, — rocky Ithaca, — the
home of Penelope and the scene of so much of the
Odyssey.   Next, Leucadia came in view, and the
white cliff down which Sappho leaped, — if she did
leap.   It is certainly a splendid place for such an
achievement.   The beautiful islands in its neighborhood lay sparkling in the light.   We were for several hours in sight of the Lover's Leap ; and then
the Albanian Hills came up along the eastern horizon, with the Acherusian Lake, the mouth of the
Acheron, the promontory of Actium, and the picturesque heights that overhang the ruined Parga.

We passed in between the island of Paxos and the coast, and as another splendid sunset approached, we came in sight of the range of the distant summits from which Corfu derives its present name. Another moonlight evening, too beautiful for perfect repose. We cast anchor in the harbor about ten o'clock, and as we were to remain until the following afternoon, I went ashore, and took lodgings at a comfortable little English hotel.

LVII.

On board Ship, at Corfu,
February 3, 1854.

ON my voyage I have been reading all the first part of the Odyssey, the scene of a great part of which is laid among these islands. To-day, at an early hour, I called on my friend, Rev. Mr. C——, with whom I became acquainted in Athens, and we made an excursion together a few miles out of the town. I had the Odyssey with me. Corfu is the Scheria of Homer, and the scene of the delightful story of Nausicaa, the court and gardens of Alcinoüs, and the adventures of Ulysses among the Phæacians. I wish you would get the Odyssey, and read particularly the fifth, sixth, seventh, and eighth books. I have no doubt that Homer had been here, and that the scenery of this island was present to his memory when he wrote those lovely passages.

It is the "last" of the Greek islands, — as Nausicaa describes the abode of the Phæacians. Its shores are steep and rocky. Ulysses leaves the island of Calypso on a boat of his own making, and sails seventeen days, keeping the "Wain" on his left; on the seventeenth the land of the Phæacians appears in sight. But Neptune stirs up a tremendous storm, which shatters his vessel. He clings to a timber, and is driven hither and thither. At last Leucothea gives him a sort of life-preserver, and advises him to swim. He does so. Minerva sends Boreas to help him on, and in two days he again reaches the land of the Phæacians. But the shore is so steep and rocky, and the waves dash with such violence, that he cannot land. In attempting it, his skin is torn, and his bones are bruised. Onward he swims, until he comes to a river, and an opening sheltered from the winds. Here he enters, and, almost exhausted, he crawls up the bank, lies down among the brushwood, covers himself with leaves, and goes soundly asleep. Meantime Nausicaa drives down to the river, accompanied by her maidens, to wash the family linen. The washing over, they have a game of ball; and in the course of it they wake up Ulysses.

Then follow the exquisite scene between the hero and the princess; the introduction to Alcinoüs and his court; the sports with which he is entertained; and the incomparable narrative which he gives of his adventures on the return from Troy.

Now the localities in Corfu correspond in a general way somewhat remarkably to the descriptions of Homer. A great part of the coast is so rocky that the impossibility of landing on it is apparent at the first sight. But on the eastern side, where the present town stands, there is an opening, with a river flowing through the valley. The springs of the river run from under a rock, and form a basin of the clearest and most beautiful water, at the distance of about an hour from the foundations of an ancient city.

We drove out to it nearly by the road that Nausicaa must have taken, passing by an ancient cemetery where numerous sarcophagi have been found, nearly perfect. When we reached the spot, behold there was a woman there, washing! — but she was not, like Nausicaa, exactly equal to the immortal goddesses, if the goddesses are particularly handsome. Nevertheless, it was a curious coincidence of a present usage with an old tradition. Near by was brushwood where Ulysses might easily have concealed himself, and a broad meadow where Nausicaa and her maids might have had a capital game of ball. I read on the spot the entire description; and the possibility, which strengthened into a probability, that the scenery I saw around me had met the eyes of Homer, and suggested to his plastic imagination that charming romance of remote and shadowy antiquity, gave extraordinary interest to the reading.

We crossed the little bay into which the river runs, in a ferry-boat, climbed the opposite height, and descended the slopes on which the garden of

Alcinoüs (the description of which I read here) is supposed to have stood. A lovelier spot it would not be easy even for the imagination of Homer himself to paint. Fruits and vines, with ever-greens, covered the ground. Especially the oranges — the most beautiful golden oranges, shining among the rich green foliage — delighted the eye and tempted the appetite. I stopped to get some of them ; two, with their leafy garniture, I have put carefully up to bring home if possible. An orange from the garden of Alcinoüs will be something worth having in Cambridge.

Having finished this most interesting ramble, and enjoyed to the utmost its classical and poetical associations, I went up to the fortress, which commands an extensive prospect, not only of the Ionian Sea and its islands, but of the picturesque mountains on the opposite coast of Epirus. Then I returned to the steamer, and at three o'clock we again set out on our voyage.

LVIII.

BRINDISI, February 4.

WE had another fine evening, and saw the magnificent scenery of Epirus, as we sailed northward through the channel that separates the island from the mainland, to the greatest advantage. I remained on deck until late. We struck off to the left, directly into the Ionian Sea, and in a short time the shores of Northern Greece, and of Corfu, the last of the Greek islands, were lost from sight. This morning the sun rose, golden and cloudless, from the sea; while on the other side, the city of Brindisi, — the ancient Brundusium, — and the low line of the Italian shore, were in sight. At about eight o'clock we anchored, and here we remain until evening; but so jealous is the Neapolitan government of foreigners, that we cannot go ashore without a special permission. My only companion is Colonel G—— of the English army, who has seen a great deal of hard service. Brindisi was once an important Roman station; but it is now a paltry village. There is nothing to be seen which we cannot see as well from the deck of the steamer as on land. We amuse ourselves with laughing at the fantastic terrors of the Neapolitan government.

LIX.

ADRIATIC SEA, ON BOARD THE ORIENTE,
February 8.

WE passed Saturday in inglorious idleness at Brindisi. At ten o'clock in the evening, we got under way for Molfetta, where I expected to land. The prevalence of northern winds for some days, in the upper part of the Adriatic, had caused a considerable commotion in the water, and the ship rolled and plunged so violently during the night, that I had hard work to keep in my berth. This morning when I came up on deck early, we were in sight of the low coast of Italy, and before long the houses of Bari and the churches of Molfetta loomed up from the sea. The waves were still violently agitated, and it was doubtful whether we should be able to enter the narrow and somewhat dangerous harbor. However, as we came near, the sea became more tranquil, and we experienced no difficulty.

Here I intended to land and cross over by diligence to Naples; but I found, on inquiry, that there was no diligence until Tuesday night, so that I should have to waste three days in a place that has not a single object of the slightest interest. I therefore made up my mind to go on to Ancona, and from that place to take the diligence or *malle-poste* to Rome. I shall rejoin P—— and the rest of the party the sooner for this; but I am afraid I shall not see Naples again, and shall have to give up Pæstum.

We left Molfetta after about an hour's detention. I had to go on shore to get my ticket and to have my passport inspected; and so I had a view of the city, which did not make me regret my determination to proceed in the steamer; and now we are within a few hours of Ancona. The weather continues fine, and the sea almost perfectly calm. It will be a week to-morrow morning since I left Athens. The voyage, though slow, has been agreeable. It has enabled me to see the Ionian Islands, and to explore the most interesting part of the principal one. I have in my mind a very distinct picture of the scenery of the Odyssey, — in fact, the voyage to Constantinople, and the voyage along the western side of Greece, have illustrated both the Iliad and Odyssey more than all the commentators of Germany. It is possible I may be detained a day or two at Ancona.

THE END.

9 783744 765916